Realms of Gold

Ritual to Romance

By the same author

The Blood Remembers
Il Richiamo del Sangue
A Tale of the Fortuny Gown

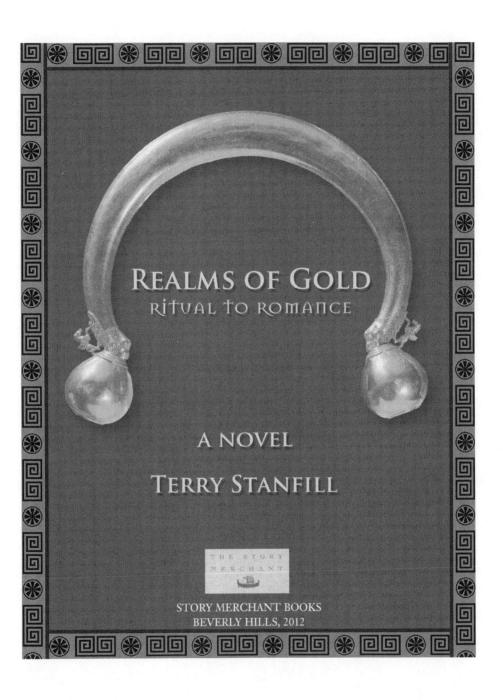

REALMS OF GOLD
RITUAL TO ROMANCE

A NOVEL

TERRY STANFILL

THE STORY
MERCHANT

STORY MERCHANT BOOKS
BEVERLY HILLS, 2012

ISBN-13: 978-0615657547

CREDITS
Image of the gold *lamella*, The Getty Museum, Malibu, California

Sketch of the Vix Krater, Michael Vickers and David Gill.
Artful Crafts, Ancient Greek Silverware and Pottery, Oxford
University Press, 1994

Image of the *pinakes* from Locri, *Museo Nazionale*, Reggio,
Calabria, Italy

Story Merchant Books
9601 Wilshire Boulevard #1202
Beverly Hills CA 90210
www.storymerchant.com/books.html

For my daughter
Michaela Sara Stanfill
in memoriam

"Much have I traveled in the realms of gold, and many goodly states and kingdoms seen."
John Keats, *"On First Looking into Chapman's Homer"*

Book I

That the man who first told the story, and
boldly, as befitted a born teller of tales, wedded
it to the Arthurian legend, was himself connected by descent with the ancient Faith, himself actually held the Secret of the Grail, and
told, in purposely romantic form,
that of which he knew.
I am firmly convinced, nor do I think that
the time is far distant when the missing links
will be in our hand, and we shall be able to
weld once more the golden chain which
connects Ancient Ritual with
Medieval Romance.
—Jessie L Weston,
From Ritual to Romance, 1920

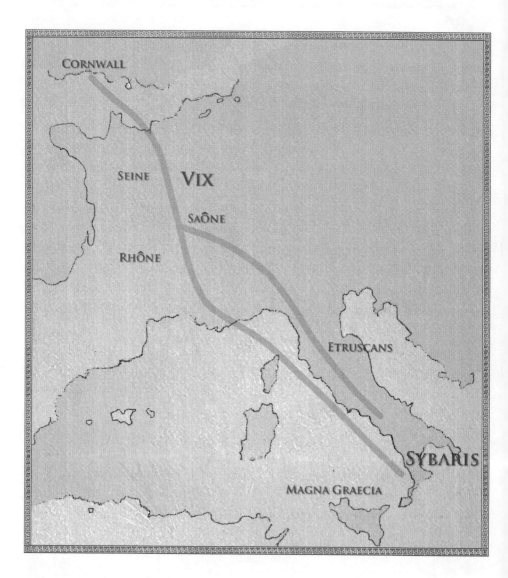

PROLOGUE

The village of Vix. Châtillon-sur-Seine, Côte d'Or,
Burgundy, 1953

It is a sunless, bitterly cold day in January when archaeologist René Joffroy and his team begin to dig. They
labor in a barren wheat field near Vix at the foot of a
hill commanding a view of the Seine. Joffroy has long surmised
that the bulging earth in the fields below Mont Lassois might
conceal an ancient burial ground. Recently, Maurice Moisson,
a local farmer and the team's foreman, turned up large fragments of limestone from a distant quarry. The archaeologist
knows the time has come time to begin excavations.

From their hilltop fortress on Mont Lassois, the Celtic *rix*,
or chieftains, controlled one of the great trade routes of the
ancient world. From Cornwall, in Britain, to Mediterranean
ports, tin and copper to be smelted into bronze was transported to Etruscans and Greeks, salt exchanged for amphorae of
wine and oil, furs and Baltic amber traded for Mediterranean
coral.

So far the team has uncovered an area forty-two meters in

diameter and about thirteen meters high. In its center they find evidence of a square chamber dug out some six meters below the surface. Wooden planks, like shutters, enclose what Joffroy suspects is a tomb. Its roof, once supported by wood beams and spread with layers of stones, has collapsed, perhaps centuries ago.

As the team clears rubble and earth from the north corner of the tumulus, Joffroy's expert eye catches the distinct gray-green patina of ancient bronze. His heart pounds and for a brief moment he cannot move. Then, his hands trembling, he painstakingly brushes earth from an elaborate volute handle shaped like the bust of a fierce, tongue-gaping gorgon. As the men continue to dig, they find that the handle is attached to what appears to be an immense bronze krater, a vessel used for the mixing of wine in ceremonial rituals. Centered on the lid of the krater is a small sculpture, a Kore, her head covered by a mantle. Joffroy knows that this great krater, the cauldron of plenty, was a symbol of immortality for the Hallstatt Celts who once inhabited this territory in the sixth century, B.C.

Soon the team makes yet another startling find, the remains of a woman about thirty years old reposing in a bier, a *charrette*, a wooden cart. Four large bronze-fitted wheels have been removed from the cart and placed along the wall of the burial chamber.

Although the skull is no longer attached to the skeleton, a golden diadem remains fixed on its brow. Scattered about are necklaces of amber and hardstone beads, shale and bronze bracelets, bronze anklets and several brooches, some studded with coral. Amidst the rubble, Joffroy also finds a silver and gold phial, two Attic bowls, one plain, glazed black with a lid. A Greek *kylix*, black-figured on a red background, is painted with scenes of a battle between Amazons and Greek hoplites, a motif Joffroy knows was popular in the Scythian colonies around the Black Sea. The Greek ceramics date the tomb to the end of the 6th century, around 500-510 B.C. He finds no indications that the tomb has ever been looted.

The archaeologist recognizes the krater's craftsmanship as Southern Italian, perhaps from Taranto, Puglia on the Adriatic, an ancient colony of Magna Graecia, Megale Hellas, Greater Greece. This massive krater has made a long, probably difficult journey to the oppidum on Mont Lassois, at last ending its journey in the earth of Vix.

The team is exuberant, but René Joffroy remains subdued, sensing that he is poised at the brink of an astonishing discovery, perhaps the culmination of his career, his own bid for immortality. He stands in wonder as he ponders *la Dame de Vix*, obviously a woman of great importance. Who was she? Princess or priestess? Or was she queen?

Giovanni
July 13, Venice, 2007

The wedding in Venice has been planned more than a year in advance so there is no way Giovanni Di Serlo can get out of going. Of course he has to be there. His conscience wouldn't have it otherwise. His cousin, Allegra Bona Dea, a lawyer for an American firm in Rome, is to marry Jonathan Evans, an investment banker from New York.

On the fifteenth of July, family and friends will gather in the ancient church of San Pietro di Castello on the city's easternmost point, the "tail" of the dolphin-shaped island that is Venice. In Italy it's often said that at weddings unmarried men—and probably women as well—hope to find the mates they have been destined for. As Giovanni scans the guest list, one name attracts him, but he chides himself for romanticizing. Still, he has to keep an open mind. What could be worse than meeting the very one and not recognizing her?

It's late Friday afternoon when he arrives in Venice from Puglia where he's been working on a dig. After parking his car in the garage at Piazzale Roma, he takes the *vaporetto* to the San Marco *pontile* for his appointment at the Biblioteca Marciana. When he leaves the library, a storm is blowing over the Adriatic, warm summer rain beating down hard: the sea has become so rough that the *traghetto* has stopped ferrying passengers across to the Dorsoduro side of the Grand Canal where he lives. Rather than walk to the Accademia Bridge to cross, he decides to stop by the Hotel Desdemona for a drink. Walking into the bar, he notices a woman reading a newspaper at a corner table. By its size and distinct clotted-cream colored paper, he recognizes it as the English version of *Il Giornale dell'Arte*, The Art Newspaper.

The woman turns the page then glances up, meets his eyes,

and stares at him almost brazenly. She looks to be in her early thirties and has a face that he remembers from somewhere. Certainly not what one would call a pretty face, but, with a bit of imagination and the right makeup, she might be described as a *belle laide*.

He moves to the bar and orders a vodka martini, then finds a place in the opposite corner of the room where he sits, with only his profile facing her. He can feel her eyes as he opens the newest issue of *Epoca* he's pulled out from the pocket of his raincoat. As the bartender mixes his drink, Giovanni turns page after page mindlessly until he hears footsteps approaching his table.

"*Buona sera*," she murmurs in a pleasing, well accented Italian.

He looks up and nods, mumbling a greeting *sotto voce*.

"May I ask if she is English?" he asks in the most formal Italian.

"I'm American. My name is Bianca. Bianca Evans Caldwell."

"So *you* are Bianca Caldwell!" he blurts out, trying to hide his disappointment. "I saw your name on the wedding guest list and intended giving you a ring at the Danieli. My name is Giovanni Di Serlo." When he offers his hand, he is surprised that hers is soft as kidskin. "Please join me," he mutters, pulling out a chair for her.

"And I noticed your name on the guest list," she responds, "and wondered if you might somehow be related to the Evans clan."

"No, I'm related to the bride, the Bona Dea side. Please— why don't you join me for a drink," he says, hoping he doesn't sound as reluctant as he feels.

She sits down primly, her back straight against the cushion.

"Are you staying here at the Hotel Desdemona?" he asks.

"Yes, I always stay here when I come to Venice."

"I'd have thought you'd be staying at the Danieli with the rest of the out of town crowd."

"I prefer to stay closer to the Accademia. I spend a lot of time there looking at paintings. My work often takes me to Venice, but these past few months I've been spending much of my free time in France—in Burgundy, to be specific." Her voice is softer, more feminine than he would have expected.

He takes a good look. Her unruly dark hair falls below her shoulders. Her skin is pale as sun-bleached ivory, her nose slightly aquiline, her eyes without guile.

Trying his best to converse, he goes on. "When I looked over the guest list I recognized your name immediately. Did you know that your great grandmother and mine were good friends? I have a photograph of the two of them in Venice. If you'd like to see it, please come by my apartment and I'll show it to you."

She hesitates, but only briefly. "It would make me very happy to see the photo."

He tries not to stare at her scuffed, down-at-heel loafers, the shabby, overstuffed handbag on her lap.

"I remember that the guest list said you were from Baltimore."

"Now New York, but my family is from Baltimore. I've lived in a lot of places but Baltimore was my home before I took a job at *Occhi e Anima*, the art journal. Mostly I cover auction sales, but sometimes my boss has me write vignettes about ancient objects and their use in ritual. My pen name is Bianca Fiore."

He feels dismay and shock. No wonder she looks so familiar! He'd seen her picture, obviously photo-shopped, in the magazine. "I'm a great fan of yours," he says, not quite meaning it. Well, he thinks, at least we'll have something to talk about. He pulls a business card out of his wallet and offers it to her.

Giovanni Di Serlo, Professor of Archaeology, University of Lecce.

"Where are you working now?" she asks after reading the card. "Archaeology has become a passion of mine."

"At the moment I'm digging in Puglia—not far from Vieste, but I have a family place here in Venice so from time to time I come to stay for a few days...I'm sure this isn't your first trip to Venice."

"It was many years ago when I was a child. We spent two weeks here."

"And what did you think of Venice when you saw it then?" he asks, expecting the usual raves.

"I hated it. But I was only eleven. Of course I love it now." She smiles broadly.

Well, at least she's honest, he thinks. Her smile is warm, genuine. Hers are American teeth, Hollywood teeth, white and straight.

"I'm glad you've changed your mind about our city—but you're not the first person to hate Venice, you know. D. H. Lawrence, for one. He called it a 'green and slimy place.'"

For a moment, there is an awkward silence. "You're a talented woman," he finds himself saying. "There aren't many people who can write about symbols and objects the way you do. Imaginative intuition is a great gift—to see far beyond what meets the eye. You are indeed the 'eyes and soul' of your magazine." He pauses, uncertain of what to say next. She looks as though she is disappointed so he hurries on. "In the May issue I particularly liked your article on the origins of the *bucrania* motif in art and architecture. The connection of the volcano with the origin of the gorgon was fascinating." He hopes his fib sounds convincing.

"I'm flattered. You obviously read my articles. And maybe even between the lines," she murmurs cryptically.

"Can you join me for a coffee at Florian's tomorrow morning?"

"I intend to be on the Piazza promptly at 9:30—for reasons of my own," she replies, her sloe eyes turning away from his.

"If I come by at nine, we can at least walk there together."

"I'll most likely be gone by then. But you can always try." She shrugs her shoulders as though she doesn't give a damn if she ever sets eyes on him again—all the while blushing furiously.

She stands up to leave. Beneath the shapeless black tunic and baggy trousers, her body seems lithe, slender, her braless breasts high as a maiden's. But her face has the gaunt look of a woman who spends too much time on introspection. And her hair! Thick hair that seems to leap out from her head like Medusa's snakes. Someone should give her advice on grooming, dressing, presenting herself to others.

They shake hands and he leaves her standing there, but feels those eyes boring through his back as he walks away and turns into the *calle* toward Campo Santo Stefano. Then bounding up the Accademia Bridge two steps at a time, he crosses the Grand Canal to Dorsoduro and walks briskly to Palazzo Bona Dea.

In the *androne*, he stops to admire his newly restored gondola just returned yesterday from the workshop at San Trovaso where it has been for the past six months. Now it is even blacker, sleek and slick, its *forcula* rubbed with wax, the seahorse brasses gleaming.

He takes the lift-for-two up to the fourth floor and, after rustling through letters and magazines, reaches for his *telefonino* to cancel his dinner reservation. Guido was saving the best table for him, just in case. When he'd seen her name on the guest list, he'd thought about inviting Bianca Evans Caldwell to dinner—now, much to his disappointment, his plan is dashed by having met her.

"The signorina isn't feeling well tonight," he explains, although explanation has never been his style. He admits that he is ashamed of himself for not wanting to take the poor girl to dinner, but spending an entire evening across from her is more than he could bear after the long, tiring drive from Puglia. Yes, he'd have to take Bianca Evans Caldwell aka Fiore one step at a time. And did he really want to be seen at the chic Monaco with a woman so badly, so shabbily dressed? Was he shallow like a lot of other Italian men, wanting always to make *la bella figura*—a good impression—walking in with a stunning woman on his arm? He picks up the photograph, one among many on the grand piano, to study the photo of his great grandmother Rose Alba with Nina Evans. No, Bianca is clearly not what he had in mind.

He checks out the refrigerator for remnants of his last stay—a slab of *bresaola*, a hunk of Parmigiano Reggiano, a box of stale breadsticks. He slices the dried beef thinly onto a plate, then shaves parmesan curls over the top and dribbles it with the green, unfiltered *extra virgine* olive oil from Puglia.

Perched on a stool at the black granite counter of his new high-tech stainless steel clad kitchen, he will eat his dinner alone. The room doesn't comfort him. He picks up a forkful and puts it down. He thought he was hungry, but the food tastes like donkey straw. He is a cad. His reaction to Bianca has shocked him. He'd always believed that he valued intelligence, that compassion in a woman was more important than mere physical beauty.

And not so long ago, he'd had a short but intense relationship with another American woman. When he first met her, he felt he'd come to the end of his search. He thought she was in love with him—and maybe she was—at least a little, but she went back home to California to her husband. He is still not quite over her, but after seeing Bianca's name on the guest list, he had begun to think there might be some hope for him.

Now that image of golden vagueness he's been carrying around since childhood is giving way to feelings of shame and guilt. He snatches the pepper grinder, twists it with a vengeance, and then wolfs down everything on the plate.

He gets into bed, earlier than usual for him, and reaches for the new issue of *The American Journal of Archaeology*. Since his late father had helped in the discovery of the remains of the lost city of Sybaris, he is intrigued by a recent paper by Claude Rolley, the famous bronze expert, on the origins of the Vix Krater in Burgundy, which Rolley now claims to have been made in Sybaris. Then he remembers his conversation with Bianca about *bucrania*. He shuffles through the magazines on his bedside table until he finds *Eyes and Soul* and turns to the ritual page written by Bianca.

Bucranium Bucranium (plural *bucrania*) is the Greek word for the skull of an ox. It is also an architectural term used to describe a common form of carved decoration on Doric temples. It is generally considered to be a reference to the practice of garlanding sacrificial oxen, the heads of which were primitively displayed on the walls of the temples, a practice with a long history reaching back to the sophisticated Neolithic site of Çatalhöyük in eastern Anatolia.

A woman kneels before the altar facing the painting on the wall, head bowed in her hands.

The *bucrania*, skulls and horns of oxen overlaid with white plaster, are placed as offerings on the altar and hang from the walls. *Bucrania* on the altar are draped with leopard skins. A stone statue of a woman with large breasts and ample vulva sits on the altar. Panthers, chained to rocks, guard her on either side.

The kneeling woman prays to the creator and destroyer of life, imploring the mountain not to rage, spit fire and bellow smoke into the sky. Our people live in view of twin peaks called Fire Mountain. Once, when the goddess was angry, smoke and ash clouded the sky.

Glowing red milk, liquid fire like molten giant snakes, poured down her breasts and turned her people into stone. And when the sky turned night dark, the earth trembled and the mountain belched flames into the skies and caused the earth to part its thighs in fields where our people sowed wheat.

So that we would never forget the anger of the goddess, she commanded us to paint on the walls of our sanctuary an image of her breasts bursting with fire. On the ceilings we painted giant birds' wings, birds like those that hover over the dead, picking the bones so clean that they can be smudged with red ochre and placed beneath the earth in the houses where our people live—above the bones of our ancestors of countless seasons past.

One night there was so much smoke in the sanctuary my hair was flaked with ashes and reeked of burning wood...

He smiles, shaking his head in disbelief—deep purple prose right out of a *romanzo* by Gabriele d'Annunzio. He puts down the magazine to reflect on Bianca Fiore. Strange that this florid, excessive writing comes from such an unprepossessing, seemingly asexual woman.

Bianca
July 13, Venice, 2007

Going to bed that night, Bianca Fiore thinks about Giovanni. When she saw his name on the guest list, she wondered what connection he might have to the Evans clan—or to the bride's family. He is the most attractive man she's ever met. In her entire life. She felt the blood rush to her heart when she first heard his mellow, intelligent voice. She likes everything about him, his carriage, his manner of dress. His English is perfect.

She orders herself not to seem too enthusiastic or ask too many questions as if she were Barbara Walters conducting an interview. Take it easy, Bianca, you might scare him away, she keeps reminding herself. And he's an archaeologist too!

She wonders if she should tell him about her reason for going to France, sure that he'll understand the importance of the Vix Krater. Never having seen such an enormous bronze vessel from antiquity, she'd stood before it transfixed. Since then, whenever she has the chance, she drives to Châtillon-sur-Seine to have another look. "Ah, it's you again," the girl at the ticket counter comments when she walks through the door. She's never told anyone about her obsession with the Krater and the woman who was buried with it, not even Sergio Battisoni, her boss at the magazine. She worries that he might want her to write about its discovery in the tomb of *la Dame de Vix*, but she isn't ready to—at least while she's working for Sergio. Some day she would find enough time and have enough money to leave the magazine to do some serious research. She would determine how and why this great ceremonial vessel made its long journey from the south of Italy to a Celtic hilltop citadel overlooking the Seine, eventually to be buried in the grave of a woman in the sixth century B.C. Who was this woman, she often wonders, and what did she have to do with the Krater? Maybe she could write a saga about the Krater and its journey to Vix, but where in the world would she begin? In Southern Italy? She's never been south of Rome. Sure—it's time to go!

$$\Omega$$

She is out of bed at seven, has her cappuccino and cornetto brought up on a tray, and waits. Don't get your hopes up, she warns herself. At the stroke of nine, church bells clang in unison with the ringing phone. She lets it ring several times before answering.

"I was just about to give up," Giovanni says.

She thinks she detects a sense of relief in his voice.

"Oh—it's you!" she replies, intent on her new "I couldn't care less" approach.

"Good morning. Bianca. *Andiamo!* Let's have a coffee at Quadri."

Glancing at her watch, she thinks she'd better hurry if she intends to be sitting at Quadri at the very same minute of the very same hour the great Campanile collapsed before Nina Evan's eyes the morning of July 14th, 1902.

"It will take me about ten minutes." she says. Even though she's ready, she doesn't want to appear too anxious.

"I'll be waiting downstairs."

Before leaving the room, she finds her great grandmother Nina's gold earrings zipped in the hidden compartment at the bottom of her bulging hand-bag along with her diary that her mother has only recently discovered in a secret drawer of an old Venetian desk. She brought the earrings and the diary because she wants a part of Nina with her in Venice. Today is surely the day to wear the earrings, she thinks, as she clips them to her lobes.

When she strolls out of the lift, Giovanni seems surprised

to see her at precisely 9:15. And indeed, up until this moment, precision has not come easily to her.

Slow down, slow down, Bianca. He will probably see haste as over eagerness on your part, she tells herself.

Giovanni is wearing chinos and a fresh shirt that matches his Viking blue eyes. In the bright sunlight she can see that his hair is already on its way to gray. If she hadn't known he was Italian, she surely would have mistaken him for a Brit or an American. She drops her key in the box at the downstairs desk. The receptionist looks surprised when he sees them going out together.

Giovanni stops at a kiosk to buy the *Gazzettino*, the Venetian daily newspaper, glances at the headlines, rolls it up and jams it into his jacket pocket. As they continue their walk he is silent. Finally he inquires, "Tell me why you didn't like Venice when you were a child."

"It was mid July, hot and humid. And they were draining the canals. My stomach couldn't take the putrid odor. Because I kept throwing up, we moved out of the Gritti, and my parents booked us into the Quattro Lanterne over on the Lido. You must know the hotel?"

"Of course. Our family cabana was on the Excelsior beach—next to the Quattro's cabanas."

"I remember how I couldn't wait to check out the water. I took off my shoes and socks and waded around. Airplanes were skywriting and tossing out white balloons—compliments of Bel Paese cheese. Children jumped in to catch them as they floated down."

He laughs. "I used to be a champion balloon catcher."

She natters on out of nervousness. "When I was a child I used to find white balloons behind the bushes in Central Park. Once, when I tried blowing on one, my mother snatched it away and told me what a nasty, filthy thing it was and never

ever to pick up one again." She turns her eyes away, suddenly embarrassed by what she has so naively told him. She rustles around in her bag and pulls out her wallet to show him the photograph of her great grandmother. They stop in the middle of Campo San Maurizio while he studies it. "Did your great grandmother always dress this way?"

"Yes, in contrast to my late grandmother and my mother, typical country club matrons always dressed chicly and never without their three strands of cultured pearls. The day this photo was taken, Nina was wearing one of her full, ankle length Santa Fe skirts and her favorite gold earrings my grandmother told me she was hardly ever without. She left them to me. Yet I've never worn them until today because I've always been terrified of losing them."

She pulls her hair back from her face and unclips an earring. "Here, have a look. Made from a late Byzantine coin— eleventh century," she says, handing it to him.

He turns it over in his palm. "Beautiful. Mint condition too, and so skillfully mounted it hasn't been ruined. Tell me more about your beloved great grandmother."

She clips the coin back on her ear. "Although she was a painter, Nina sold very little of her work. A gallery in Paris gave her an exhibit in the early Fifties. Most of her paintings were burned when a fire destroyed her old house in Connecticut."

"Do you own any?" he asks, with what seems a great deal of interest.

"Yes—a tiny watercolor, about the size of a file card-of the Campanile. I wish it were with me to show you, but it's in my apartment in New York. My mother still has a few of Nina's large paintings, so if you're ever in Baltimore and would like to see them, I can ask Mom to show them to you."

He is silent as they walk through Via XXII Marzo, past a

window of Fortuny style pleated silk dresses, a spectrum of colors from whiter than white to an intense magenta, dark as blood. He waits patiently as she checks out the window display. From the corner of her eye she catches a glimpse of Frette, the luxury linen shop. Whenever she walks down Madison Avenue past Frette, she stops to look in the window at beds made up with opulent linens, 100% Egyptian cotton percale sheets cooler, smoother than the finest silk, bordered with sea foam blue or peach embroidery. Or beds heaped with lace-trimmed, weightless goose down pillows and rolls to tuck behind pampered necks. She is well aware that her aging foam rubber pillow crumbles like stale bread whenever she squishes it too hard, that she sleeps between slick, synthetic-smelling mostly polyester sheets that Luisa, her helper, buys for her on Houston Street, always trying to save Bianca's money.

Why, she ponders now, is there such a vast chasm between the way she lives and the way she yearns to live, between the way she looks and the way she longs to look?

Since the skies are blue, bright and cloudless, Quadri's tables and chairs are already set up for the usual weekend throngs, most of whom can't afford to spend the eight euros for a cup of coffee. Tourists are scattering birdseed to already overfed pigeons waddling and pecking in the Piazza. Although it is early in the day, guano stuck with feathers is spattered all around the *pavimento*. Her stomach does a turn.

Giovanni chooses the table. When they sit down, she turns her chair sideways so she'll have a good view of the Campanile, as well as of the bell-striking Moors over the entrance to the Merceria, the narrow shopping street that angles its way toward the Rialto Bridge. She surreptitiously checks both ears to make sure her earrings are still there.

When she was fourteen, her grandmother had given her Nina's bracelet of twisted gold chains, linked with seed pearls and dark blue enameled cylinder beads. She'd lost the bracelet a few days later and still reproaches herself for it.

The waiter takes their order for cappuccinos. She hopes Giovanni hasn't noticed that she keeps glancing nervously at her watch. By now it is almost 9:30 and she's suddenly sorry she hasn't come here alone. Now she'll have to share what should be a private moment with a stranger, however appealing, however interesting, and even with a family connection to Nina.

"I hope you'll forgive me if I read a few pages from Nina's Venetian journal while we sit here."

"Go right ahead. I have my newspaper, and besides, in a way, I feel as though Nina is part of my family history because she was my great-grandmother's friend."

"Of course—you have the photo you're going to show me." She fumbles around in her shoulder bag for the diary, sets it on the table and wonders what he's thinking as he watches her stroking its soft leather. She turns to the entry marked, Venice, 1902, excuses herself and begins to read.

Venice,
the 11th of July, 1902, my first visit to Venice

After a week in Venice, I, Nina Evans, who have always preferred painting to writing—the eye before the word—intend from this day on to keep a diary of my most private thoughts. Ever since Father passed away last year, Mama has been sad, yet at least here in Venice she seems more cheerful. But how miserable I have been, breathing in the evil stench seething up from dark canals. This morning as I looked out from my balcony across to Ca' Rezzonico, the palace where my favorite poet Mr. Browning once lived, I saw a filthy white wig tied with black ribbon afloat amidst the garbage. I was glad no one heard me gag.

On July the 9th we boarded the Orient Express in Paris and arrived for the Feast of the Redentore, just before the yearly spectacle Mama was determined not to miss. As we neared Venice, a storm blew in from the Alps, hailstones and rain pelting the windows of our compartment, nature's fitting welcome to this wet, dank place. When we stepped off the train at Santa Lucia Station, we were met by the Countess Bona Dea's major domo, all done up in full livery with gold and crimson epaulettes. I could tell that Mama was impressed. The Countess is her old school friend, Margaret Norville, who has a pretty daughter, my own age. We have already become friends.

At last, when the storm passed, surly porters, babbling in baffling Italian (the likes of which I had never heard at school), escorted us to the Countess' gondola. We drew the curtains of the felze to keep the mist from our clothes and hair and to give us privacy, two women traveling alone. The ancient Palazzo Bona Dea, where we are staying, leans over the Grand Canal across from Palazzo Barbaro, owned by the Curtis family, old friends of Father's. On arrival we found their gilt-edged calling cards. Mama fairly swooned with delight because Mrs. Curtis has invited us to dinner with Mr. Henry James, the famous writer.

Bianca smiles inwardly. Even though she never knew her, she sometimes feels she loves her great-grandmother even more than her grandmother. Maybe even more than her mother. She turns the page.

July 12, 1902

How homesick I am for my cozy dormer bedroom, with its wisteria vine wallpaper and broderie anglaise curtains crisscrossed against shiny windowpanes. On the Fourth of July, Father's family must have gathered for the annual clambake. I remember the vast lawns where I played croquet in my bare feet. Now, as I wriggle my toes, I can almost feel the stubby blades of grass tickling my soles. Here, behind the palazzo, there is a shady garden where grass grows rank and harbors furry black spiders and bugs that suck my blood, where lizards dart in and out of stone crevices so fast I wonder if I have really seen them.

Mama scolds me every day for not yet unpacking my watercolors and brushes. I have yet to under-stand why I do not, as she does, find Venice the most beautiful and challenging of cities to paint. With its rose-copper streaked sky and rare nimbus light that sends poets into rapture, its imposing monuments and decayed palaces, Venice should be the joy of every painter. Strangely, for me it is not.

Bianca looks up to find Giovanni gazing at her intensely. She blushed. "I'm being terribly rude," she says.

"No, you warned me. I'm just admiring your intensity. Please continue."

She turned back to her great-grandmother's journal.

Same day after dinner

This evening I wrapped my waist in a wide sky blue ribbon, then tied it into a big butterfly bow—not exact-ly a bustle, but at least a bit of commotion behind me as we made our evening stroll. I feel that in certain ways Mama does not like to see me growing up.

Tonight we dined on the terrace of the Hotel

Monaco e Canal Grande with the Countess Norville and the writer Gabriele d'Annunzio and his friend the actress, Signora Eleanora Duse. Duse's eyes have purplish crescent moons beneath them. Her voice is soft and low. Every now and then she would toss her head back and laugh at Signor d'Annunzio's witty remarks. But his eyes were always trying to pin mine to his. He made me so uncomfortable I could not enjoy the granzeola, spider crab picked out and served in its own round pink shell.

During dinner my mind wandered off as I listened to the harsh cries of gondolieri, the high tides lapping the deck. As I gazed across at the church, Santa Maria della Salute, I wondered how many hundreds of thousands of wood piles have been driven deep into the silt to support what looks to me like a giant wedding cake.

July13, 1902

This morning as Mama and I walked across toward the Hotel Danieli to meet the ladies from the Towson Reading Club who will discuss The Flame of Life, Signor d'Annunzio's scandalous new novel about Venice, I overheard the Countess Norville telling Mama that the book is about Mr. d'Annunzio and Miss Duse.

At last I feel normal. This afternoon we took tea at Florian's. While listening to arias from Rossini and Verdi, I opened my box of watercolors, unfolded my little easel and began to paint the tall brick Campanile that seems to me a sword thrusting high into the sky. Mama says my painting is charming, rather in the style of Mr. Childe Hassam, Grandfather's friend. Tomorrow I shall certainly return to paint the four horses above the portals..

July 14, 1902

After 8 o'clock Mass at San Marco. Another hot and humid day. I sit here writing. It is such a muggy morning, even my lightest batiste frock weighs heavy.

Now I sit at Quadri, writing and sipping strong black coffee with lots of sugar, for the first time enjoying the bitter beneath the sweet. Meanwhile, Mama is shopping in the Arcades, most likely purchasing embroidered sheets and lace tablecloths for my trousseau. How I wish that I could convince her that, at sixteen soon to be seventeen, I have no interest in marriage. But she persists in ordering fine linens wherever we go. If this makes her happy, then I am too.

Mama is taking so much time shopping. Pennants droop on the tall bronze flagpoles in front of Saint Mark's. There is not even the slightest breeze to unfurl them. I wait for the bronze Moor's hammer to strike the quarter hour. Now I shall put down my pen to play my favorite game. Supposing.

Bianca turns at least five blank pages before the writing continues.

Vienna,
September 14, 1902

The kind lady doctor asks me to re-read my diary. Then she asks me to try my hardest to remember what happened that day.

I seem to recall that I began, at that first strike of the hammer, to play my favorite game, Supposing.

Supposing, I imagined, that the four bronze horses poised above the front portal were to gallop off into the sky—alighting on the clock tower where the Moor, hammer in hand, strikes the time on the massive bell. Supposing...the horses circle Saint Mark's golden domes, flying over the flagpoles, higher, higher until they soar into the heavens circling the tall bell tower.

I remember staring at the Campanile, staring hard. Then, right before my eyes, I saw it curve like a huge red snake, as bricks, thousands of bricks, collapsed in clouds of pink dust. I can still hear the Campanile's bellow, the death cry of a huge, wounded dragon. What had I done to it?

I must have fainted. When I woke up, a man stood over me. Even though it was a warm July day, he wore a black silk cape, and, on his head, a wide-brimmed black slouch hat. But the strangest thing about him was that he had neither eyebrows nor lashes.

Vienna,
September 15, 1902

This morning my kind doctor advised me to take up my brushes again. "Paint the Campanile as you remember it after it collapsed on July 14, 1902, at exactly nine-fifty two in the morning," she urged me.

Now I shall pick up my brush and try to recreate that moment.

But I will never paint what I saw that day in Sicchia.

Although Bianca has read this entry before, she still feels goosebumps traveling along her arms. Nina was born in 1886, so she was only sixteen when she began to write in this diary. She must have penned this last entry in the Viennese hospital. Or maybe in some kind of sanitarium. And the watercolor of the collapsed Campanile she had painted at the doctor's urging—where is that painting now? She wonders if Mom has ever seen it. In her own little miniature painting, the Campanile is still standing. And who was the eerie-black caped man? And Nina's words, those mystifying words. *I shall...try to recreate that moment. But I will never paint what I saw that day in Sicchia.*

When she finishes reading she heaves a deep sigh and then hands the diary to Giovanni. "Look at this beautiful binding, how soft and supple it is."

He takes it from her and examines it with the painstaking care of a man long accustomed to handling fragile, timeworn objects. "They don't make leather goods like this any more," he says, as he gives it back to her. "Not in Venice, anyway. But there's a place in Naples where one can still get a diary like this."

"I'm glad you didn't ask to look inside," she says. Her comment doesn't appear to faze him.

"Bianca, was your great-grandfather, Nina's husband, an American?"

She feels she has to tell him the truth. "I only recently learned that Nina never had a husband. She bore her daughter, my grandmother, out of wedlock when she was very young," she says feeling her blood rush. "And then Nina never married, she... "

"She sounds like a very independent woman, a woman far ahead of her time. In those days it was a real stigma for a well-bred young woman to bear a child out of wedlock."

"My mother told me that her family and friends thought Nina was eccentric, but they loved her and tolerated her eccentricities. She was always full of energy and most people had a hard time keeping up with her. Right up until the time she died she never stopped traveling, learning. Just before I was born, she was killed in a plane crash over the Tamaklan. She was in her eighties. I sometimes try to imagine the stark fear she must have felt when the plane spun out of control. Whenever I allow myself to do so, it terrifies my heart." Her eyes are pooling with tears; she wipes them away with the back of her hands, then rustles around in her bag for a wad of tissue.

He covers one of her hands with one of his and, with the other, takes out a fresh white square from his pocket.

"Although I don't look like Nina in the slightest, I think part of me is very much like her. How I wish I'd inherited her golden looks—not to mention her spirit and originality. Her reckless courage." She heaves another long shuddery sigh and blots her eyes with the proffered handkerchief.

"How are you feeling at this moment?" he asks.

"Sad. As though there's something I must tend to, something she might have yearned for, something left undone. Unfinished business, I guess."

"Do you mean something you must complete for her? Or something you must discover about her?"

"Maybe both," she replies. Anxious to change the subject, she says, "Giovanni—tell me—how do you feel about American women?"

"I've always liked them. Their independence, their frankness. But then, you're not the first American woman I've known, Bianca." He smiles wryly.

A vision flashes into her mind of endless Miss America contestants, all with long blonde hair, big breasts bouncing, parading down a runway, followed by movie stars posing in their slinky dresses on a red carpet.

"The relationship with my American friend went nowhere. After she returned to California I threw myself into my work. Mostly in Apulia and Calabria where we'd made some important archaeological discoveries. I decided that I wanted to get out of architectural restoration and back to the field-back to the business I was trained for. Digging. I missed the blood, honest sweat and tears, the precise science of a dig—and the elation of discovery."

"Where are you working now?"

She catches him glancing down before he looks up right into her eyes.

"I prefer not to discuss my project. At least not yet."

He begins tapping the table nervously but perceptibly as he looks at her with critical—or are they amused—eyes?

Maybe she is boring him, irritating him, she thinks.

"The dig has been closed until spring. Right now I have other things on my mind. You know, Bianca, I've wanted to contact you ever since I read your first column. I was intrigued by what you'd written. Your writing reminds me of Gabriele d'Annunzio or one of the other nineteenth-century Italian writers."

She realizes she should reply to his compliment—if it is a compliment—but instead she checks her watch. It's 9:48. Four minutes to go. "I'd love to talk about my work later, but if you don't mind, I'd like to sit quietly for only a few moments to read and reflect on Nina's Venetian diary. It means so much to me." She stops, not wanting to say more about the Campanile.

"Of course! I would want you to. It gives me a chance to catch up on the local news." He pulls out part of a rolled-up *Gazzettino* from his jacket pocket, and as he turns to the Venetian local news page, she notices his porphyry signet ring engraved with a crenellated turret.

Now, in just a few minutes, it will be the very time when

one hundred and four years ago the Campanile collapsed. Her heart races.

"Only one more chime to let you know that it will soon be striking the hour," he says.

More tears well up as she imagines Nina sitting here at Quadri, in the summer of 1902, jarred out of tranquility and into terror as the bell tower collapsed. Now they watch as the Moors begin to toll the hour. Ten o'clock. After those few moments, she wipes her eyes.

Surely he could tell that it means so much to her: he had to have noticed how moved she was, but all he says is, "Come on, Bianca. Why don't we leave? My apartment is across the Canal, on Dorsoduro. I'd like to show it to you—and the photograph of Nina Evans and Rose Alba Bona Dea, our great grandmothers. We'll take the *traghetto* across."

She hesitates—but only for a moment.

He pays the bill, and they push their way against the weekend crowds to the dock next to the Gritti Palace Hotel and wait for the gondolier to ferry his passengers back from Dorsoduro to the hotel.

Giovanni pulls out some coins, hands them to the gondolier, and helps Bianca step into the boat. While she sits on the back bench, Giovanni stands tall and straight to balance the boat's center. "Venetian men rarely sit when they cross the Grand Canal on a *traghetto*. They don't consider it good manners."

The two oarsmen, one in the aft, one in the fore, back the boat out of the slip all the while chatting with Giovanni in Venetian dialect, all z's and x's to her ears. Reaching Dorsoduro, she stands, taking the gondolier's extended arm to help her step on to the wooden stairs leading up out of the water. Her foot slips on a mossy plank and then catches. She hears a gentle thud. She looks down to see one of Nina's gold earrings bounding off the boards and disappearing into the murky darkness of the Grand Canal. She raises her hand to her ear. Unable to move, unable to utter a sound, she stares into the water.

"What happened? Are you all right?" Giovanni grabs her.

"Nina's earring! Gone! Fell right to the bottom! Why, why did I ever wear them?" She fights the tears. "Why did I even bring them with me? I should have known better than to trust myself! I *lose* things."

The gondolier becomes impatient. "*I signori passeggieri* want to leave. Would you please step aside?" Giovanni leads her into the calle and puts his arm around her shoulder. She finally gets a grip on herself. "You mustn't blame yourself, Bianca! Don't despair. We can try to retrieve the earring. As soon as we get home, I'll call the shop in Mestre where I buy scuba equipment. They have a team of professional divers. We'll find someone to go down to search for it."

"What an optimist you are! With changing tides and passing boats, I should think the chances would be very slim." She unclips the other earring and zips it into the secret compartment of her purse, her only consolation being that she still has one. Maybe this is an omen that she should not become involved with Giovanni. She wonders what Nina would think of him, but more than that, what would she think of her?

Ω

He unlocks the wrought iron entry gate to the Palazzo Bona Dea. They walk into the dimly lighted *androne*, the palazzo's entry hall, with water access to the Grand Canal. A gondola rests high on a platform, like an altar. "It looks as though you're making an offering to Poseidon," Bianca says. "Maybe I ought to make one too so we can find my earring in his Adriatic."

He smiles. "These days we use the gondola ritually only in September, for the Regatta Storico. It's been at the *squero* over at San Trovaso being repaired and painted." As the elevator lifts them to the third floor, she enjoys his closeness, smells his spicy citrus cologne, and, in spite of the sadness of her loss, feels tremors where for a long time there have been none.

He opens the door. "Please make yourself comfortable."

Collapsing in an armchair, she feels rather shaky and weak. Yet she is able to take pleasure in the setting and the warm, jeweled sunlight spilling in from old stained glass windows facing the canal. The rooms are not so large, the ceilings not so high, as she knows they must be on the gilded, frescoed floors below, especially two floors below, on the *piano nobile*, the grandest, most formal *stanze* where Venetians receive their guests.

On one wall hangs a large portrait of a dark haired brooding woman.

Giovanni sees her studying the portrait. "She's Eleonora Duse, the famous Italian actress. One of her lovers was the writer Gabriele d'Annunzio. They used to keep company in a nearby palazzo."

"Nina writes about Duse and d'Annunzio in her diary!"

He nods. "They were very much a part of the early twentieth century Venetian scene." He picks up a phone book and says, "Please excuse me. I'll be back in a moment."

She takes a long, assessing look around the room. The library is furnished with early nineteenth century pale wood Beidermier furniture. A guitar case is propped against one wall. Two worn but comfortable Genovese velvet sofas are separated by a coffee table with a scagliola top, a silvan scene of Orpheus strumming his tortoise lyre surrounded by deer and cavorting nymphs.

Antique prints of Greek vases, some red figure, some black,

cover two walls from dado to ceiling. Her mind flies back to the black-figured images of Amazons fighting Greek hoplites painted on the ceramic *kylix* found with the Krater and *la Dame de Vix*. She knows that the subject of Amazon women fighting armed soldiers was popular around the area of the Black Sea, especially with the Scythians.

"We're in luck!" Giovanni announces when he returns. "The divers are ready to search around eleven o'clock tonight. The timing couldn't be better—a full moon but no more storms predicted so there shouldn't be a lot of movement in the water." He hands her a fragile Venetian glass of fizzy San Pellegrino.

She takes a long swallow. "Do you think there's any chance they'll find it?"

"Fifty-fifty. Definitely worth the try."

"How much do they charge?"

"Three hundred euros."

"I'd expected it to be about that much. Even if they don't find it, we will have tried."

"And you'll always remember the experience."

She nods. "Yes—an experience worthy of Nina's earring."

"Bianca, I have a four o'clock meeting in Padua, but I'll be back after dinner. Obviously I won't be going to the pre-nuptial dinner tonight."

"Neither will I."

"Why don't I pick you up at ten forty-five. We'll walk over to watch the divers."

She hesitates, then starts to get up.

"Please…I didn't mean for you to rush off. I still have a little time. May I offer you some Pinot Grigio or an aperitivo? Or maybe a vodka? An unusual brand given to me by a Ukrainian colleague. You'll like it, come on—it will do you some good after the shock you've had."

"I usually don't drink hard liquor, but I'd like to try the

vodka, thanks. I should be leaving fairly soon. I have a lunch date at...at Harry's Bar." Harry's Bar is the only restaurant that comes to mind. She hopes he didn't notice her hesitation. It always bothers her to lie, even to protect herself.

She quickly changes the subject. "Are those prints of Greek vases by Sir William Hamilton?" she asks, knowing full well that they are.

He hands her a small *latticino* glass of vodka. "Yes—my grandfather pulled apart a copy of Hamilton's *Recueils des Vases Etrusques* and had the plates framed. I would never have done such a thing myself, but I must admit I enjoy having these on the walls. My grandfather—and my father, also an archaeologist, specialized in Greek ceramics. They dug with the University of Pennsylvania when they searched for the lost city of fabled Sybaris—about forty years ago."

"Sybaris! My boss is always talking about Sybaris. Do ancient ceramics interest you as well?" Why has she asked such a dumb question when she knows he knows she knows the answer?

"Of course. Every archaeologist of Southern Italy has to know Greek pots. But more than that, I'm working on a theory about the rapid change from black-figure to red-figure pottery in the Hellenic world. It took place around 500 B.C., perhaps a bit earlier. I've always wondered what brought about this sudden stylistic change."

"What are your conclusions?" Now she really is curious.

"Let's say I have a revolutionary hunch, but it's too long, too complicated for now."

"Can you at least tell me whereabouts in Southern Italy you're digging?" She tries to avoid his eyes realizing that she's beginning to sound like a TV interviewer.

"My secret—at least for the time being," he replies, pouring himself another drink.

When he smiles, she notices that the corners of his lips turn up, like the mysterious smile of a Greek kouros.

Her mind starts working on a scenario. She wonders if he might be involved with the Mafia, trading in illegally unearthed treasures. *The Art Newspaper* frequently publishes articles about antiquities smuggling in Italy. Sergio has a fit when he reads about Italians dealing in purloined patrimony. She has to listen to him yell and curse whenever he hears about museums accused of buying stolen objects with fake provenances.

"You know, Bianca, you have such an incredible faculty to envision the past lives of objects and their ritual uses. Has anyone ever told you that you have a bicameral mind?"

"What's in heaven's name is a bicameral mind?"

"I took a course from Julian Jaynes when I was at Princeton. He believes that in ancient times people followed the instructions of inner voices in their heads and had visions from a more highly developed right brain. These hallucinations were attributed to ancestors, chiefs, or kings. Eventually they were attributed to gods. Jaynes calls the highly developed right brain the 'bicameral mind.' In essence, you have a highly developed right brain. You have a real gift."

"Have you ever thought that this so-called bicameral mind of mine might be tangled up with a vivid, lurid—even pathological—imagination?"

"What is imagination then if it isn't a journey into the depths of the unconscious to encounter ancestral memory? Archaeology is a science, but I'm convinced there's room for intuition, another function of the right brain. I often envy Schliemann, who allowed himself to be guided by intuition. But Schliemann also had a beautiful and intelligent Greek wife, as well as Homer and the *Iliad* and the *Odyssey*, to guide him. Unfortunately, I don't have a saga or epic poem to guide me—not to mention a beautiful Greek wife."

She turns her eyes away from his; she gets the message.

As they are preparing to leave, Giovanni asks, "Bianca, did your grandmother ever speak about a woman named Margaret Norville?"

"Margaret Norville? No—I don't recall that she ever spoke of her-but here's another coincidence."

"Coincidence?"

"I'd guess you'd call it that. Her name is mentioned in the diary I showed you." She pulls it out from her shoulder bag. "Nina wrote that her mother and Margaret Norville had gone to school together in Maryland. After Margaret Norville was windowed, Nina and her mother travelled to Venice. Nina was sixteen years old."

He smiles, takes her hand and holds it gently. "Let me explain then. During the summer of 1902, Nina's mother, Signora Evans, rented a floor in this palazzo." He pronounces the words slowly, deliberately, watching their effect on her. "She rented it from Margaret Norville, the Contessa Bona Dea, who was my great-great-grandmother. You are at this very moment sitting in Palazzo Bona Dea. Margaret never remarried but had a lover, an Italian writer, a would-be Gabriele d'Annunzio."

"You're telling me that this is exactly where my great-grandmother Nina stayed during that visit in 1902? When did you learn all this?"

"As a child, I heard it from Margaret Norville's daughter, Rose Alba Bona Dea. It was Rose Alba who was the childhood friend of Nina Evans, your great-grandmother. Even when I was a young boy, she'd tell me about the young Nina Evans from Baltimore, a real American beauty with long golden hair and sapphire eyes, who'd come to stay in the Palazzo—right at the beginning of the twentieth century. Yes—she was your great-grandmother, Nina Evans," he emphasized,

He picks up a silver framed photograph from the piano

and hands it to her. Here is my great-grandmother, Rose Alba, with her arm around Nina." She studies the photo, so moved she instinctively leans toward him, eager to embrace the man who is a descendant of Nina's childhood friend. As she's about to reach out, he clasps both her hands in his; she feels him pull away slightly. She would much rather have hugged him and kissed him on both cheeks as though he were a long lost relative.

"Earlier you mentioned that Nina had a daughter out of wedlock."

She nods. "My grandmother only revealed her illegitimacy a few years ago, when I began to show an interest in family genealogy. She told me there was a scandal about Nina getting pregnant soon after she returned from Italy, then refusing to marry the tall, dark, handsome Baltimore ne'er-do-well womanizer who was the baby's father. Her mother took her to the family home in Vermont where my grandmother was born in June, 1903. Not too long after, they moved to Santa Fe and never returned. Unfortunately I've never learned the father's name. It's been a family secret for three generations. My grandmother eventually returned to Baltimore where she met my grandfather. And because my Dad was a Navy Captain who taught at Annapolis, we lived there until he retired."

They talk about their families until Giovanni checks his watch. Obviously he doesn't wish to be late for his lunch date, and she wants to see the exhibit at Palazzo Grassi. Giovanni is sorry he can't accompany her; at least that's what he tells her. "I'll come by the hotel around ten-forty-five. We'll walk together to the *pontile* to search for lost gold."

Giovanni
July 14, Venice, 2007

That night he arrives at the Hotel Desdemona precisely when he said he would. The moon is full, the sky clear and star-strewn. Lights shine from the Palazzo Barbaro on the San Marco side of the Grand Canal, making the water gleam. He takes her arm as they head for the *traghetto* landing.

When they reach the *pontile*, they find the divers testing their equipment and batteries for the lamps' high beams that will shine light at the bottom of the canal. The divers are slight and skinny, shiny in their black wet-suits and wearing bug-eyed goggles, like nightmare creatures painted by Hieronymus Bosch.

Giovanni speaks to them in Venetian dialect. They tell him they plan to dive in one at a time, each submersion being ten minutes. The older man will go down the ladder first. He turns to Bianca. "Signora, please—can you give us a description of the earrin"

"Better to show you." Bianca retrieves the remaining earring and hands it to him.

"*Va bene*—now at least I know what I'm looking for. Okay-let's time it, Raffaello! It's exactly twenty to eleven."

The younger diver sets his watch, then pauses to look into the water—making the sign of the cross and murmuring a prayer to San Antonio, patron saint of lost objects. Only then does he back down into the blackness of the Grand Canal.

"*Buona fortuna,*" Giovanni shouts as the diver's head breaks the dark surface.

A few moments later a *vaporetto* passes stealthily, sending silent ripples in its wake as it sidles up to the Salute's *pontile*.

Seven minutes pass. To Giovanni it seems like an hour. If the divers haven't found it by now, he fears that the coin will be lost forever.

Bianca remains silent as the divers make their search with underwater spot lights. He wonders what's going on in her mind, she seems so far away.

"Remember, Bianca, that Venice was once essentially Byzantium. Did you ever think that your coin might have been in the treasury of an early doge? From my work I know that many of these palaces around us still have architectural elements from the 11th century when your coin was struck. If the divers don't find your earring, you've given a gift, an offering, to the Adriatic."

Before she has time to respond, the younger diver surfaces. "*L'ho trovato*," he shouts, as though he was used to performing a ceremony of miracles every night. He scrambles up the ladder, unzips his pouch, then holds up the shiny gold coin as though it were a Communion wafer. "*Ecco, Signora*," he says as he hands it to her. "Your *orecchino prezioso* from the mud of the *Canale Grande*, now cleansed by the sea. Tonight was your lucky moon!"

She presses the earring to her lips, then zips it into the compartment of her handbag. "I'm not taking any more chances," she declares, as she slips the straps over her shoulder, hugging the bag against her body.

A crowd has gathered around the pontile. "*Bravissimi!*" they shout. Bianca throws her arms around the slippery black-masked phantoms. "Grazie mille, grazie infinite. What does it look like down there?"

"Mussels and mud. And bottles. Lots of bottles, mostly broken. They've probably been tossing them over these balconies for centuries. Your earring gleamed like a lighthouse beacon in the mud."

Giovanni pulls out his wallet and starts to pay the divers.

"No—don't please—that's very generous of you—but paying them is my responsibility." She gives them 300 euros plus.

The divers seem almost apologetic for accepting it and refuse the tip, but she insists. "You must take it. This is the best money I've ever spent in my entire life. And I'll be grateful to you both for the rest of it."

Giovanni takes her arm and they cross the bridge, heading straight for the hotel. They say their goodnights under the glass canopy of the entrance. He wants to kiss her cheek, at least like a brother, but holds himself back. He senses she isn't in the least attracted to him—nor is he to her.

Instead he finds himself saying, "Bianca, one of these days you should consider coming with me to the dig. You might enjoy having a look at our excavation."

Bianca

Back in her room, she flops on the bed, reliving every moment of the earring episode. Then her mind turns to tomorrow's wedding. She hadn't wanted to come. She doesn't even know her cousin well—they haven't seen each other in years. But there was no excuse since she'd already been in London for the annual board meeting of the magazine, and her aunt, the groom's mother, knew it. Besides, her mother would have been embarrassed and disappointed if Bianca didn't attend in her place, and, since Mom had recently had back surgery, Bianca felt committed to represent Nina's part of the Evans family. So always the dutiful daughter, here she is alone, but not quite as miserable as she thought she'd be. At least she's met Giovanni, although she chides herself for thinking about him too much. *Don't set yourself up for heartache, Bianca.*

Fretting about both the wedding and Giovanni keeps her from sleeping. So she does something she seldom does—gets up to find her Halcyon sleeping pills from Zitomer's. Whenever she's jet lagged, they always give her six good hours of sleep. There will be plenty of time in the morning to finish the piece she'd meant to hand in to Sergio. Then she'll go straight to the beauty spa for the ten o'clock appointment the concierge made for her for the works—hair, skin, face, nails—and make up.

Weddings are not the happiest of events for Bianca. Indeed, she dreads them. She's been going to so many lately, mostly cousins from her extensive Roman Catholic family in Maryland. The Evans clan is very much like, but not as famous as, Maryland's Carrolls of Carrollton. Her older brother who lives in California will carry on the Evans side and so will his sons. This makes her mother happy because she senses that her daughter, at the rate she's going, will never have children.

Ω

She wakes up with a jolt and leaps out of bed. It's 1:45! How could she have slept through the clanging bells of La Salute! There go all her good intentions about looking her best. She's done herself in—sabotaged herself. She should have known better than to take the damn Halcyon. She rushes down to La Bellezza, the beauty spa only a few steps away in the *calle*. "Saturday closing 1 PM" says the sign. No time to find another place and no time for panic. She runs back to the hotel, shampoos her long, thick hair and wraps it in a towel. What a stroke of luck to have the wall dryer work! Her travel dryer burned out in London, and she hasn't had time to buy another.

Holding the dryer with her left hand, she tries to apply makeup with her right. She never wears much makeup, and today she'd intended to go all out, but now there's time for only a slap dash job. Her hair is still damp when she pulls on her bra and panties. She grabs a pashmina from her suitcase—it looks like rain today—and her beat up raincoat won't work over the dark green chiffon dress, her mother's choice. Since walking is faster than taking the *vaporetto*, she pushes her way through the throngs toward San Pietro di Castello and arrives just as the wedding gondola is being moored at the *fondamenta*.

Ω

The bride's father is waiting while his daughter adjusts her veil. When he takes her arm to escort her to the great portal, the crowd cheers: "*Che bella sposa! Buona fortuna!*" Bianca watches as the maid of honor, dressed in lavender blue organza, adjusts the bride's train and drops the tulle veil over her face. Bianca is relieved that there isn't time to feel sorry for herself. She rushes in to find a place in the back row. The church is packed, it seems, with the entire population of Venice. Since there are few pews in San Pietro, folding chairs have been set up from the majestic entry portal almost all the way to the altar. Here the invited guests will find their places. She catches a glimpse of Giovanni sitting in one of the front pews on the bride's side. Even though the invitation stated that there would be special front row seats saved for family and friends of the bride and groom, there's no way she's going to walk down the aisle alone to claim one.

It's quite a while since she's been to Mass. She takes a deep sigh, releasing her feelings of pent-up guilt. As she sits there. admiring the beauty of San Pietro, once the cathedral of Venice, her mind keeps flashing back to Nina and her diary, to the image of her earring gleaming in the black mud of the Grand Canal. She gives prayers of thanks to the Virgin Mary and to St. Anthony of Padua, the saint who sometimes helps her find lost objects.

Everyone stands as the chords from the immense pipe organ boom out the wedding march. The bride and groom move slowly to the gilt throne-like chairs covered in brocade the deep crimson of crushed pomegranates. Then the joining together of these two people, these two souls, begins. Bianca wonders how they found each other. Her mother insisted that it wasn't an arranged marriage. Was it just chance or was it destiny? She prefers to think that it was destiny, but then, what is the difference between them?

When the ceremony is over, the bride and groom, all radiant smiles, walk down the aisle to the joyful flutes and trumpets of the Venetian *Aria da Festa*. The crowd follows to the tree-shaded grass *campo* to hug and kiss the newlyweds and shower them with paper confetti. Not wanting Giovanni to feel that he has to have her in tow, or feel responsible for her because their great grandmothers had been close, Bianca dashes out of the church and makes her own way through the narrow *calle* to the Hotel Danieli.

Ω

She is one of the first guests to arrive. At the entrance to the dining room a table is set with tiny *ecru* envelopes, guests' names arranged in alphabetical order. In every envelope is a table number. "And there are also place cards—so no wives and husbands sit next to each other," comments the woman who introduces herself as the wedding consultant. *Wedding consultants even in Italy!* She peeks through the not-quite closed doors of the elegantly decorated dining room. All the tables are centered with tall glass cylinders filled with long stemmed white roses and cloyingly fragrant Casablanca lilies. She's sure she'll be badly seated—probably tucked away in some dark corner. She couldn't be so lucky as to have Giovanni by her side or, at the very least, seated at the same table.

Wandering the reception room with a glass of prosecco, she looks in vain for someone who might be interesting to talk to, or even better, someone who might find her interesting. Bianca has long been aware of her insecurities, but speaking up isn't one of them. Twice she makes an attempt at introducing herself and twice she's dismissed with a nod and a *noli mi tangere* glance. Across the room Giovanni is chatting with some attractive people, one elegant young woman in particular. Bianca turns her back on the group, knowing that she has lately developed the bad habit of staring and she doesn't want to make him feel uncomfortable.

Because the bride, groom and the bridal party are having their official photos taken, the reception goes on far too long. She sits out the wait in the corner of the adjacent lounge.

When dinner is finally announced and the dining room portals thrown open, she finds her table—not a bad table—in fact it's nicely placed not far from the newlyweds, and not too far from Giovanni. At least he's in plain view. The man on her right, probably in his late fifties, is a Venetian who cultivates a fish farm so they mostly talked fish and *acqua alta*. He is vehemently against plans for the construction of the MOSES project which would prevent high tides from flooding the city. Not good for the balance of nature in the lagoon, he tells her, which she understands to mean, not good for his fish farms. On her left is another Venetian, a cousin of the bride, who lets her know within the first few minutes of conversation that he is descended from a Doge and his family is listed in the *Libro d'Oro*. His eyes keep darting around the room as she makes an attempt at conversation, but she gives up. It's hopeless.

The typically multi-coursed, marathon Venetian wedding dinner takes up an entire page of the menu. The feast begins with antipasto, then asparagus risotto, *branzino* with artichoke sauce, thin slices of roast veal with vegetables followed by *salatina*, all grown on the island of Torcello. Just before the dancing is to begin, a squad of waiters wheels around a silk-festooned chariot centered with a seven-tiered rum custard and whipped cream wedding cake. The cake is so delicious it makes up for the boring company. When she tells the waiter how much she enjoyed it, he returns with another even larger piece which she greedily and guiltlessly polishes off.

The orchestra, imported from Naples, plays all the favorite romantic songs—the theme from *Summertime, Anima e Cuore, Luna Rossa*. After the bride and groom's dance, their guests join them on the dance floor and, almost at the same instant, Bianca's dinner partners leap up to table hop. Rather than sit alone, she leaves for the ladies' room. At least she can comb her hair, and as she does, she tries not to look at herself too critically in the mirror she can't avoid. Her hair is clean and lustrous and, despite not having a major makeup job, she thinks she doesn't look so bad, after all—pink lipstick and blush-on help—and the mascara makes her eyes sparkle.

She considers not returning to the dining room but then, on the way back, she hears Giovanni's voice behind her.

"Bianca, would you do me the honor of a dance?" he says gallantly. She doesn't tell him that she hardly ever dances, and then only at company parties, although she loves all kinds of music. Her heart pounds as he leads her to the crowded floor. The woman soloist is singing *Al di la*—"the world beyond"— she feels the tension leave her body as his arm goes around her, even though he keeps her at a slight distance.

Afterwards, they return to the still deserted table and sit down to drink a prosecco together, mostly talking about music they like—or dislike.

"I enjoy singing old Neapolitan songs with my guitar," he says. "My friends and family usually ask me to play and sing at weddings, but they didn't this time. What a relief!"

She isn't sure he means what he says.

"I'd love to hear you sing sometime. I noticed you had a guitar in your *salone*."

"I'm rarely without it. Now—when do you leave Venice?"

"I have a reservation for New York on the late afternoon flight from Malpensa. I plan to leave Venice on an early train to give me enough time to get to the airport without too much worrying."

"My car is at the Piazzale Roma Parking garage. Why don't I drive you to Milan? I have an appointment there on Monday morning."

"That's very kind of you." She hesitates for a moment. "A ride to the airport *would* make things so much easier."

From out of nowhere a young man appears brandishing a

guitar. "So you thought you were going to get away without singing, Giovanni," he calls out, holding the instrument aloft for all to see. Cheers and enthusiastic applause.

She senses that Giovanni knows he has no choice. "Carlo! How the hell did you manage to get my guitar, I'd like to know."

"Graziella, your cleaning lady. She hopes you're won't be too angry with her. Please don't be."

Giovanni laughs, "Graziella is a good soul and means well."

As he makes his way up to the orchestra stage, the room becomes quiet. "I'm not going to begin with my usual *canzone Napolitane*. Instead I'll sing *'Ah Camminare,'* written for a Broadway musical from the Sixties. I sing it in honor of Jonathan and my dear cousin, Allegra, his beautiful and accomplished wife. Allegra's grandfather, who was a singer in the cast, had a place in Greenwich Village, where the newly-weds will live. I hope that when Allegra and Jonathan take an evening stroll in the Village, they'll remember these lyrics. The name of the musical is"-a long pause—*"Bravo Giovanni."*

Guests clap and cheer. "Bravo! Bravo Giovanni!"

He begins to sing in a husky Neapolitan way, the kind of voice Bianca wouldn't have expected but she catches most of the words.

> *Di sera, a camminar'*
> *Con tanto amor*
> *Con tanto amor e canta*
> *Di sera a camminar'*
> *O mio tesor*
> *O piccolo fiore,*
> *E che fa*
> *Ah camminar'*
> *Con tanto amor,*

E canta
Di sera a camminar'
O mio tesor
O piccolo fiore
E che fa?
E la passione mio e un sogno d'oro
Non so perche
Quando con te....ah camminare.

Lots of applause, guests blotting their eyes at the tender, appropriate lyrics.

Bianca convinces herself that Giovanni looked straight into her eyes when he sang *"o mio tesor, o piccolo fiore e che fa?"* As if to say Bianca Fiore, this song is also for you, *piccolo fiore, little flower.* Or is it just her rampant, romantic imagination working overtime?

Then he goes on to sing some classic Neapolitan songs much to the delight of the guests, Italian and American. What a different Giovanni from the formal and sometimes distant Giovanni she's been with these past two days.

After wishing Allegra and Jonathan many years of happiness, it's time to leave. She reaches for the confetti placed at her table setting—a little bouquet of white sugared almonds wrapped in white tulle and tied together with a satin ribbon. As she stands to leave, a hefty older woman at the next table shouts, "Tarantella! Tarantella!"

The Neapolitan band strikes up *C'e la luna mezz'o mare.*

C'e la luna mezz'o mare
Mamma mia me maritari,
Figghia mia, a cu te dari
Mamma mia pensaci tu
There's a moon above the sea,
Mama mia, I want to marry,

Daughter of mine, who's your choice?
Mama mia, my choice is yours!
C'e la luna mezz'o mare.

She's watched guests dancing this tarantella at Italian-American weddings in New York, along with *Hava Nagila* and the inevitable conga lines. Tonight even the most sophisticated guests jump up—hopping around ridiculously, she thinks. Giovanni doesn't ask her to join in and she's relieved. She knows herself well enough to realize that she would be two left feet and gangly, dangling arms. Yet there's something about the music that strikes a chord within, stirring up something inside her. She wonders why, she's not even Italian!

Then he surprises her by insisting he walk back with her to the Hotel Desdemona. This time, after they say their good nights and *ci vediamo domani*, he kisses her on the cheek as if she were his sister.

Giovanni
July 16, 2007

At ten o'clock on Sunday morning he's waiting at the parking garage where he picked up his Range Rover packed full of equipment and archeological paraphernalia. Bianca arrives wearing an ill-fitting charcoal gray trouser suit, obviously not the Armani it pretends to be, but more like the kind of outfit worn by American nuns. It does nothing for her face.

"Bianca, *Bianca, Basta grigio.*" He wants to tell her, "With your looks, your coloring, you should stay away from that shade of gray."

They hit the road and, by the time they drive past Bergamo, he hears his stomach growl. The thought of a warm *piadini* stuffed with melted mozzarella and ham makes his mouth water. "Let's stop at the next Autogrill and get something to eat."

She's silent as they make their way through the Veneto. Finally she speaks. "I've been thinking about it all morning— about visiting your dig. I might even be of some help to you. I'm prepared to give it a try—but the best way for me is not to have any pre-conceived ideas or half-formed images of what might be helpful to you. Before I write my articles for *Eyes and Soul*, I incubate visions. Sometimes I even tie a scarf tight around a mask because my visions are stronger without even a sliver of light. In total darkness I see colors, shapes, tiny details. Sometimes the pictures are so detailed, so vivid, I can almost reach out and touch them. It's like having a link to the past—you might say it's like virtual reality in my head."

"Do you enjoy doing this? Or do you do it because it helps you with your work at the magazine?"

"Both. I like escaping life by placing myself in a distant world. What isn't in front of my eyes is sometimes more real than what is. Within me I hope to find what it is I need to know for my work and for whatever else I write."

By one, they are famished and stop at an Autogrill where they have a picnic in the vehicle, munching hot-off-the-grill *panini* and gulping down light beer. Giovanni buys two Magnum bars-thick, dark chocolate coating rich vanilla ice cream. Although last night her blood sugar had reached a high and then dropped very low after a double portion of wedding cake, when he asks if she'd like a bar, she replies, "Sure, why not?"

Then she steers the conversation to Sybaris. "Is your dig anywhere around there? You mentioned that your father dug with the University of Pennsylvania team when they discovered the exact site of the vanished city. I must admit that the suspense is killing me. Can't you tell me now just a little about your recent finds?"

"I'll be happy to. We have at least an hour before we arrive at Milan airport—plenty of time. So sit back and make yourself comfortable—but please don't fall asleep on me."

"I'll sit back prepared to be enthralled," she says, knowing full well she will be.

He begins. "During the summer I keep my boat at the marina of Sybaris. It was only a couple of weeks ago—in fact, June 29, the Feast of San Pietro and San Paolo—when I sailed into a little cove, not far from the mouth of the River Crati. I'd always noticed in the distance a strange looking hillock rising above a flat terrain, and that day I finally decided the time had come to satisfy my curiosity. But when I anchored my boat and went ashore, I was disappointed to find that the mound wasn't an ancient tumulus, but a dump for local trash—rusty car parts, heaps of plastic olive oil containers—now mostly grown over with dune grasses.

"The countryside beyond seemed so peaceful. I remember

white longhorn cattle grazing, the hum of cicadas in the hot, still afternoon. I was thirsty but I wasn't quite ready to get back to my boat. Besides, a kilometer or so away, I could see the rise of another hill, this one crowned by tall cypresses and umbrella pines, partially obscuring what appeared to be a habitation. I trudged up the unpaved road toward the trees and finally came to high, stone, ivy-covered walls surrounding an old dwelling. A typical *masseria*, a fortified farm. I pushed the half open gate and looked at the house. Rather large it seemed to me for a house of a *contadino*. The windows were shuttered tight, and it seemed as though the place might be unoccupied. By then my throat was parched so I walked around looking for a water pump or a well. As I passed an old barn, I noticed that it was still attached to the house. The door being slightly ajar, I pushed it open and looked down into a sort of cellar, what we call a *magazzino*. There were deep steps leading to a storage room crammed with empty wine barrels, rakes, shovels. But when I aimed my flashlight across to the opposite wall, I couldn't believe what I was seeing. I thought I might be hallucinating from heat and thirst. I moved closer to have a look.

"I don't know how long I stayed there, gazing at that wall. Finally I climbed back up to the house looking for someone who might tell me more about what I'd seen. I tried the door. Locked. I knocked, banged, yelled. Finally the door opened. An old woman peered out. She didn't seem unfriendly, only a bit frightened. She offered me a glass of water. I thanked her and asked about what was on the wall. She was upset that I'd seen it and begged me not to tell anyone. I promised her I wouldn't, assuming that she'd lived in the house for a long time. But then she told me that she'd moved here from Taranto only about six months ago. Her son is the owner of an oil refining business. He wanted a *masseria* out in the country—so he and his wife bought this place from a *contadino*.

Her son, who enjoys working with his hands, intended to restore it slowly, even though he could well afford to do otherwise. So the old woman became the custodian of the new property, and her son and his wife, who still live in Taranto, drive down almost every weekend to work on their project.

"I must have an honest face because, when I asked the woman if what I had seen on the walls had always been there, she relented and told me more. It seems that when they began restoration, her son noticed the walls of that part of the house were very thick—almost five feet. He was curious. He began to hack away some of the stones to use for an exterior retaining wall. When he'd hauled away about two feet of masonry, he saw that there was a separate double wall behind-the wall of another building. A vacuum had been created between the two buildings. That meant that there was no air, no light, much less moisture, so that what was on that wall had been fairly well preserved.

"I asked the woman if her son had called the authorities of the *Belle Arti*. 'Oh no,' she reassured me—'the *sopritendenza di monumenti* might very well have made us leave the house. That always happens to people when they find things on their property-they take it away from you.' Then she told me, '*Per carità!*—swear to me that you won't tell anyone about this. If you do, I'll put the *malocchio*, the curse of *la Tarantina's* evil eye, on you.' She raised her fingers and made the sign in my face. I must admit that I'm enough of a superstitious southerner that I took this seriously. Since then I've been conflicted by my allegiance to the *soprintendente*—and my promise to Concetta, the old woman, whom I've come to know and like. And there are other reasons—my own—for not wanting this to get into the newspapers. Not yet, anyway.

"But you haven't told me what was on that wall."

"Because you write about objects and ritual you of all people will be intrigued by my discovery. But I won't tell you what it's about; I'd like you to come see it for yourself."

"It will be a long time from now, Giovanni, if ever. With my various deadlines I don't know when I'll have the time to return to Italy. Someday I'd very much like to see your find—and also to visit the excavations at Sybaris."

"As soon as you're ready, I promise to drop everything to drive you there." And braving it for the first time, he impulsively puts his arm around her. "I'll most likely be coming to the antiquities auctions in early December. We could get together then and talk about a trip to Sybaris."

"Giovanni—you've been so kind, so caring--but there's something else going on between us that I don't understand."

He pulls his arm away gently. From the moment he'd set eyes on Bianca Evans Caldwell, he knew there could never be anything romantic between them. No. It would never happen—he'd never let it happen. Better to set things straight right away. After a long moment he says brusquely, "I don't know what you're talking about." He needs to let her know that she shouldn't be taking his invitation to Sybaris, or to anywhere else, as an invitation to bed.

Bianca

Because the plane is late, Bianca prefers to wait a while before going through security. As they stroll through the airport shops, she stops to admire racks strung with silk designer scarves. She points to a Gianni Versace foulard, a silk-screened pattern of his famous Medusa logo.

"I like this one," she says, pulling the bag from her shoulder ready to take out her wallet.

"I like it too," he responds, untying the scarf from the rack. "This will be a present from me."

"A present for me?" She is genuinely surprised.

"Of course for you—to remind you of...Venice." He feels a little guilty for having spoken so sharply to her earlier. After paying for the scarf, he wraps it around her neck and ties it loosely under her chin. The earth tones light up her face, taking the edge off her pallor. "There's a mirror behind you. Look at yourself. See how becoming it is."

"I don't need a mirror. Thank you, Giovanni, It will be a precious possession—a remembrance of the Evans-Bona Dea weekend in Venice. How happy I am that I didn't go straight back to New York after the meeting. I was tempted not to go to the wedding, but something inside urged me on."

"My own story is the same. I was obliged to go," he says, taking her hand. "I almost canceled with an excuse that I would be out of the country, but for me there was simply no excuse."

"We were destined to meet one another—to become friends. I don't want to leave without saying I'm sorry about what I told you this afternoon. I feel that my remark might have put you off."

"What was it you said?" he questions, as though he's forgotten.

"I told you that there was something between us that I couldn't understand." Her eyes are dark pools. When she turns her head, he sees a glistening tear trail on her cheek.

"I may have reacted too strongly," he replies, trying to soften the blow a little. It has never been easy for him to reject women—and he has rejected plenty.

She begins to wipe away her tears with the border of the scarf, then she hastily uses the back of her hand instead. At that moment the loudspeaker blares out the New York boarding. She blinks back more tears and puts her hand on his arm. "Goodbye, Giovanni."

He feels those old pangs of separation—even with this plain woman. Worse yet, he can't bear to see her cry. He remembers his mother crying when he was a little boy, being frightened by her tears, by his helplessness to comfort her.

They say their goodbyes at the gate and promise each other to keep in touch. She kisses his right cheek, his left, then his right cheek once again. He wonders why she kissed him three times. Russian style.

Bianca

She's lucky the plane to New York is half empty. She pushes up the dividers allowing her to stretch out across three seats. With her safety belt fastened securely, her head resting on three pillows, she shuts her eyes tight vowing to wipe out those visions that keep haunting the caverns of her mind—but to no avail. *Blood behind the black curtain. Slaughtered goats. A man clutching a club. A cloven hoof held high.*

She writhes in her seat, opens her eyes, and tries to talk herself back to calmness.

You're okay. Take it easy. Don't worry. You're on the plane. But her heart keeps pounding double time.

When she closes her eyes again, the vision has vanished. She sees herself standing inside her own head. She hears herself breathing in, letting it all out, hoping, praying that the frightful images will never return. They are dangerous visions, visions she has no business having. Maybe the nuns were right. Where inside her is all this darkness coming from? But, no. She is no longer the one summoning the visions: now the horrible phantoms are seeking her out.

The flight attendant interrupts. "What can I serve you? We're offering a very nice red, a Burgundy from the Côte d'Or. Our white is a Chablis."

She starts suddenly. "Thank you! May I please have the Burgundy." *How come, Bianca? You rarely drink red wine.*

She pays the flight attendant and pours herself a glass from the bottle, then takes a sip that tastes of black raspberries and passion fruit. She tries leafing through the pages of a home decorating magazine, *How to Display Your Collectibles*, relieved to be engrossed in something normal and safe. She begins to muse about how she might furnish her apartment on the cheap. The way it looks now there's no way she could ever invite Giovanni to drop by for a drink. He probably imagines that she lives among a collection of rare, exotic objects, the kind she writes about for *Eyes and Soul*. If only there were time to browse the downtown Broadway antique shops, she might come across a Welsh cupboard to display Nina's antique Bianco Ginori. The plates would be the focal point of the living room, and maybe she could find a deep, comfy sofa instead of the pair of sagging love seats her mother bestowed on her when she moved to New York from Baltimore.

With newfound zeal to organize her life (and to keep the visions at bay), she vows to spend the rest of the weekend going through old cardboard file boxes overflowing with outdated work; and, when Luisa comes on Thursday, she can help her figure out what to stow away in the almost empty basement storage bin she's never bothered to use.

And then she'll look for a drinks tray table, the kind one sees in refined English country houses; she'll stock it with vodka, sherry, Campari, an ice bucket and crystal glasses for cozy little dinners. And there will be a tea tray with a sturdy stoneware pot and brown sugar crystals like bits of chipped amber.

The mellow Burgundy and planning her apartment transformation seem to have calmed her: she feels her limbs relax. As she searches her bag for some Kleenex to wipe her damp forehead, she finds the map of France, already folded to show Burgundy, the Côte d'Or, the area surrounding the little town of Châtillon-sur-Seine where she'd gone just before the London board meeting. It must have been almost ten years ago when, by taking a detour, she found the Vix Krater in the local museum. She's been back to see it at least four more times.

The night before her discovery at Vix, she'd had a dream about Nina that from time to time she re-reads in her computer dream journal.

I'm riding in a small cart or wagon. Nina, looking ahead, straight ahead, is sitting by my side. We are approaching the most beautiful sight imaginable-as if we're driving along a quay that projects into the water. Across we see a brilliant panorama. The wide view takes my breath away. I talk to Nina's spirit that is radiating from her body. She is transparent almost, but still very clear. I tell her that everyone thinks she's dead, but I know she never died at all. "Look ahead," she says. Now I can see tall towers and turrets and dazzling water. I turn to her—it's like arriving at Avallon I say. Then I look again and Nina has vanished.

She daydreams about Avallon for a few minutes. Wasn't it Avallon where King Arthur was supposedly carried by his loyal soldiers after he was wounded in battle? Avallon is not many kilometers from Châtillon-sur-Seine and the museum of the Vix Krater. She gazes at the map, at the green shading of woods, mountains, scenic roads. She studies the hairline squiggles of rivers and tributaries, trying to pinpoint Source-Seine, the site claimed by the City of Paris, which marks the beginning of the great river flowing through Paris to the English Channel. Here, ancient Celts worshiped their goddess Sequana. She'd visited the site more than once on her visits to Châtillon-sur-Seine. And then she finds Sens, the cathedral city named after the Senones, an ancient Celtic tribe of Burgundy. Sens is less than thirty miles from Troyes, where the river widened enough for important commerce. She measures the distance with her eyes, then, checking the mileage, she finds that it's about thirty miles from Troyes to Vix and Mont Lassois, once a Celtic trading post. And Avallon is so close by, only a long day's ride to Troyes. Troyes. What was Troyes famous for? She remembers the famous medieval Fair at Troyes. Troyes as in Chrétien de Troyes, the Medieval poet who was the first to write about King Arthur and the Grail legend. The Krater flashes before her eyes. Chrétien was from

Troyes! The Grail Legend. The Grail. Avallon. The Krater! Chrétien de Troyes!

In a lightning burst, she realizes what she saw at the museum at Châtillon-sur-Seine. Why this epiphany comes to her at this instant she'll probably never know. Since she's so used to her imagination flowing from vision to vision, since she depends on her visions for guidance and makes a living writing about them, there are some things she just knows. She's certain she's now been handed arcane knowledge from a divine source. Feeling shivers, she pulls the blanket up to her chin. With eyes closed, she sits back to ponder her revelation. Why had it never come to her before? There is no doubt in her mind that she has discovered the very source of Chrétien de Troye's Grail story. The Vix Krater, the actual, tangible source for the Story of the Grail and its pagan Celtic origins. She has found the Celtic Cauldron of Plenty, the Cauldron of Immortality, buried with *la Dame de Vix*. How many Celts must have seen and celebrated this immense bronze vessel, dipping their cups into it, drinking deeply from it? How many bards must have sung about it, how many storytellers woven tales about it? For centuries until it finally surfaced as *Le Conte du Graal*, the Grail Legend from Chrètien who lived in nearby Troyes.

She promises herself that the minute she returns home she'll begin her research on the Vix Krater, and Troyes. When she gets home she'll read Chrétien's *Romances*.

And Chrètien. She racks her brain. She knows so little about him. And why was he the first to tell the Grail stories as we know them today? She remembers reading about Chrètien in Jessie Weston's book *From Ritual to Romance*. Since her job is writing about objects in ritual, often she memorizes certain passages important to her. She takes another swallow of wine and closes her eyes as she gropes for Weston's words, hoping they'll return to her at this moment of dazzling clarity. She takes a deep breath, drawing out the lines from memory, soft-ly whispering each word aloud.

That the man who first told the story, and boldly, as befitted a born teller of tales, wedded it to the Arthurian legend, was him-self connected by descent with the ancient Faith, actually himself held the Secret of the Grail, and told in purposely romantic form, that of which he knew.

She pauses, and, trying fiercely to push the rest from her brain, entwines her fingers tightly, pressing them hard against her chin until Weston's words float to the surface of con-sciousness.

I am firmly convinced, nor do I think that the time is far dis-tant when the missing links will be in our hand and we shall be able to weld once more the golden chain which connects Ancient Ritual with Medieval Romance.

The Krater, *la Dame de Vix*, Chrétien de Troyes, the Grail story, Avallon. The missing links. She's found them! She's con-vinced. Totally, irrevocably convinced. No one, no one would ever be able to make her believe otherwise. Leaping from her seat, she opens the overhead bin for her laptop, boots it up, and begins to write.

Chrétien
Vix, Burgundy, France, circa 1145 A.D

After a long day's journey, a woman and her young son arrive at Vix, a village at the foot of Mont Lassois. They tether their horses and stop to rest by the old fieldstone bridge. Ancient oaks, their branches thickened with lichen and mistletoe, cast flickering shadows over the riverbanks.

The boy quenches his thirst from a flask of sacred water filled at the nearby source of the Douix, a sanctuary of Sequana, the old goddess of rivers and springs. He picks up a pebble and tosses it across the narrow stream that will soon become the Seine, the same river that flows by his home near Troyes; but at Troyes, the Seine courses broad and stately, its quays and docks crammed with all manner of boats and barges laden with tin ore from Cornwall.

From a pouch at her waist, his mother takes an object bought from a peddler at Sequana's shrine, a small limestone figure carved in the shape of a serene-faced, bare breasted woman with double fish tails. A *melusine*. As she admires her curious keepsake, the boy reminds her that he has seen another such creature carved in a stone capital in the crypt of the Church of the Magdalene in Troyes.

Before long, mother and son begin their ride up the winding road to Mont St. Marcel. As they near the summit, the boy jumps from his horse to look out over the surrounding valley, its fields spread with a blanket of ripened wheat. In the distance he can see the already widening Seine teeming with punts and rafts.

When darkness begins to fall, they reach their destination—a cottage shaded by a copse of tall trees. It belongs to the Wise Woman. The traveling woman is her daughter, the boy her favorite grandson, Chrétien. The Wise Woman is cared for by her niece, the homely, still unwed Blanchefleur, almost the same age as Chrétien, her cousin thrice removed.

The lad is tired, his body aches, his stomach rumbles. Blanchefleur has cooked up a pot of barley. He gulps his share down with bread and goat cheese, and, when his stomach is full he climbs a ladder to the alcove. Stretched out on a straw pallet and warmed by chimney stones, he lays his head against a coarse blanket and closes his eyes. As he begins to drift off, strange images flash through his head, but they quickly fade when he hears his grandmother whisper, "Has Chrétien fallen asleep yet? We have much women's work to do this night."

"You must not worry," his mother replies. "He will not hear us. I have stirred a dose of poppy and yarrow into his porridge."

"My daughter, you have yet many words to commit to memory. Let us now begin as I fear it will not be long before my soul passes to the Otherworld."

Chrétien struggles to stay awake. He wonders why his grandmother, who has often told him stories, does not want him to hear these.

The old woman draws a deep breath and heaves a profound sigh before she begins to intone in a voice strangely unlike her own.

Listen, daughter, as I sing of who we are,
Of how we came to be.
I sing this song as it was sung to me

In the voice of my mother
And all mothers before,
In the morning of time,
On our distant shore.

She pauses. Then Chrétien hears his mother recite the words exactly as his grandmother has chanted them.

The boy's heart hammers in the darkness as the Wise Woman goes on.

I tell this story as my mother told it,
As did hers before
Back, back, back in time,
Before the seasons of my life,
Those seasons before hers.
Night had fallen
And the ramparts of Vix
Opened for the Woman.
From strange lands she came,
Crossed seas, came up rivers
To the River that flows through our village
A woman wearing raiment never before seen,
The King met her at the city gates,
Bade her tell her story,
And this is what she sang:
     From across the seas I come.
     From a sanctuary so rich
     Our maidens offered thirsty travelers
     Fresh water in golden cups
     Until the maidens were taken
     By the enemies' men,
     When the outrage was done,

And the battle won,
These wicked men changed the river's course
To run over the golden city.
And so the land of wheat and bulls,
Of purple and gold,
Became Wasteland.

The old woman stops to sip from her cup of tisane.
"Aunt, what happened to the outraged Woman?
Where did she go?" Chrétien hears Blanchefleur ask.

Over the mountains she fled
Fled from the flooded land,
Her heart as wild as the waves,
Crossed seas, sailed up rivers
Her spirit journeying.
And when at last she reached our gates
The people knew she was the Queen
We'd waited for.
And queen she was until she left this world.
So she was buried with her cart.
Around her neck, her amber beads, her golden
    torque.
Still she lies by her Sacred Cauldron,
Cauldron of plenty that will never empty,
Cauldron of life after death.
From her we claim our descent.
We hold the secret of all who come here to seek it.
Our women are the guardians of the Grail
That lies buried in the earth of Vix.

BOOK II

Bianca
New York City

The taxi turns the corner of 75th Street by six o'clock. Bianca pays the driver and asks for a receipt, intent on turning over a new leaf with her expense account, all part of The Improved Bianca. She lugs her rolling bag down the steps to the door of her basement apartment and rummages in her handbag for the tiny squeeze battery flashlight she always carries on her key chain. She drags the cart over the doorsill, then turns on the light. She gasps.

Books, papers, magazines, CDs, DVDs, tapes strewn about, drawers dumped out, chairs, tables upside down. The TV still sits on its stand, the stereo and video equipment on its shelf. Her heart feels as though it will leap right out of her chest. She runs straight to the kitchen. Just as she feared, Nina's cookie jar from Rhodes, with its lovely image of a double-tailed mermaid, lies shattered on the floor. She stoops to pick up the fragments. Even in her desperation, she counts the seventeen pieces before she finds a plastic container and carefully places them inside, consoling herself that she knows a ceramics curator at the Met who moonlights by restoring broken objects. She's relieved that Nina's earrings are in the felt sack safely pinned to the inside of her bra. Then she goes to the bedroom. Nina's little painting of the Campanile is gone!

She feels violated—hollowed and sick. But she won't allow herself to collapse.

Should I call Sergio? Or Giovanni? Mom? The voice inside her shrieks, "Call the police!"

Ω

"Looks like an inside job to me," Officer De Vita tells her.

"Think hard, Ms. Caldwell. If they haven't taken your TV or your appliances, they were probably after something else that has nothing to do with resale value. What do you think the burglar—or burglars wanted? What other valuables do you own?"

"A new laptop, a pair of gold earrings, a diary left to me by my grandmother—and my passport." She reaches for her purse. "But they're all with me—right here in my roll—on bag, and they've been with me during my entire trip to Venice. When I'm in New York I keep them in a safety deposit box at the bank."

"Anything else?"

"Some antique plates my grandmother left me. But they're still in the kitchen cupboard. And a very small framed water-color of Venice painted by my great-grandmother. But it just occurs to me that it wasn't where it should have been the day I left, I'm assuming that my helper put it away somewhere."

"Do you have any enemies, Ms. Caldwell?"

"I never felt as if I did, though from time to time I get a nasty letter from a reader accusing me of black magic or witch-craft. But my boss never shows them to me. I only learn about these crank letters from his secretary."

He raises an eyebrow and continues to probe her about *Eyes and Soul*, her column, her relationships with colleagues, with Luisa. "Think hard. Maybe someone in your office wants some of your work. Most likely information from your person-al computer. From what you've told me, you must have lots of fascinating stuff in that little laptop of yours."

"You're not implying that the burglar could be someone from the magazine, are you?" She hears her defensiveness. "There's no way I'll talk about my job or my colleagues."

"Whoa…Hey, lady— I'm not implying anything! If you don't want to cooperate, that's your decision. Our switchboard rings its head off. We usually don't have time to bother with this kind of stuff. This happens to be my old neighborhood so I decided to take the call."

She feels sheepish and assures him that not cooperating never entered her mind.

"I see that there's no knob handle on either side of your bedroom door."

She hopes he doesn't notice her blush. "It's been that way for almost a year—I keep meaning to get it fixed."

"Have you ever seen this before? I found it on the kitchen counter."

She looks at the scrap of paper. On it is written in a spindly, shaky, old-fashioned Italian hand, Sacra Corona Unita.

"Sacred Crown United? I wonder what that's all about."

"Sounds like someone from the Mafia left this little bit of information for you. Perhaps as a warning. Sacra Corona Unita is the name of the Mafia organization in Puglia. I'll keep the message as part of the police report."

"A warning for what—I have no idea what this is all about."

"Well, keep your eyes open if you ever go to Italy again. Didn't you tell me that you were in Venice?"

"Yes, for a wedding. I met a lot of Italians there." She immediately thinks of Giovanni, but she doesn't mention his name, then wonders why she wanted to protect him. Protect him from what?

Ω

After Officer De Vita leaves, she double bolts herself in, makes sure all the windows are locked, and heads for the bedroom to clear up the mess. She opens the suitcase and pulls out her raincoat. And instead of throwing it over a chair as is her habit, she puts it on one of the puffy pink satin hangers her mother sent her, most likely hoping that they would encourage her to hang up her clothes. When she begins to pick up old underwear strewn about the floor, a black spider scurries along the baseboard. She watches in horror as it disappears. She continues her search for the painting. *Not here, not there, not anywhere.* She won't give up. She's convinced that Luisa has hidden it in a safe place. Her heart still knocking, she rummages inside the roll-on for her eye mask and ties it on tight. Breathes in, blows out, three times. This time the black curtain fades to whitest white.

"When did you see the watercolor last, Bianca?" the voice inside her asks.

"The night my mother called me before I left for Italy."

"Where do you think Luisa might have put it?"

Nothing appears on the inner screen. She hears only the sounds of her breathing, her heartbeats. All she can think of is Zitomer's. Zitomer's! Remember to renew your prescription at Zitomer's. She'd worn her trench coat to the pharmacy!

She yanks the coat from the hanger and pummels and squeezes until she feels the frame. The painting is still buttoned up in the inside pocket of her raincoat where, before leaving for Italy, she'd absent-mindedly put it! Nina's watercolor of the Campanile has traveled all the way to Venice, then back again, in the coat she'd folded into her suitcase and never once worn. She feels like singing as she pulls out the painting and presses her lips to the protecting glass.

$$\Omega$$

The bed is stripped, sheets and pillows tossed on the floor, feathers all over the place. She gathers up the sheets and begins to make the bed, trying her best to square each corner. Even when she lived in the all white room, she was scolded for never tucking the corners neatly enough. Looking at the crumpled sheets, she is suddenly fed up with tops that don't match bottoms that don't match pillowcases. From now on the Brand New Bianca will buy matching sets.

Ω

At nine, she finally musters the courage to get into bed, where she worries about those three words, "Sacra Corona Unita" on the slip of paper. A message from the Mafia? She doubts it. *What's the Mafia to do with me?* Get some sleep, she urges herself. What's there to be afraid of? No one was harmed, nothing's been taken. She's more terrified of her own dark visions than of a burglar. Or of the Mafia, for that matter.

Now she's sorry she ever met Giovanni. If she hadn't, she would have stayed on in Venice, roaming through the Accademia, gazing at Saint Ursula's sweet face turned upward to heaven, as she dreams of angels under the tasseled *baldacchino* of her bed. Or she could have stood in wonder before Giorgione's *La Tempesta*, the courtier leaning on his staff as he observes the half-naked woman nursing her baby under a tree, and in the distance, beyond the castle, the sky dark with storm clouds. What would happen if a lightning bolt hit that tree, she wonders. Whenever she looks at *La Tempesta*, a curious run-for-cover feeling comes over her.

She staggers to the kitchen and makes coffee by heaping espresso crystals into her favorite mug and sticks it under the boiling water tap. The mug has a faint hairline crack but she can't bear to throw it out. By now she's ravenous, and since there's no milk, she pours Rice Krispies into a bowl and eats them dry.

She goes back to bed and wakes up at five with the word *sinope* repeating itself over and over in her head—*sinope*. To her, it sounds like the Italian word for mustard, but no, that's spelled s-e-n-a-p-e. She's sure there's more to this dream, something about entering new rooms, but sinope is all she can remember. What is sinope, she wonders. She looks it up on Google. Sinope. In Turkey. At the southern shore of the Black Sea. She heaves a great shuddering sigh, the kind of sigh that makes her feel good about herself, as though she's somehow touched a distant place within her soul.

$$\Omega$$

By noon the place is beginning to look like Thursday, as though Luisa has just left. She looks in the hall closet where Luisa has stocked the shelves with toilet paper, Kleenex, and soap. Even before the break-in, the flat never *ever* looked this neat. She keeps walking in and out of the rooms, admiring them. She doesn't feel quite at home with such orderliness. Maybe it's better for her work, living and writing in chaos, but someday she'll fix up the place so she can invite Giovanni for dinner, or at least a drink.

With her coat hanging in the closet, clothes tucked into drawers, sweaters folded neatly and stored in hotel laundry bags, scattered books now shelved and categorized, the place looks forbiddingly barren, like that all white room on Boar's Hill. She thinks about adding some personal touches to make it look less sterile, to transform it into a cushion-comfort bower where The New Bianca Fiore might welcome her would-be lover, Giovanni.

On Wednesday afternoon, just before the bank closes, she rents a safety deposit box for Nina's diary, the watercolor, and the earrings, taking no chances in case the burglar turns up again. On her way home from the bank, as she walks up Lexington Avenue, she notices an advertisement for still another Starbucks Coffee shop, soon to be opened. She stops to look at the green and white logo. Is she seeing things or is it a mermaid, framed by her wide-flung tails? Yes—there she is with a five pointed star above her forehead. She is so much like the *melusine* on the shattered Rhodian jar! Why, she wonders, was this image chosen as the Starbucks logo, and why has she never noticed it until today? She decides that when she has time, she'll do more research on the origin of the *melusine*.

Ω

The Monday after she returned from Italy, she's at her office desk by nine. Neither Sergio nor Leonardo has turned up. Sergio has most likely spent the weekend in East Hampton. As for Leonardo, she hardly knows anything about his private life, except that he worked for an art and architectural design magazine before Sergio hired him.

Leonardo, her immediate boss, is the new jack-of-all-trades at the magazine. Administrator as well as Editor-in-Chief. Like Sergio, he is Italian-born, but has lived in Manhattan since childhood. He and Sergio were classmates at Columbia.

He calls her into his office before noon. Leonardo can't be more than forty, but with those spectacles, his shiny bald pate and snub nose, he looks like a Dominican priest who might be more at home in a brown, rope-tied habit. But Leonardo always wears too tight designer jeans and never a tie, in studied contrast to Sergio's Cerutti haberdashery look.

Leonardo doesn't look up from his desk. "How was the rest of your week in Venice?"

"Interesting. I arrived home Monday night."

He glances up, seemingly surprised. "Why so soon? Work? Problems?"

She bites her lip. Mind your own business, she wants to say.

"When I walked in the door last night, I found that my apartment had been ransacked."

"My God! What a shame!" He makes a clucking sound. "Terrible coming home to that." He leans back and stares at her as though he expects a reaction.

She stares back boldly.

He takes a cigarette from his pack, then slips it back in, slaps his hand over the pack, and almost squeezes it flat. "I'm trying to kick the habit. Doctor's orders. Quitting cold turkey is driving me crazy. By the way, I thought Sergio said that you were staying on in Venice."

"And didn't you tell me you were going on to Rome?"

He nods. "I spent Saturday night on the Via Appia Antica—at my widowed aunt's villa. She's had a slight stroke so she doesn't get out much. I came home Sunday. Lots of work to finish up. Now what about your expense accounts? Do you have them ready yet?" He begins shuffling papers around.

She speaks confidently. "Over the past two days I caught up on six months' worth."

His jaw drops. "Are you kidding?"

"You were right to keep reminding me. I can't have my own money tied up in travel expenses that mount up to losses because I don't claim half of them. I wind up cheating myself." She hands him the envelope.

He looks up, peering at her over his spindly Armani glasses. "Good girl. I'll look them over—then Wanda will cut a check for you."

An hour later Leonardo calls her into his office. "I have a question to ask you about your accounting. I see that you took your Venice hotel bill as an expense."

"Sergio told me I could. He also encouraged me to stay a few extra days if I wanted to, but I decided to come home after the wedding."

"Fine. But then you've cut yourself short on your meals in Venice. You're only cheating yourself when you do this. You should get exactly what's due you."

"I didn't have to pay for any meals."

"Who did then?"

So that's what he's getting at. "I don't think it's any of your business."

He grins and raises an eyebrow. "Hey—don't tell me you finally found yourself a man."

Bianca
New York City, late October, 2007

From time to time Sergio comes by to cook dinner for her. In the kitchen drawer she keeps the recipe for one of her favorites, Le Cirque's spaghetti primavera. Now and then she pulls it out to read, but that's as close as she ever gets to cooking. This is something she intends to change—just in case Giovanni ever appears on her doorstep. Since Grace's Marketplace is only a few blocks away, she goes by to stock up on all things Italian, from pasta, cheese, and biscotti to even a CD of Neapolitan songs sung by Roberto Murolo.

At exactly three she checks her e-mail and finds a message from Sergio.

Ciao, Bianca. I'll be stopping by around six o'clock with some gorgeous white truffles and fresh porcini. I'm going to make you a risotto like you've never tasted. A tutt' all'ora, tesoro.

Her heart sinks. He's back in town again. The last person she feels like seeing tonight is Sergio. She planned to order in some Chinese, and after dinner she wanted to read more about Sinope and the Black Sea, where traces of an ancient, submerged city were recently discovered by Robert Ballard, the underwater archaeologist and discoverer of the Titanic wreck. She'd also come across a story in The New York Times about Dr. William Ryan and Dr. Walter Pitman, geologists from Columbia, whose theory is that the Mediterranean, thousands of years ago, had burst through the narrow Bosporus valley pouring itself with cataclysmic force into a large sweet water lake destroying all life and causing the inhabitants to flee for their lives. What was once a benign body of sweet water became the Pontus Euxinus, the inhospitable, dangerous saltwater sea, the Black Sea.

Ω

The doorbell rings at six thirty. With her eye pressed against the peephole, she squints at Sergio's Ferragamo necktie. Her first instinct is to keep the door locked, but the instinct flies by unheeded so she opens it.

"Hi—how did things finish up in London?" Sergio stayed on after the board meeting.

"Better than I thought, so I came home early," he replies in his perfect, beguilingly accented Columbia University English. He then proceeds to straighten his new "cheetahs lolling among the daisies" necktie as if it is a signal for her to admire it. "The Bergamo lab should give us better color repros at a cheaper rate. And if they don't work out, I've got a printer lined up in Bari who supposedly does fantastic work. But you know how I hate dealing with those *terrone*. I guarantee you that in no time we'll beat *Franco Maria Ricci*. Eyes and Soul will become the most beautiful art magazine in the world...and because of you, Bianca, the most fascinating one." He smiles broadly. Sergio smiles a lot ever since his teeth have been resurfaced.

"You've got a long way to go before you beat *Franco Maria Ricci*." She has no trouble at all speaking up to him.

"Let's walk over to Grace's together. I need to buy a few things to make our dinner."

She is surprised because Sergio rarely goes out in public with her. He claims he doesn't want it to get back to his wife.

"I've already done the shopping."

"How did you know what to buy?"

"I'm a quick study. You should know that. You'll be happy to hear about my decision to learn to cook. I stocked up today at Grace's—all the ingredients to make risotto, pastas. San

Marzano tomatoes, Parmigiano Reggiano—extra-virgin olive oil..."

"You're telling me no more take-outs from Word of Mouth, no Chinese, no more pizza deliveries?"

"You heard what I said."

He produces a truffle grater from his pocket and opens a bag containing a glass jar. A huge earth-cloaked truffle is nested in a bed of rice. "I bought it in a little shop in Bergamo Alta. So far the best of the season. They had a lot of rain this year."

"It must have cost you a fortune."

He winks. "Let's say we're enjoying it compliments of the magazine. Have a sniff. I'll be right back."

She puts the jar to her nose and inhales, convincing herself that she can smell the truffle's musky ripeness right through the glass.

He takes off his coat in the bedroom and tosses it on her bed, then rushes to wash up in the bathroom. *"Merda!"* he shouts when he returns. "Why the hell don't you take that poster off your mirror? How can you live without a mirror in your bathroom?"

"Because I don't like looking at myself. The only time I do is when I have to and that's not often." Last year when her mother had given her an elegant silver compact for her birthday, she returned it to Tiffany's for credit, relieved that it hadn't been engraved *BEC*. Sergio wraps himself in her new apron and begins step by step to show her how to make risotto with porcini. *"All'onda,* Venetian style so when you pour it, the risotto ripples like waves, each short, swollen rice grain still hard to the bite, all bound up in a loose, creamy sauce. When you hear the rice clinking against the sides of the pot, then, only then, do you add the hot broth," he says as seriously as she's ever heard him speak.

She stands by watching him stir, every now and then taking her turn. In nineteen minutes when the risotto is perfect to the tooth, he adds freshly grated parmesan and some heavy cream and beats it quickly. He spoons it reverently onto Nina's gently warmed Bianco Ginori plates, then, rubbing the hard fungus knob against the sharp teeth of his truffle grater, he crowns the rice with a heap of wispy, putty-colored flakes.

Instead of just digging into his risotto, the way she always does, Sergio flattens his with a fork, patting it into a "cake." Then he begins by eating from the outer, cooler edge to its warmer center. Venetian style.

She puts the plate to her nose to sniff the truffle. "Such a strange, animal smell. I read somewhere that it's probably the same chemical as civet or…."

"Truffles are supposed to have aphrodisiac qualities," he says, raising his eyebrows, as if to suggest "even if they might not work for you."

"This has got to be the most delicious risotto I've ever eaten," she exclaims after savoring the first forkful. "I'd call it sybaritic what with truffles almost worth their weight in gold."

He nods. "They cost more than $2,000 dollars a kilo in New York."

She gasps, remembering his cost-cutting admonitions to most of her colleagues.

"But of course I buy them near Alba—where there's a black market for white truffles. I get them a helluva lot cheaper—you bet I do!" he announces proudly.

"I wonder if the Sybarites ever ate truffles," she muses aloud, once again remembering that Giovanni said his father had dug with the looking for the site of the fabled city.

"I'm not sure if truffles were found in the Suth, although oak trees certainly grow in Southern Italy. And there sure are plenty of lazy pigs down there to sniff them out." He slaps his knee and laughs, obviously delighted with his own joke.

Sergio always makes fun of Southern Italians—*terrone* he calls them, regarding them as inferior beings. "A race apart," he often says disdainfully. It always makes her angry when Sergio derides the South. Especially Puglia and Calabria. He often speaks about how he believes the North should secede from the rest of Italy. He is all for the creation of a separate new state, Padania.

"How come the Sybarites were so rich?" she asks.

"Location, location, location. The Italian boot narrows as it reaches the ankle. The Sybarites had a very short land route from the Adriatic side of the Italian peninsula, across the mountains—from the eastern side of the boot to the Tyrrhenian Sea. If weather conditions were good, it could be traveled with pack animals in just three days, connecting with Etruscan traders who sailed along the west coast south from Etruria to trade with Sybaris and Poseidonia, also founded by Sybarites. Both became important trading posts for the entire western Mediterranean."

"I'm amazed, Sergio. You seem to know an awful lot about Sybaris."

"Hey-a few years ago I saw that show on the Greeks in South Italy at Palazzo Grassi."

"O.K. So tell me more about what you learned."

"At the port of Sybaris boats from all over the Mediterranean were unloaded and the goods hauled away on pack mules or wagons headed over the mountains to the Tyrrhenian Sea and the cities of Neapolis or Poseidonia. There, the Sybarites would trade with the Etruscans or they would send cargos of amphorae of wine and olive oil via the sea route to Massilia, ancient Marseilles. From there, the goods would travel up the Rhone and its tributaries to the Seine, which flows north to empty into the English Channel. The Greeks and Etruscans bartered for tin and copper from

Cornwall, both alloys necessary for making bronze. The other city states of Magna Graecia had to send ships all around the heel and toe of the Italian boot up the Tyrrhenian Sea. This route was more dangerous and took longer, lessening their profits and giving the Sybarites a huge advantage."

"Since the Sybarites didn't have to sail all around the toe of Italy, they made more money. Is that what you're saying?"

"You've got it, Bianca. It was this short trade route that made the Sybarites super rich. But they were already wealthy from cattle and wheat, wine and fruit."

She closes her eyes and envisions the trim ankle of the Italian boot. Finally she rises from her chair. "Excuse me. I'm going to get my atlas—to find Sybaris."

"Sit down! You don't need any atlas! Sybaris is in Calabria. On the instep of the boot—down the coast from Taranto–on the Ionian Sea. Ancient Sybaris was supposed to be at the mouth of the River Crathis. Near the sea, but not on it. Now the sea has receded to about three miles away."

"For an arrogant northerner who's always making fun of the South, you've certainly learned a lot about Southern Italian history. You took it all in. I'm impressed."

He sits back in his chair and fixes his eyes on hers, as if commanding her to believe him when he senses she doesn't. "When I was growing up we had no choice. We had to study Greek, as well as Latin. We read the ancient historians, Herodotus, Athenaeus, Diodorus Siculus."

"One of these days I might even do some research on whether or not your Sybarites ate truffles," she replies, spearing the last swollen grains of the risotto with the tines of her fork. The rest of their dinner conversation is all about the next issue of the magazine—until Sergio sidles over and starts stroking her shoulder.

She shrugs it off.

"I've missed you, Bianca."

"I was hoping you enjoyed being back in Italy with your wife and kids."

"Bianca Fiore, *piccolo fiore*, my little white flower, why don't you ever take me seriously?" He squeezes her hand so tightly, she yelps.

"Why? Because you're married! To a beautiful woman who so far has given you two perfect children and another on the way."

Besides, she isn't the least bit attracted to her boss. Sergio is a nuisance but she's learned that he's relatively harmless. She's known him for three years, and then she'd worked in the mailroom for more than two years before Sergio bought the magazine. Later on Sergio discovered what he considers to be her special talents. Despite his benign hounding, he's occasionally generous to her, a quality not shown to other staff members.

She leans back in her chair to give Sergio the full attention he demands. "Haven't you read what happens to men who keep on making advances to colleagues? Especially when they do it in the office?" she inquires.

"American women are such hypocrites—suing their bosses for being nice to them. That would never happen in Italy."

Better to change the subject, she decides. "You know—I'm not sure I like Leonardo. There's something about him that bothers me, but I just can't put my finger on it."

"Well—keep your fingers off him, then," Sergio chuckles at his own joke and at the same time removes a hair from the sleeve of his Brioni custom suit sleeve. He studies the long blonde strand, then, blowing it into the air, chortles. "How do you like your new desktop?" He walks around the desk to gaze over her shoulder. "I wanted you to have the best, Bianca. You deserve it. Milan circulation had another survey made. They hate to admit it, but you're still the reason for our upward circulation and increased advertising revenues. Our little Bianca Fiore has become quite a star in Italy. They love all those over-the-top rhapsodies you dream up." He laughs. "The staff over there doesn't know that I changed your name from Caldwell to Fiore. You're so damn good, they think you've got to be Italian."

He pats her shoulder. "Hey—you know I love your kind of looks—but it's better that you remain mysterious. That's your big draw, Bianca. Your mystery. You're my most precious commodity. Why are you turning red?"

She was born with a systemic problem with blushing: she blushes when she's happy, blushes when she's sad, embarrassed, or whenever she feels the slightest emotion. Or whenever she thinks about sex. Because her skin goes from far too pale to red, people always notice. It's been a life-long curse to have her face so blatantly betray her feelings.

The phone rings. Sergio leaps up. "It's probably for me. I left your number on my answering machine."

Saved by the telephone. She often wonders what would happen if she allowed herself to be seduced by Sergio. Or if she'd ever feel enough desire to seduce him.

"*Ciao*, Leonardo," he says grumpily. He doesn't move a muscle as he listens. "OK, OK." He murmurs something in Italian, then says, "I haven't seen it. Don't worry. I'm sure it's..." He pauses, looks up at Bianca. "I'm sure it's somewhere in my desk. I'll come right over."

"What's so important it can't wait until Monday morning?" she asks after he hangs up.

"You heard what I told him. He needs information for a client in Rome. And he couldn't find the manila folder. I'm sure it's around. I'd better check my office."

She glances at her watch and adds six hours forward from

New York time. "It's already way after midnight in Italy."

"Leonardo is working with the night shift."

"I didn't know there was one."

"I told you I made a lot of changes in the Milan office."

She finds Sergio's coat and graciously opens it for his arms.

"I'm not happy leaving you with dishes to wash. And I hope you do wash them, Bianca."

"Sure—while I do the washing up, I'll play my new CD. Domingo and Kiri Ti Kanawa. *La Rondine*."

"Good girl! Start some new habits. I'll call you tomorrow. *Ciao, cara*." He kisses her on each cheek, opens the front door, then dashes back to the kitchen for his precious truffle grater.

After piling up, then guiltily leaving the dishes and pots in the sink, she falls into bed remembering Oxford and the loneliness of those years spent away from her family, wondering sometimes why she'd ever been there in the first place.

Bianca
June, Boar's Hill, Oxford, 1996

The room is white-as white as the dress of the young woman who stands lost in thought as she gazes out the window. Her room overlooks a garden planted with herbs and trellised roses enclosed by high clipped yew hedges. In its center a small fountain spews a single jet upwards toward a cloudless azure sky.

It is here, at this peaceful place of prayer and meditation, that she's learned about her visionary gift. The woman turns from the window and fixes her eyes on the blank white wall above her desk as though to see her reflection in a mirror. She adjusts the white veil covering her head.

Soon her mother and father will be coming up the staircase to greet her, to embrace her and bid their farewells. Her heart aches because her brother, so far away, could not be with her on what would be the most important day of her life.

She opens a drawer and takes out her journal, a thick, lined notebook that she has kept every day since she left home. She has been told that from this day forward she will not be able to keep this journal. She has been told her visions are dangerous. Evil. She often wonders why her name is Bianca when there is such darkness inside her.

Her heart begins to pound. Sweat beads her forehead. She has had her doubts before, but they would always come and go.

Now from the tower she hears insistent tolling, bells clamoring, bronze against bronze. She closes her eyes tight, welcoming the black screen and whispers, "Tell me, Nina—I beg you, Nina, please help me decide."

Above the din of the bells, she hears Nina's voice. "Bianca, the veil. Take it from your head. You must return with your parents."

She slowly lifts the veil, lays it across the chair, then passes both hands over her dark hair cropped close to the scalp.

She hears a triple knock. The door opens.

Her mother, her father, and the Mother Superior enter, ready to escort her to the chapel.

Although she feels the quaking within, Bianca's voice is strong, unwavering.

"I'm sorry, Sister Catherine, I cannot go through with it. I'm not ready to take final vows. I doubt that I ever will be."

The distinguished, gray-haired American naval officer and the pretty blonde woman throw their arms around their daughter. They are so happy, so relieved, that there will be no good-byes.

Bianca
November 21, New York City, 2007

It is six o'clock on the morning before Thanksgiving when Bianca gets up to go to the loo, then crawls right back into bed to try to get more sleep. She's feeling the usual holiday-hollowness, an overwhelming sadness. Every year as she approaches her December birthday, the autumn emptiness intensifies. She hasn't heard from Giovanni. Maybe he's forgotten all about getting together here in New York during the December antiquities sales.

After what seemed like an endless day at the magazine, she rushes to D'Agostino's to shop for the Thanksgiving dinner she's determined to cook for herself. By the time she returns home and puts the groceries away, it's still early. She flops on the too short, too soft sofa and channel surfs until she sees Julie Christie's face. Ray Bradbury's *Fahrenheit 451* again. She's seen the film three times, once not very long ago. And each time she remembers sobbing at the final scene, not understanding why it always strikes a powerful chord within. The scene is about memory and the people who have become "books" in order to preserve for civilization all the printed books that have been burned by storm troopers.

The film is almost over.

The setting, a birch forest at the end of the railway line-characters from books walk by reciting their lines. "I am Anna Karenina," one woman says. "I am A Tale of Two Cities," a young man utters.

Night falls. It's beginning to snow. A young boy sits beside his grandfather, repeating the lines recited by the dying man. His grandfather has become a book, and now, knowing he will soon die, the old man is passing his story on to his grandson.

Tears roll down her cheeks and, as she watches this scene,

sadness washes over her, feelings she can't account for.

When the film ends, she closes her eyes. Good. No visions. It is still early. She turns on the laptop, thinking about the seventeen pieces of broken crockery, the fragments of Nina's Rhodian jar, now out being mended. It's a good time to begin her next assignment for the magazine. She won't wait for a suggestion from a reader: she'll write about the *mixoparthenos*, the goddess with twin tails of a snake—or of a fish.

The *Mixoparthenos* and the Black Sea

The Freeing of the Waters

Listen for I tell you who we are and how we came to be.
I tell this story as it was told to me,
To my mother before me and all the mothers before,
Back to the beginning of time when nurslings
Were not safe at their mothers' breasts.
My people once lived by the edge of a lake,
A bounteous lake, clear and fed by fresh streams.
Long-legged birds nested in the marshes
Where I would gather reeds and grasses to weave into
    baskets.
It was the year the crops rotted.
There were too many mouths, too little grain.
Winter winds blew early.
Hard rains beat down day after day.
Was our double-tailed goddess
Angry with our people?
Or had her son, the River God, sent endless floods,
To ruin the grain stored in the caverns?

And then one day when my brother and I were threshing wheat, we heard a sound that broke the stillness of the day. A deep roar of the giant, angry god filled our ears. An unearthly sound like none we had ever heard, at first a distant rumble ever growing louder, like the sound of countless herds of galloping horses.

Day by day we watched the salty water rise. Dead fish floated to the surface. We could no longer drink our once sweet water. Those who had boats for trade or for fishing pulled anchor. Some of our youngest and strongest ran for their lives in search of safe ground or toward the rising sun.

Men and boys felled trees for rafts and dugout boats; women twisted rope or gathered food and culled wool for sails. When the rafts were tight with pitch, we climbed aboard, bringing animals, seeds, wheat, roots of trees, and our carved stone image of Milouziena.

We fit in as many as the wide boats would hold and wept as we deserted our land, our homes, the bones of our ancestors. Our rafts and boats held twenty women and children, ten men. The younger men and lads poled while the women consoled the children. We prayed for winds to carry us to higher ground. For days, borne by breezes and currents, we floated on the rising lake. Our rafts drifted between forests of tall trees emerging from high water. With water turned to brine, we shared the milk of our goats, and nursing mothers gave their breasts to children and the sick.

At last when we were about to lose hope, we saw crags of white rocks in the distance, hills green with trees we knew were pine, for we could smell the sap on the breeze as our sails billowed with the wind. Flocks of white sea birds hovered, flapping their wings and swooping as we waved and shouted with joy. Soon we would set foot upon the land and give thanks to our goddess of earth and water who brought us safely to this distant shore.

Bianca
Thanksgiving Day, New York City, 2007

This is no day for bleakness and self pity. She looks at the purchases she made yesterday at D'Agostino's—turkey breast, bag of stuffing mix, can of cranberry sauce, two sweet potatoes, pecan pie, and a can of Reddiwhip. That should fill the emptiness.

She turns on the stereo and listens to Rachmaninoff's Symphony No. 2. Over and over again she plays her favorite Adagio. There's something about this Second movement, the limpid clarinet solo, the flutes and plaintive oboes, that makes tears well up in her eyes, puts her heart in focus.

I shouldn't be so afraid, she tries to convince herself. *I will, I must, enter those locked rooms of my mind. The music gives me the courage.* She closes her eyes. She sees her again, the same woman.

A woman with long thick dark hair pulled back and tied in a cord. She's riding a horse across the steppes. The horse gallops over the windswept earth, and as she rides I see gray grasses gradually turning into fields of green wheat, wheat rippling, bending in the wind. I see it in the glaring sun, ripening to gold, ready for harvest.

Ω

At eleven, she puts the turkey breast in the oven, along with a pan of stuffing and scrubbed sweet potatoes. Before long, the kitchen is filled with aromas it has never known—at least not since she moved in. When turkey and fixings are ready at the same time, she takes a moment to congratulate herself. *Brava, Bianca*, she says aloud.

She finds the CD of the Bulgarian Women's choir singing Thracian harvesting songs from *Le Mystere des Voix Bulgares*. At one-thirty precisely she pulls up a chair to a folding card table covered with her only plain white sheet, now centered with chrysanthemums and dried wheat stalks spilling out of a straw cornucopia. Her place is set with one of Nina's *antico bianco* Ginori plates.

She thrusts the steel blade through the turkey breast and feels strangely disquieted as she carves two thick slices. She spoons stuffing on a heated plate and sets a slice of jellied cranberry sauce next to it. The sauce gleams faintly like a giant cabochon ruby. As she admires the effect, the "ruby" melts into a puddle. *The Krater. Wine is spilling over its edge, dribbling over the frieze of armored hoplites, parading horses, sliding over the gorgons' tongues.*

Some moments later, when she opens her eyes, the Krater is gone. She touches the turkey on her plate with her fingertip. Cold. Since her microwave oven isn't working, she dumps the plateful of food into a garbage bag, sticks the turkey breast back into the fridge. She goes to the medicine cabinet for two aspirins, falls on the neatly made bed, and cries until there are no more tears. She's now worried that she's going over the edge. But she forces herself to get up—and then she does something unusual, at least for her. Instead of leaving the dishes piled up in the sink, she tugs on some plastic gloves and washes, dries, and puts them away.

In the early evening she turns on Rachmaninoff's Adagio again, boots up her laptop, and sits down in front of it. Closing her aching eyes, she leans her head back against the chair and listens. When she hears the melody of the clarinet solo, the woodwinds, her mind begins to descend. She is overcome with feelings—feelings she doesn't understand and visions seem to be floating up into her consciousness. Part of her fights them, trying to hold them back. Another part yields, longing to see more.

I shouldn't be afraid. I know it will be dark. I know the jar-ring black moth flutters about in these rooms. Rooms I will enter. I have made up my mind. The haunting melodies of Rachmaninoff give me the courage.

She begins to write.

I see hooks and eyes, fasteners of ivory or bone, attached to fab-ric, rust and mustard colored woven fabric. Why am I thinking this—why does my mind light upon hooks and eyes?

Then I see a hand unhooking the fasteners, a turgid breast exposed, a baby's lips eagerly searching for the teat. The child is wrapped in shiny fur, like otter, with silvery hairs.

When the woman smiles at the baby. I can see her sharp teeth. Her dark hair is long and matted. She has a tattoo on her cheek. I try to make it out. The baby turns its head, seeking the other breast. But there is no other. Her chest, on one side, is flat and scarred.

Is she an Amazon? She would have given her child to someone else to nurse if she were. Who is she? Where is she? Near the Black Sea?

Suddenly she feels drowsiness overtaking her. She saves the document and turns off the computer. She goes to bed think-ing about the woman of Vix, buried with the golden torque and the black figured *kylix* of Amazon women fighting Greek hoplites. Who was *la Dame de Vix*? And who is this frightening woman with the tattoo on her cheek? Moreover, does she have anything to do with the woman buried with the Krater? Or—does she have something to do with me?

Ω

"Zatoria." It must be about three o'clock when she wakes up with a word repeating itself in her head. She lies there in the dark, spelling it letter by letter in her mind. Z-A-T-O-R-I-A.

Zatoria. Is it a place like Astoria? Or a woman's name? It has a Russian ring to it. She seldom forgets names or words that sound so loud and clear in her dreams. When they pierce the fragile, eggshell surface of consciousness, they stay with her forever. But what kind of name is Zatoria?

There's one way she might be able to find out. Switching on the desk lamp, she takes her habitual swig of Evian before turning on the laptop and, wiping the sweat from her forehead with her sleeve, she enters "Zatoria" in Google search.

Names appear on the screen, names of actual women from Virginia, Michigan, Sweden. So the name really exists. There's also a place name, a town called Zator, in Poland. She finds it on the map—not far from the Ukrainian border, near the Black Sea. She hadn't just "dreamed it up." And "ia" is a Greek suffix, Zatoria, like Astor and Astoria! Maybe she should call one of the listed telephone numbers. But then what would she say to the woman who answered? "Your name, Zatoria, came to me in a dream?" Or—"When I woke up this morning I heard Zatoria ringing loud and clear in my head, so I decided to check you out on Google?" Of course the woman would think she's crazy. But then she mightn't be too far wrong.

She switches off the computer and the lights and crawls into bed. Staring at the ceiling, a cloudy starless sky, she whispers, "Zatoria, Zatoria, how far back in me do you come? Why do you haunt me? Who are you—what are you trying to tell me?"

Then she jumps out of bed, turns on the lights, heads straight for the computer. She switches it on, then cradles her head in her arms and closes her eyes tight, waiting for the visions, the knowledge to translate the darkness.

Zatoria

I, Zatoria, tell this story as my mother told it to me,
As did hers before,
Back, back in time,
Before the seasons of my life,
Those seasons before hers.
I do not read. I do not write.
It has never been the way of my people.
All knowledge must be stored in the head
So that it will live within our souls through
    countless lifetimes.
My mother taught me the legends of our tribe, my
    father the wisdom of the everlasting soul.
Countless moons have come and gone since my
    father's people left the birch forest where
    white butterflies flutter, where shamans gather
    golden mushrooms spotted like fawns.
I bring you a branch of the birch tree,
Sprouted green, spring sap sweet as honey.
Listen as I tell you of who we are and how we
    came to be,
Back in time I will lead you, before the seasons of
    my life,
Back to the time when Giants roamed the earth
And nurslings were not safe at their mothers'
    breasts.
When we came to worship the double-tailed
    goddess
Twin mountains belched fire into the sky and
    boiling black rivers
Like writhing snakes ran down their breasts,
Turning all into shiny black stone that sea traders
    carried away on square-sailed boats.

The Hellenes called me Zatoria, but Zato was the name my mother gave me. I wear white, the color of the robes of the shaman, Zalmoxis, the man my mother claimed to be my father. I was born out of their union offered up to Dionysos.

Year by year my mother's people moved westward leaving the steppes, planting fields with wheat and barley we sold to the Hellenes who had built their cities on our land along the Pontus Euxinus. My mother was the storyteller of our tribe. She rode stallions and fought as well as any men. Every spring she led us to the river's mouth near the polis, Olbia. She sold wheat to sea traders plying the sea in flat barges collecting their golden cargo.

While my mother haggled my little brother and I gathered up bones of sea otters that feed in the marshes. I spent hours scratching on them the magic signs my mother taught me. My brother painted symbols with red powder ground from madder roots.

My mother paid no heed to my brother, let him do as he pleased. With me she was strict since I would someday follow her as the leader of our people, the one who led our horses, oxen, wagons in the direction of the setting sun, to new land, new fields, and to the forests we would clear and build cabins for the wintering over, near pastures where our cattle could graze, leaving their droppings to enrich the earth, making our wheat grow tall and burst with seed.

I remember that fateful year when winter came early. Horses were tethered, axes sharpened, trees felled, and soon the clearing was dotted with log huts lined with bark peeled from silver branches. We gathered twigs and tied them into bundles to cover the roofs of our sheds and those of our livestock. Horses can endure cold, but oxen cannot. Then we made ready for the long days ahead.

We huddled by the fire, carving or sewing or braiding marsh rushes into mats while we listened to the elder women tell stories of our people, of our goddesses, Tabitha of the hearth, of the double snake-tailed Argimpasa, the goddess my mother's people call Milouziena, goddess of the harvest and of springs and rivers. During those endless days I took to my memory many stories.

No great task for me as it always seemed part of my very nature. As days turned warmer new fields were ploughed by our oxen, their broad necks to the ground, swaying as though their huge bodies felt the rhythms of the grain goddess beneath them.

Soon our men and boys prepared the furrows to receive the seed. With their iron-tined forks, they pushed into the earth, lifting, pausing, lifting as if to offer each forkful to the bright sun, before turning its blackness under. And the young women stood by, singing in sweet, high voices hymns to Milouziena, pleading with her to make our crops fruitful. Their voices aroused the men to use their planters and spill their seed into the soil. Then the grain maiden would be brought forth to mate with the grain king. And after, their lives would be offered up to Milouziena. From time to time I was clutched with fear that this would someday be my fate. And at other times I wanted to spend my life like those women before me, planting crops, learning the stories of our tribe. I was too young to know that there were other worlds beyond the cycles of planting and harvest. I had hoped we would stay on by the river at the edge of the forest for more of the night sun's waxing and waning, but, after the grain ripened and the season of warmth and light turned short days into long, then we would push on to other land, as my mother's people always had.

Beyond the marshes by the river lies the Hellene's polis of Olbia. Great stone figures of Milouziena flank the city gates. Once Milouziena was goddess of the earth and had only a single tail, but the Great Floods caused the sea to take our lands, so she became double-tailed, one part of the earth and one part of the water—with the starry sky above.

The Hellenes tell their own story of Herakles, father of our people and the Milouziena, the Hellenes call *mixoparthenos*, the mixed maiden. Milouziena stole the mares of Herakles while he slept under a tree in the dark forest. Herakles searched for his horses in vain. At last he found them in the cave of the beautiful Milouziena. She promised to return his mares if he would bed her. Herakles could not resist her, planting his seed in exchange for his mares. From this union Milouziena bore Herakles three sons, Skythos, Gathyrsos and Gelonos.

My mother was of the tribe of Gelonos. The Milouziena is our emblem. Herakles gave her a bow, a belt and a small gold cup and showed her how to string the bow and how to wear the belt. To this day my mother wears a golden cup tied at her waist with a leather thong. On her cheek is a scar hidden by a tattoo of Milouziena.

Sometimes the goddess's smile is sweet as she gives us blessing; sometimes we see her as a gaping tongued, leering maiden, whose glance turns men to stone, like the rivers of molten mud that flow down Fire Mountain.

My years by the Pontus Euxinus were too few, it was my fate to leave this place. I was not destined to live the life my mothers did before me.

Ω

Yanking the damp mask from her eyes, she wipes away her tears and shakes her head hard to clear it of darkness. There is no way she can continue to live like this, visions and dreams looming up. Her mind is spinning out of control. Visions are taking over her life. She closes the laptop and lays her head on its consoling warmth for a few moments, then reaches for the phone to call Giovanni.

Book III

Giovanni
Lecce, Puglia, the Day after Thanksgiving, 2007

He is shaving when he hears his cell phone ringing through his briefcase. Another one of those early morning crank calls and hang ups he's been having lately! "*Caspite*—go ahead, ring, ring your head off," he shouts. But when the vibrating sound becomes too much for his nerves, he pounces on his briefcase as though it were something he wants to kill.

He's relieved to hear Bianca's voice.

"I'm calling you because I've been scared ever since I came home." She tells him about the break-in. "I don't know what to do. And there was a scrap of paper on the kitchen counter. On it was written Sacra Corona Unita."

"What! Are you kidding me?"

"Why would I be? The detective who came by told me it was a Mafia symbol."

"He's right, the Mafia of Puglia. Why would anyone want to come by your apartment and tear it apart? Poor Bianca." He hears his feeble attempt at consolation. "You must have been terrified! You're sure you're not missing anything then?"

"I have very few possessions to miss."

Strange. He imagined Bianca Fiore living amidst a plethora of ancient artifacts and icons, like the ones she writes about. "What do you think the burglar wanted?"

"I've no idea. Besides the diary and earrings, another of my most precious possessions was with me—Nina's watercolor, the miniature of the Campanile in Venice."

"A miniature of the Campanile?" He pauses, then says? "Do you know when she painted it?"

"On July 13, 1902. She writes about it in the diary I showed you. It's why I wanted to sit in the Piazza until the clock struck the very hour of the very day the Campanile collapsed."

"You're positive about that date—the 13th of July, 1902?" He mutters something about being relieved, but hopes she hasn't noticed.

"Are you still there, Giovanni?"

"I hope you've put your valuable earrings and the painting in a safe place."

"I took them to a bank safety deposit box."

"You did exactly the right thing. You must take good care of them since they mean so much to you."

"After almost losing one of Nina's earrings in the Grand Canal, I swear I'll never wear them again until I can find a jeweler to put on safety wires that can be hooked over my ears."

Strange that he suddenly remembers her ears. Pretty ears, small, like moon shells in ammonite.

"Giovanni, I can hardly wait for you to come to New York. I've been wanting to talk to you about something important— a startling discovery I've made."

A long silence.

"I'd like very much to hear about it, but I'm sorry, Bianca," he responds and he means it. "I'd planned on calling you tomorrow to say that I won't be coming for the December Antiquities sales. I have to go south to checkout some work on the field. Flooding rains have caused mudslides and cave-ins on one of our digs. We've had some real setbacks. Why don't you think about taking a sabbatical and joining me in Italy?" A hollow invitation since he's sure there's no way she'll ever leave her job.

Another long silence.

"I can't just pick and fly to Italy again. Sergio will fire me. I need to work—and to write. Besides, I like my job even though I'm not crazy about my boss. I'm disappointed. I was looking forward to your visit."

He hears the tremolo in her voice. He apologizes again

and pulls out a cigarette, hoping that she won't cry. Even though he can't see her face, it bothers him to hear women weep. He cuts the conversation short by telling her that he has to rush off to an appointment.

"If you decide to come, just give me a ring. If I don't answer, leave a message. I'm always checking. I'll be in Milan for two days and then fly to Naples on Thursday. Why not meet me there? Think about it, Bianca."

He takes a long, deep, unsatisfying drag, wondering if all this is worth it.

Bianca
November 27, New York City, 2007

She's relieved when Monday workday is over. The temperature has dropped to below freezing, and the wind blows against her as she walks up from the subway at 59th and Lexington Avenue. In the darkness, early Christmas lights flicker in shop windows along Madison Avenue. When she reaches Pratesi, she stops to admire the forget-me-not embroidered sheets in the window. Maybe if she's careful turning in her expense accounts, someday she might be able to splurge on sheets like these.

At 72nd and Madison, she turns east, thinking she'll stop at Grace's Marketplace for more of those now-in-season *tarocchi*, Sicilian blood oranges. As she nears the corner of Third Avenue, she sees a man in a long black cape standing at the stoplight. Pulled down over his face is a slouch hat like an old fashioned Borsalino. The hat hides his eyes and nose. A muffler covers his chin and mouth. He seems faceless. He reminds her of the man in the old Sandeman Sherry ads. Or of the description of the black cloaked man in Nina's diary. She shivers. And not from the cold.

As she crosses Third Avenue, she thinks she hears his tread behind her; her legs take longer strides toward Grace's. But before she pushes open the door, she turns around. He's across the street, his head bent. Then he disappears around the corner.

She steps inside the market, and even in her fear she takes note of the aromas of rising yeast, aged parmesan, citrus peel. Leaning against the take-out counter, she searches her pockets for a tissue to wipe her damp forehead. Is the figure in the black cape a vision, a phantom from Nina's diary lodged in her mind like a bullet in her brain? Or has she been followed by a flesh and blood man?

"Who's got number eight?" shouts the clerk behind the deli counter.

Ω

That evening she can't get the stranger out of her thoughts. It's making her neurotic That night she has an urge to call Giovanni, but in Italy it's early morning. Why bother him, she thinks, dismissing the idea as she carefully washes and dries dishes. Keeping busy seems to keep the visions at bay, and what suddenly gives her courage is discipline, this new-found dedication to order. She yearns to transform herself into a woman not only Giovanni can admire but she can admire too.

Ω

Just after she's gone to bed around one in the morning, she hears the doorbell ring. She won't answer it. Officer De Vita might have been right. Maybe someone is after her—or something in her apartment. The bell rings four more times. If she had a panic button, she would push it. Without turning on the lights, she tiptoes to the door and waits until the ringing stops. After a few long minutes she peers through the peephole. Nothing. Moving to the window, she sees the back of a man in a black cape crossing the street. Now she's convinced that her visions are crossing over into reality. She grabs the phone. Six hours difference. In Italy that means seven in the morning. She dials Giovanni's cell phone and leaves a message. She's coming!

Zatoria

One night before the spring harvest my mother killed the king of our tribe, the man who would have taken me as the maiden whose life he would offer up in the grain ceremony. That night the King entered our cabin, a dagger clutched in his hand. He had come to kill my mother and maybe to kill me, but my strong mother grasped his dagger and thrust it in his heart. When he was dead she wiped the blade clean and put it in her pouch. She ordered my younger brother and me to make ready to flee while she gathered up food. We pulled on deerskin leggings and boots; my hands shook so that I could hardly wind the gut strings around my ankles. Blood gushed from the dead King's body; she threw a blanket over him, made a torch from dried branches, touched it to the hearth's glowing embers, then to the bloody blanket until flames leapt around him. We waited until the fire swept over the rooftop, then mounted our horses and made our way toward Olbiopolis and the dwelling of Zalmoxis, my father. A half moon shone upon us as we rode. The wind and the wolves howled around us. Tears froze on my cheeks while my heart pumped in terror.

Ω

The next day Bianca finally gets up the nerve to speak to Sergio in his office. He seems to be avoiding her.

"I hope you and your family had a Happy Thanksgiving," she says, trying her best to be polite and interested.

He nods. "I decided to take the family to Zurich, after all.

Oh, Leonardo told me that you had a robbery when you returned from Venice. Why am I'm just now hearing about it?"

"Break in, yes. Robbery, no. I didn't find anything missing. "

"Well, that's good news!" he responds brusquely. "Now let's talk business. Leonardo tells me you finally turned in your expense accounts."

"That's right, Sergio." *Now I'll have more than enough for a plane ticket and cash to take out from the ATM machine.*

"Good girl. You've got quite a bit of money coming to you."

"What is this 'good girl' business? Leonardo says the same thing. You both speak as if I were a child. I resent it." She can't believe her new found spunk.

He smiles. "Come on—we only want to take care of you, Bianca."

"I can take care of myself."

"Not from what I've seen so far. When are you going to let me come by to cook dinner for you again?"

"I'll have to check my calendar." She heads briskly toward the door. "I'm so busy now it will have to be after Christmas. Last night I decided to fly to Naples."

"Hey—Napoli—why Napoli? What's the matter with you? You don't seem like the same girl—excuse me, person—I used to know. What the hell has happened to you?"

"I met a man."

His jaw drops.

"Noooooh.—I don't believe it. Who's the lucky guy?"

"Someone I met in Venice. I can't wait to go back."

His tone becomes oily, seductive. "Bianca, Bianca, *Finalmente!* Don't you remember the first time I sent you to Venice to write a story on that eleventh century throne—the one with the Kufic writing in San Pietro di Castello? How you couldn't wait to get the hell out of the city. Christ! I remember how shocked I was when you took the train back to Milan the same day, after I'd told you to stay for a few days, all expenses paid. What the hell has suddenly made you change your mind about Venice?"

She grabs the doorknob. "It's a long story. Sergio. You wouldn't understand. I'm going to my travel agency to book my flight."

He leaps from his chair. "Wait a minute. You can't do this to me!" He kicks his desk chair so hard it spins around carving a circle in space. He follows with a tirade of Italian curses. "What about my next issue?"

"You're in luck." She hears herself speaking calmly. "I almost finished the February assignment last night."

"At least you've done that!" He gives her a sour smile. "What's it on?"

"The *mixoparthenos*. Or *melusina*—or whatever you want to call her. Or how about the Saga of Zatoria? Take your pick."

"What the hell are you talking about? Who is Zatoria?"

"That's what I'm going to find out."

"Why don't you tell me a little about your boyfriend."

"He's my business."

"Suddenly everything is your business. After three years of taking care of you, feeding you, being like a...a brother to you—you give me one day's notice that you're going to Naples. What the hell do you want from those stupid Southerners? They're a different race down there. A race apart. Or didn't you know that?"

"You're dead wrong, Sergio. Ovid and Gabriele d'Annunzio and Dante Gabriel Rossetti were from the Abruzzo, as were the great philosophers, beginning with Pythagoras and Benedetto Croce. And what about Carlo Levi and Lampedusa and *The Leopard* in Sicily? The first Italian universities were in the South. You must have forgotten that. I could go on and on! I may not know much about Sybaris, but I do know there was a great civilization in the South while your Italians in the North were still living in rude huts." Her fingernails dig into her palms. "I'm going to take a leave of absence. I just decided, and don't try to make me change my mind."

"You'd better get your head examined! You can't walk out on us this way. I need you right here. I've got to leave for Italy in a week, and I won't be back until after New Year's. And you tell me you're taking a leave of absence? After all I've done for you!"

Her shoulders pull back squarely, her spine straightens, she speaks calmly. "I won't be taking a real sabbatical since I'll be writing for the magazine as I go along. But if you don't like what I write during my time away, maybe someone else will publish it. And if I decide not to come back—well—go find someone else." She hands him a sheet of paper. "Here's my proposal. You can read it at your leisure. Ciao, Sergio. And please say ciao to Leonardo."

She walks out the door, picks up her check from the bookkeeper, and heads straight to Bloomingdale's for make up lessons and new clothes.

In the late afternoon she calls her mother to tell her that the travel agency said she had enough mileage for a round trip to Italy, and was able to get her a reservation on the 15th of December.

And more importantly, to let her know that she plans to visit her new friend, Giovanni, Allegra's cousin. She can tell from the tone of her mother's voice that she's thrilled. "My dear girl, I'm so happy you're taking some time off—just go and enjoy yourself. And for heaven's sake, please don't worry about me. Just give me a ring now and then or send an e-mail. I finally got myself a computer."

kylix (or *cylix*, pl. *kylixes* or *kylikes*)
Greek. A type of wine-drinking cup with a broad relatively shallow body raised on a stem from a foot, many with painted decoration in the Black-figure or Red-figure styles of the 6th and 5th century B.C. The word comes from the Greek *kylix* "cup," which is cognate with Latin *calix*, the source of the English word "chalice."

When we arrived in Olbiopolis my mother learned that the Thracian shaman Zalmoxis would soon depart from Olbia to the south shore and Sinope. Then he would set sail for Lokri in Megale Hellas. I was eager to greet my father and wondered if he would recognize me as his daughter, or better still, accept me. My mother said that we must wait until he has spoken to his followers on the agora, and then we would approach him. What if he denied I was his child, but why would he want to?

When at last we found Zalmoxis, he embraced me for he knew at once that I was his. My mother pleaded with my father to take me with him, and my brother would stay on with her. And when he agreed, she looped her precious amber beads around my neck. Then, plucking the gold plaques from her tunic, she slipped them into a small sack already heavy with dolphin coins to pay my passage to Sinope and Lokri

Epizefiri. In my deerskin bag, wrapped in straw, I kept my only treasure, the *kylix* my mother and Zalmoxis drank from in the feast of the Thracian God, Dionysos. Painted on it is a scene of women fighting Hellene hoplites.

At dockside, shifty-eyed men with curly black beards and crooked noses took us aboard their blue-sailed boat. I have seen tears in my mother's eyes, but have never seen her cry or weep as I often do. My little brother threw his arms around me and sobbed. My mother and I wept with him. We all knew that we might never see one another again.

Giovanni
Naples, December 15, 2007

His plane from Milan lands at Naples airport half an hour before hers is due from New York. He waits patiently for that first glimpse, wondering if her looks will still shock him. True, her soft, pearl-glazed fingers are lovely, but, with that wild mane of hair, those ill-fitting clothes looking as though they'd never known an iron, she leaves him cold. He admits to himself that he's put off by the idea of sexual contact with Bianca Fiore. At the same time he feels an urge to claim her, control her. But then she doesn't seem the kind of American woman who would be dazzled by wealth. Or, for that matter, by his titled, aristocratic friends. Once again, he scolds himself for his shallowness.

His mother, a brilliant tree botanist, has never set store on her own looks or her son's. If he ever marries, Silvana Santopuoli will not be the typical Italian mother-in-law who makes sure his wife irons his shirts meticulously, who makes sure she caters to all his creature comforts. He's probably no different from many Italian men, spoiled rotten by Mama. He knows himself well enough to sense that he's using Bianca for reasons of his own.

Passengers begin shuffling out from the Customs Hall. When the plane seems completely unloaded, he wonders if she's changed her mind--but then he's sure she would have called. In his entire life he's never been stood up. He gropes for his cell phone to be sure this isn't the first. Then, when he looks up and finds her standing there, he surprises himself by feeling strangely relieved. He throws one arm around her shoulder, drawing her close to his side. He kisses her formally on both cheeks, breathing in her scent of almonds crushed with cream and carnations.

"I hoped you'd recognize me with my hair drawn back."

Her smile dazzles. "It's very becoming this way," he mumbles. Are his eyes deceiving him, or is he becoming used to her? His eyes sweep over her, admiring her lean, straight-line grace.

She's wearing a black belted suit that shows off a long-waisted narrow rib cage. Slim, well-cut trousers enhance long legs he notices for the first time. Although she spent the night on the plane, her clothes look fresh. No, she isn't at all the plain, untidy woman he remembered.

"I'm happy to see you, Giovanni. I don't know how or where to begin ..."

"First you must get some rest." He takes hold of her precious, roll-on computer bag wheeling it behind him. Slung over her arm is also a hanging bag, and, as though this time she intends a longer stay, they pick up a suitcase in the claim area.

"What's our plan?" she asks as they walk toward Hertz. Unconsciously he's drawn his hand through her arm, entwining his fingers with hers.

We'll pick up the car and drive on to the *castello* in Sicchia, about sixty miles."

Her face reveals a mixture of seriousness and excitement. "Is that the castle you told me about? The one built by the sons of Simon de Monfort?"

"Yes—it's been in my mother's family for over a hundred years, but she rarely goes now. After my father died, we spent our summers there while my mother researched Sicchia's trees."

"Sicchia? Nina mentions Sicchia in her diary! What sort of trees grow there?"

"Sycamores, beech, birch, pine, ash."

"Oaks?"

Why, he wonders, is she suddenly so interested in arboriculture?

"When we arrive we'll have a short rest, then a light supper. If you like, we can have a walk in the morning—but you should go to bed early." He loads her beat up Sport Sac bag and roll-on in the back of the SUV along with his old but well cared for leather valise and his guitar case.

"You'll meet the family's long time retainer. Anselmo, who takes care of the *castello*, must be the third or fourth generation of the same family. He'll cook a simple dinner for us. Then early tomorrow we'll be on our way to Sybaris."

Bianca
December 15, 2007

From Naples they drive north on the *Autostrada del Sole* and exit on the road to Isernia, driving through a valley looking up to patchworks of brilliant green winter wheat, blue-green broccoli-rape and squares of dusty pink, precisely tilled earth, ready to be furrowed and seeded.

They arrive in Sicchia, in the Molise, by mid afternoon. Ascending on the turning, twisting switchback road, they finally reach the hilltop village and a small but impressive turreted stone *castello* a few kilometers off the main road. Giovanni stops at the gate and presses the buzzer. The gate yawns open and they drive into the cobbled courtyard and park by the castle's heavy oak portals. The door knocker makes loud thumps when Giovanni slams it hard against the wood. They are greeted by an elderly, gray-haired man wearing a brass-buttoned jacket with gilt shoulder tabs. When Giovanni introduces Anselmo to her, she offers her hand. Muttering a greeting and only vaguely smiling, he excuses himself to unload their suitcases.

They enter a hall where stag antlers line the walls along with old swords and muskets. A flag is embroidered with a garland of oak leaves and olive branches tied with a blue ribbon. "The coat of arms of Sicchia," Giovanni explains. In one corner stands a tall mahogany pillar, wider than a grandfather's clock, with a large concave disc made up of hundreds of faceted glass tesserae set into its face.

"I've never seen a lamp like it. Is it for reflecting candle-light?"

He nods. "Margaret Norville's lover, a writer, purportedly brought it from Krakow and used it for ceremonial purposes. He was a strange man, detested by her family. From all accounts he had bizarre tastes. The *contadini* still talk about wild, decadent parties with his Roman friends when Margaret wasn't around. He wore a black cape and a slouch hat—like local men in the village, even when he was away from here."

She shudders—and feels a frisson of fear shoot through her, *the man in a black cape who'd followed me home. And the words in Nina's diary. But I will never paint what I saw in Sicchia.*

Anselmo materializes from nowhere with a silver tray and two glasses of prosecco which they gratefully accept. After clinking glasses, she returns to the subject of wild parties, and, as nonchalantly as she can, asks, "How and why were his parties decadent?"

Raising an eyebrow he gives her an oblique look, as if to say, "Try using your imagination." Then he takes her arm. "Come, I'll show you to your room." She follows him up the narrow stone staircase, all the while envisioning the black-caped man, and, at the same time, wondering how the white linen stair runner manages to stay so clean. When they reach a small landing with two facing doors, he opens one. "This is for you."

A four-poster bed centers the small, butter-yellow room. Carved, gilded grapes and vines cling to its twisted baroque posts. The only other furnishings are a painted green commode festooned with flower garlands and matching bed tables. Crisp curtains are drawn across lead-mullioned windows. Although the cozy room retains old world charm, it also seems fresh and modern, the sort of bedroom she wishes she had in New York.

"My mother re-decorated after she inherited the castle—now it's authentic Colefax and Fowler." He grins. "This room used to be quite weird."

She laughs. "Please describe it to me. Or would you rather have me envision it?"

He seems reluctant.

"Go ahead. I want to know what it was like."

"Okay, if you insist. The ceiling was a deep red-purple. the bedspread and curtains purple velvet. There was a painted frieze around the room just below the ceiling. It read *lux est bonum sed carpe tenebrae*. Light is good but seize the darkness."

Strange, that's just what I do! Shaking her head in wonder, she replies "What a curious conundrum."

He shrugs—"No more curious than The Writer. The room used to be crammed with furniture—shelves crammed with bits and pieces of junk. A wide *cassone*, painted with mythical beasts, griffins and grotesques, stood against the wall. My mother sold everything but the antique bed brought from Venice by Margaret Norville. Then she used these simple local Abruzzi cottons to decorate. Now it's time you had a rest."

She won't give up. "Did Margaret ever have any children by this man?"

He gives her a sideways glance, and shakes his head. "She had only one daughter, my great-grandmother Rose Alba, your great grandmother Nina's childhood friend."

"Did the eccentric writer have any children?"

"That's another story." He checks his watch. "I'm tired from the drive. And you must be from your long trip. Anselmo will serve dinner at eight."

He leaves and goes into his room. No, Giovanni isn't ready yet to share a room with her, but then maybe he'll never be, no matter how hard she tries.

Ω

In the oak-beamed kitchen, Anselmo has set the table with sturdy earthenware bowls and pewter utensils. In the great hearth a crackling fire spits, sparks. Burnished copper pots and pans hang on whitewashed walls. Giovanni dips a ladle into a steaming tureen, filling their bowls with minestrone that they eat with crusty bread and ewe's milk cheese. "Simple and delicious, but hardly a Sybaritic feast," he says.

"A few weeks ago, when my boss and I had dinner together, we talked about Sybaris and truffles. I remember wondering if the Sybarites ever ate them."

"Tuscany was ancient Etruria, the land of the Etruscans. They still hunt for truffles there. And since the Sybarites traded with Etruscans and aped their manners, we can safely assume they also ate their truffles. Especially since the Sybarites were always on the look out for special recipes. Athenaeus tells us food was so important to them that they planned their banquets a year in advance." He laughs. "Customs haven't changed much in Italy, have they?" Then more seriously he adds, "Sybaris was rich from growing wheat in a vast and fertile plain. The Sybarites were also renowned for raising bulls—the famous coin of Sybaris has a representation of a bull on its face. They also sacrificed many bulls—and sacrifice and feasting usually went hand in hand. The people from nearby Kroton didn't approve of this. At least Pythagoras, their leading philosopher-mathematician, didn't. Eventually, historians say, Sybaris was destroyed in part because of their decadent habits, Etruscan habits. Until my father and grandfather dug with the University of Pennsylvania team in 1968, no traces of the place were known. The city was buried beneath many meters of mud and silt-maybe eight meters. It will take years for it to be completely excavated, probably not in our lifetime."

"When exactly did this happen?"

"In the sixth century B.C."

"The late sixth century B.C. has become an interest if mine. Since I saw you last I've been doing some research on that period—and the Middle Ages—mostly on north-eastern France. Now I can hardly wait to visit the site."

"Unfortunately, there's little to see. Digging is seasonal and slow and so far not that much has been uncovered, though they have found some very nice Roman mosaic floors from Thurii, a city eventually built over submerged Sybaris about a hundred years after its fall. The Greek historian, Herodotus, lived in Thurii.

She's rapt as he speaks.

"I'm afraid I'm boring you—telling you more than you ever wanted to know about Sybaris."

"No, please go on—I *want* to learn more about this fabled place. You're a gifted story teller, Giovanni, an academic one. You *know* so much!"

Encouraged, he continues. "I remember being surprised to learn that Sybaris was a city—a polis—larger than Athens. The Sybarite Greeks welcomed and included foreigners, something the citizens of Athens did not do. To Athenians anyone who did not speak Greek was a barbarian. Not so in Sybaris. Besides wealth from wheat and wine and bulls, they were made even richer by a short trade route across the narrow end, the trim ankle, so to speak, of the Italian boot. While other cities of Magna Graecia had to send their boats around the straits to arrive at the westerly Tyrrhenian Sea, braving storms and pirates, the Sybarites could send their trade goods in a short overland trip, a trip of only a few days, now just a few hours. In very little time, they would arrive in Poseidonia, a Sybarite city known today as Paestum."

"You've explained this so much better than Sergio, my boss at the magazine."

When she mentions Sergio, she sees a strange look cross Giovanni's face, but he continues. "The Sybarites, loving luxury, traded with the Milesians for purple dye. When Sybaris was destroyed by Kroton, the citizens of Melitus, in what is now Western Turkey, went into mourning. There must have been tremendous resonances throughout the entire Mediterranean world at the fall of the city. Herodotus tells how Miletus wept for Sybaris and for the loss of their most valued customers. The devastation of such an important economy had to have affected commerce throughout the Mediterranean, and beyond. It could even have caused sweeping changes in taste, almost like self-imposed sumptuary laws. I have my own theory about ceramics from Greece or Greater Greece, Puglia and Calabria."

"What kind of theory?"

Giovanni hesitates, then after a long sip of Sangiovese, and clearly born to teach, goes on with his history lesson. "Sybaris was a gold-loving polis. My friend at the Ashmolean, Michael Vickers, believes that in Greek ceramics, clay imitated metal. Red clay represented gold, black clay, silver. Michael believes that these ceramics were used as grave goods, or as disposable utensils to use in feasts, stand-ins for the real thing—valuable gold and silver objects. In my hypothesis, after Sybaris, the Golden, no longer existed after 510 B.C. Trade fell off all over the Mediterranean. There must have been alterations in what was considered beautiful and appropriate. That's just about the time ceramics went from being black figure to red figure. In other words, from a background of red, signifying gold, and a design in black, signifying silver, to just the opposite. And from then on, the taste was for the black background with the design in red. With the fall of Sybaris, a lot of gold was lost and probably there was much less gold traded so ceramic style changed. That's my theory in a nutshell."

"Well—I think I understand. Your explanation is that a black figure represents silver on a gold pot, later to become a gold figure on a silver pot, silver being a metal of lesser value."

He takes her hand in his and squeezes it gently. "You've got it! And this sudden change came just after the fall of Sybaris. Some day soon I'd like you to tell me all about Sybaris."

"How do you mean?"

"By doing whatever it is you do at *Eyes and Soul*. By using your visions."

"But archaeology is a science. You, of all people, shouldn't have to be reminded of that. Besides, the Archaic period in Italy has always been Sergio's territory. He's never let me write about Etruscan art or artifacts—or about anything south of Rome. He's always joking that everything south of Rome is Africa. If I ever get to work on anything Italian, it's always Northern, or of a much later period."

"You mean that he chooses exactly what he wants you to write about? You have no say in the matter?"

"Well, lately I have been choosing my own subjects—and I'm open to suggestions from readers. But Sergio is—or was—my publisher, after all. If you're really interested in my help, knowing so little about the south of Italy should make it easier. For me the South is still untrammeled territory. I'll have to use my imagination."

"Do you know what Einstein said about the imagination? Please permit me to quote him.

'Imagination is more important than knowledge. For knowledge is limited to all we now know and understand, while imagination embraces the entire world, and all there ever will be to know and understand.'"

"Okay. If Einstein says so, I'm convinced. When and where do we start? And when will you show me what's on the wall in the *masseria*? The suspense is killing me."

"Right now it's time to get some real rest." He rises from the table. "If we intend to arrive at Sybaris at a decent hour tomorrow, we should get an early start. You must be tired."

Why, she wonders, has Giovanni pointedly evaded her question about showing her his discovery?

Ω

She considers taking a shower before going to bed, but she barely manages to wash her face and brush her teeth. She's even too weary to open the larger suitcase for her nightgown and crawls naked between the linen sheets. The crisply ironed pillowcase, still smelling of hay and sunshine, feels smooth and luxurious." Turning over onto her stomach, she clasps her pillow tightly. Visions take over. The man in Nina's diary looms up, the outline of his cape still visible against the black velvet screen, black on black. He looks like the same man who followed her near Grace's Marketplace, the same man as Margaret Norville's lover who'd once lived in this *castello*.

As she becomes drowsy, she sees the room as it must have been when Nina was here as a young girl. Purple velvet walls glowing from flames of many candles, some very tall like the long tapers that used to cost fifty francs to light at Lourdes. Branches studded with pinecones festoon the stags' antlers hanging on the walls. At the foot of the bed, a chest as wide and as long as a coffin, is painted with devils brandishing pitchforks.

Nina lies inside on purple satin, her fair hair spread out upon a white pillow, a Pre-Raphaelite beauty by Burne-Jones or Dante Gabriel Rossetti. A dress the color of sprouting green and around her neck a golden torque, the golden torque at Châtillon-sur-Seine, the finials worked with winged horses.

Nina's eyes are closed, but Bianca sees her lashes quiver. She is relieved that Nina is alive.

A man appears from out of the shadows, flings his cape on the purple bed, falls upon the coffin—upon Nina—whose eyes open wide with horror. He pushes his hips hard against hers.

Nina screams. He moans. Blood stains Nina's pale green dress. A dark hand snuffs out the candles one by one.

Her heart jack-hammering away, Bianca sits bolt upright, sickened by the relentless image of Nina in the coffin. Was this vision beyond the realm of the real world, or was it the by-product of her own imagination? She flicks on the lamp. Only three o'clock. She thinks about taking a sleeping pill, but they might make her feel worse—besides Giovanni might be cross with her if she oversleeps. Instead, she pulls the bedspread up to her chin and tries drawing the black velvet curtain across the screen in her head. But it won't budge. Finally she jumps out of bed and takes two aspirins. This is one vision she can't and won't record in her computer journal. She doesn't fall asleep until almost dawn.

In the morning, Anselmo packs their luggage into an old Lancia Giovanni exchanged for his Range Rover and they are off by eight o'clock. When she shakes Anselmo's hand and thanks him, she senses his relief at their departure. She thinks to herself it's perhaps a burden for him to get the house ready, dinner prepared, without any help.

Traffic is light. She's still groggy and, after the vivid, frightening dream about Nina being raped by The Writer, she doesn't feel the least bit talkative.

As they pass field after field of white longhorn cattle, Giovanni begins his daily lesson. "There's some argument about whether or not they're the descendants of the ancient cattle of Sybaris. I like to think so." He laughs. "I must confess that I've been thinking about stopping for mozzarella, so fresh it drips warm milk. But I don't want to appear to be yet another a food obsessed Italian."

She barely acknowledges his remark. Food is the farthest thing from her mind: Zatoria is the closest.

Lokri Epizefiri, Apulia, Magna Graecia

In the culture of Ancient Greece and Magna Graecia, a *pinax*-plural-*pinakes*. A "board" or tablet of painted wood or terracotta, marble or bronze serving as a votive object deposited in a sanctuary as an offering to Demeter and Persephone and Aphrodite.

Zatoria

We had not many days in Sinope. When the winter winds calmed, we set sail for Lokri, not such a long journey and land is never out of sight as our boat hugs the shore. The blue sails billow in the spring breeze and we arrive at Lokri Epizefiri in only seven moons. As the boat meets its moorings in the harbor, the vast sea is as flat as a pool of melted silver. On the docks grain is everywhere, sacks spilling wheat, bound for cities I have never heard of. Women wrap straw around clay pots, the *kraters, kantharoi* and *kylixes* the Hellenes use for drinking and feastings and as offerings in the graves of the dead for their use in the afterlife. The Lokrians worship at two temples renowned across the seas, the temple of the Kore, Persephone, daughter of Demeter, the Hellenes' harvest goddess. Beyond the city, on the edge of the sea, stands the temple of the Cyprian Aphrodite. These temples are of such beauty they say they rival those in Olbia or Athens.

At the great temple of Persephone, the women leave clay pomegranates and *pinakes* as offerings to Mother and Daughter. The Lokrian women have rights they do not have in Athens. They have taken it upon themselves to return to the rule of women. Unfaithful wives found with lovers, or *hierodule*, and women who had lost favor with citizens, abandoned Athens to found this polis, Lokri of the Sweet Breezes. Here, a child bears the name of the mother's family, not the father's.

This is the year few children were born to the Lokrian women. Many men succumbed to high fever and some who survived could no longer sire a child. The young men had gone off to wage war with the Persians, while Lokrian merchants plied the seas trading coral, wine, and oil for the tin and amber of the Hyperboreans and for wheat from the people who live along the shores of the Euxinus.

The women of Lokri took matters into their own hands. They knew they had to dedicate themselves to Aphrodite if the Lokrians were to continue to increase in number. A woman who wanted a child would offer herself to the goddess. On a night of her choosing, she would come to the temple to loop a garland of myrtle across Aphrodite's stone image and sing hymns to her beauty. Then she would go forth with any passing stranger who might please her.

The temple to Aphrodite, the Cyprian born of foam, Savior of men, sits on a neck of land that juts out into the bright sea. They say it pleases the violet-crowned goddess to look out over the loud-moaning sea, and, with her sweet moist breath, calm the waves to make the voyage safe and swift for sailors. There, young boys, beginning to feel their manhood, offer up their seed against the stone folds of her gown.

Ships from many ports moor close by and love-starved men come to shore seeking the pleasures of the Lokrian women. Childless women come upon tall, golden-haired giants from the Hellenes' Massilia, or the pale-faced, blue-eyed Hyperboreans, or dark-skinned sea traders who entice them with coffers of fragrant spices, ambrosial balsams, and flasks of cedar oil to burn, making the air thick and sweet around the temple.

Night has fallen and the Lokrian lighthouse torch burns its flames around the temple of Aphrodite. The sea trembles looking toward her image. Tonight the goddess is draped with a garment of *byssus*, gold-embroidered. The fair Ortygia left this offering, having made a large fortune from the beauty of her own body.

In the portico of her vast temple, doves nest everywhere, leaving droppings in the eaves and gables. Other doves with clipped wings, fat with grain, waddle, pecking at the offerings to the goddess. They say that the cooing of doves is like the sound of a woman moaning with pleasure in the arms of her lover.

In the most sacred space, women prepare them-

selves for the ceremony they call the *hieros gamos*.
Pyxides filled with perfumed red unguent for the lips
and breast tips, fine brushes with soot-black powder
to line the eyes, and golden powders to dust on face
and body. With her *peplos* loosened, a woman is
ready to dedicate herself to the goddess of beauty
and love. For the poets sing that on these nights nothing is sweeter for these women than desire and their
mouths spit honey.

Book IV

And the Lady Blanchefleur loved Sir Percival every
day with a greater and greater passion, but Sir
Percival showed no passion of love for her in
return, and then Lady Blanchefleur was
greatly troubled.
—Chrétien de Troyes, *Le Conte du Graal*

Giovanni
December 16, 2007

On their way to Foggia, Giovanni suddenly stops to get something from the trunk. She opens the window and watches him scanning the horizon with binoculars. Finally he jumps into his seat and they drive off.

"You never told me you were a bird watcher."

He shakes his head and laughs. "Bianca, Bianca you're blessedly naïve! If there are any *tombaroli* out there, I can usually spot them with these powerful glasses. December and January are the best months for tomb looters and this is one of their favorite areas for probing and plundering. The ground is wet from autumn rains, so it's easier for them to screw their long metal rods into the softened earth to probe the soil. And they also wear masks so they can't be identified with a telephoto lens. Sometimes they even pay the farmers to plow the earth or use farm equipment to carve furrows seemingly for seed planting. Now they've even begun to use dredges and deep plowing to make it look as if there's legitimate agricultural work going on."

He reaches for the map from the door's side pocket and hands it to her.

"Where are we now?" she asks.

"Not far from Canosa, once the stronghold of the ancient Daunians."

"Who were they?"

"People of Celto-Illyrian stock. from around the Danube, a horse-riding elite warrior aristocracy. They made their way across Europe to the Adriatic to settle the East coast of the Italian peninsula around the ninth century B.C.—before the Greeks arrived on the scene. We'd know more about the Daunians if only their tombs had not been so unmercifully violated and evidence destroyed forever—there are still some *tombaroli* around here who smash less salable but still valuable artifacts.

"In 1980 an untouched tomb was found—the Tomb of the Willow Branches. What they discovered in the tomb were tightly braided willow branches, most likely used in rituals, in the Orphic Mysteries. Orphism was strong here in the South—due to the influence of Pythagoras and the belief in the afterlife, a new concept for the Greeks."

Bianca
December 16, 2007

After stopping for a *panini* at an Autogrill, they arrive at the marina of Sybaris and the Hotel Oleandro. Giovanni seems worn-out and goes straight to his room for a siesta. Bianca is shown to a tiny room with a view facing a basin of luxury pleasure craft and moored sailboats with battened-up sails. The silver sky has darkened to pewter gray with a light mist falling, fog creeping in.

She unpacks her fancy never-yet-worn nightgown. Even though her mother once let it slip that she thought her daughter would never marry, Bianca knows hope still springs eternal in Mom's breast--probably more hope in hers than in her own. When she checks the gown for washing instructions, she's relieved when she reads the tag—100% polyester. Her mother knows better than to have bought silk. Real silk needs to be ironed. Bianca is determined finally to wear the nightgown on this trip and promises herself to rinse it out ever every other night and let it drip dry.

Get rid of your fantasies about him, she keeps urging herself. *A romance will never develop between us. He's already made that very clear.* But then she rationalizes—*maybe he's just as lonely as I am. Did you ever think of that, Bianca?* She keeps re-mending herself, keeps correcting and improving the text she writes in her head.

She slips into her nightgown and crawls between the crisp sheets smelling as fresh and salty as if they'd been washed at sea and flapped dry on a mast. She closes her eyes, relieved that the black curtain is still drawn tight against the visions. She nods off thinking about the ancient Greeks in Italy, wondering when they'd first sailed to these shores. The last thing she hears is the deep, muted sound of a distant foghorn. She falls asleep envisioning Nina's gold earring gleaming in the mud at the bottom of the Grand Canal.

Ω

When she wakes up, words echo in her head. "Sila, Sila, Sila, Sila." She turns on her computer and writes "Sila," the last word she "heard" as she entered consciousness. Then she records what she's "seen" in her dream.

She looks at her watch. It's almost five. She throws on her clothes and walks downstairs.

Giovanni is in the lounge playing his guitar. She recognizes the Adagio from Rachmaninoff's *Symphony No 2*. He looks up, then abruptly stops.

"Don't stop—please go on. I love that melody. I listen to the Adagio all the time—especially when I write."

"A few years back Eric Carmen added lyrics."

"Can you sing them for me?"

He hesitates as if he's just about to say no. "I can sing them all right—but I've sung them far too much these past few years."

"Are you sick of them?"

He shakes his head, then slapping his hand hard against the guitar, he begins to pluck its strings. He looks right at her. This time she knows the words will be for her, Bianca Evans Caldwell. Not for Bianca Fiore.

> *No use pretending things can still be right*
> *There's really nothing more to say.*
> *I'll get along without your kiss good night.*
> *Just close the door and walk away.*
>
> *Never gonna fall in love again.*

I don't wanna start with someone new
'Cause I couldn't bear to see it end
Just like me and you.

No I never wanna feel the pain
Of remembering how it used to be.
Never gonna fall in love again....

Her hopes are dashed. His heart is definitely tugging in a different direction from hers. Now she understands why he didn't want her to hear the lyrics—on second thought, he may have decided to use them as defensive armor. So she'd get the point—know exactly where she stands. Maybe it's easier for him to do it this way, in a song.

Hurt by his rebuff, she thinks that for his sake and hers, she'd better change the subject. "I just had the strangest dream. I don't always remember afternoon dreams, but this one is so vivid I wrote it in my computer journal."

"Tell me about it." He pauses. "If you want to."

She isn't really sure that she should share it. But, then, from the disappointed look on his face, she relents.

"My dream was about a woman whose husband wants to abandon his girl-baby in the forest because she isn't perfect." She smiles and shakes her head. "A puzzling dream because my own father never expected perfection from me or my work. To the contrary, it was my father who always encouraged me to use my imagination. My mother never understood it. I think it scared her."

"I'd like to read what you've written. It has the ring of a mythic tale."

"Sure...perhaps later on this evening you can come to my room."

"Better yet, why don't you bring your laptop to the lounge while we're having a drink before dinner?"

He's put her in her place. She bites her lower lip, hoping that maybe he'll forget about the dream and what he obviously thought was a blatant invitation to read it in the too close comfort of her room.

At eight o'clock he calls. "I'll be in the bar. Don't forget your computer."

She changes into a mid-calf black skirt, white cotton shirt and black cardigan and pins up her hair loosely. She unfolds the Versace scarf. She never once wore it in New York, but tonight she will. Spreading the scarf out on the bed, she stops to admire the silken image of the beautiful Medusa. This is not the ugly, frightening Gorgon whose glance turns men to stone. She loops and ties the scarf around her neck and looks in the mirror. Yes, Southern Italy is different, she's beginning to feel. Maybe Sergio is right. Maybe it is a race apart. Stranger yet, she's beginning to feel that she's a part of this race apart.

Giovanni

He's pleased that Bianca is wearing his gift. With her hair off her face and her subtle makeup, she looks quite attractive. He orders vodka on the rocks and sits by her side, watching intently as she boots up the laptop and scrolls through to her journal. She turns the screen toward him so he can read the entry.

Sila, the word Sila, repeats itself in my head.

I descend step after step to a basement apartment, not the one I'm living in now, but another I recognize from having lived there a long, long time ago. I knock on the door. A woman opens it.

I enter a room where I see a young woman, her stomach swollen as though she's about to give birth. The woman stumbles and falls. "Are you all right?" her husband asks. "Where does it hurt?" The young woman answers, "In my womb." Her husband shakes his head. He does not want to raise an imperfect child.

[Cut to another scene] I follow the woman who explains that she has given birth to a red-haired daughter. The woman is fearful for her child. Her husband exposes the baby girl in the forest but a she-bear finds her and suckles her.

Now the daughter is grown. Her hair is long and red, thick and wavy. Men surround her. They are building a ship, making plans for a voyage. The young woman is excited because she will be sailing with a group called the Forty-Nine Men. She will be the only woman on board. The red haired woman seems happy with the prospects of this sea journey.

Ω

He reads Bianca's dream three times before he finally speaks, "Bianca, do you know what you've written here? Do you have any idea at all?" From the look on her face he can tell she's puzzled.

She shrugs. "I tried not to read too much into it." Laughing self-consciously and blushing, she says. "A dream about a woman with forty-nine men? Freud would say this dream was obviously sexual wish-fulfillment for a frustrated old maid." Her face flushes even deeper.

He shakes his head in disbelief. "Surely you've read the tales of Jason and the Argonaut and the Golden Fleece."

"Of course I know about Jason's quest. When I was in college I read *Medea*—the tragedy—about the sorceress so angry when Jason deserts her that she avenges herself by killing their children-and destroying his new lover. Never a story I liked or identified with."

"Did you not know in the legend there was one woman who sailed with Jason? And forty-nine men? Fifty people sailed on the Argonaut. Forty-nine men and one woman."

"The woman's name?"

"Atalanta."

"The mythic huntress who raced? As in the 'swiftness of Atalanta'?"

"When Atalanta was born, her father abandoned her in the forest but she somehow survived."

She shakes her head in disbelief.

"Did you not know that Sybaris and Kroton were founded by Achaeans and Troezenians? And that the Troezenians were from Argos? Jason and his men were probably the first Greeks to settle these shores. One of the first Greek temples was built in Krotona, a temple to the goddess Hera Lacinia. We are near the Sila Mountains. What were you thinking about before you fell asleep?"

"I only remember asking myself who were the first Greeks to settle in Southern Italy. I can't remember anything after that."

"In your dream you were given the answer. Incredible!

What an ability you've been given! Now you can probably understand why you should be my guide. Have you read *The Iliad*?"

"Yes—in bits and pieces—but never all at once, nonstop from start to finish. I've always felt lacking in the Classics, although I read a lot on my own for my magazine assignments. Sergio keeps me so busy with my stories and covering the auctions, I hardly have time for anything else. I think he's afraid that I'll run out of visions for the vignettes."

"Why do you stay on?"

"It's a job, fairly well paid. Besides, he believes in me."

"He may, but he obviously sees you as a circulation booster. He uses you."

"Is that so very different from what you're doing?"

He feels his face warming. "Bianca, would you answer a question for me?"

"What is it?"

"When did all this begin? When did you learn about your extraordinary gift?"

"I'm not ready to tell you. Not yet. And you're not ready to tell me about your discovery—so we're even."

"Well, let's order some dinner then," he says curtly and beckons the waiter.

He wonders why he is making the same mistake all over again, falling for another woman who has visions and dreams fraught with curious details and meanings. They say the same mistake happens again—and maybe even again. He is the prime example. No, he's going to keep this woman at arm's length. He could be her best friend, but he will never be her lover.

Bianca

They finish their dinner in silence. Giovanni shifts about in his chair, gloomily taciturn as if she is boring the living daylights out of him. In self-defense, she allows her mind to wander, letting it descend as far as it will go without her mask.

I ponder which door to open. I see door handles. One is silver, the other bronze gleaming like dull brass with strange markings. I choose the latter. I wonder, is it Scythian or Thracian? In a clearing of the woods, a shaman holds aloft a long pole cut from a sapling pine topped by a golden cone. The leader of the tribe holds it high for all to see. Then, with the pine cone's tip, he marks the man in the center of the circle where they are to gather. The man is wound like a human spool with ox-hide strips sewn together, each no wider than a finger. The strips are slowly unwound to mark the shaman's circle.

A woman is watching the ceremony. She is someone I've seen before, still wearing her long coat of animal skin, like golden sable. The garment is edged with shearling or fur—I can't make it out. Now I see it. It's red fox. She turns her head, and the glow from the blazing fire throws light on her face. I see the tattoo on her cheek. It's clearer now. It's a tiny melusine.

A man leaps up. He wears wings of rawhide, thin as parchment, stretched on a frame and fastened to his back. He dances around the glowing coals. Shamans with antlers on their heads sit around a fire under a large cauldron. Men in goatskin capes stand around a wide circle formed by thongs of ox-hide.

The tall woman places her baby in the center of the circle. Young men, brandishing spears and clanging metal shields, dance around the child, their shouts fending off evil spirits. A figure in a white eagle mask pushes his way toward the center just as someone in a raven mask attempts to reach the child as though he wants to kill it. But the raven is frightened away by the white eagle and clashing cymbals and drumbeats.

The woman clutches moss in her hand—green moss she has ripped from logs that lie in the forest. She tosses the moss into the cauldron. She throws in some sacred muscaria. With her other hand she grasps the long pole topped with a golden pinecone.

A shaman with antlers takes a sip of bull's blood from a two-handled cup and passes it to the other men in the circle.

The shaman comes toward the woman and raises the kylix. *She takes it in her hand and puts it to her lips. The cup is painted with a design of Amazons fighting foot soldiers.*

A few moments must have passed before she feels a tap on her shoulder. Giovanni is leaning forward against the table. "You seem light-years away." His touch slams the door on her mind's distant place. "Maybe I am," she tells him, rising from her chair. Then reflecting for an instant, she says cryptically, "Whatever it was you discovered on the wall, I've been wondering if it's still there."

He raises an eyebrow. "What do you mean? Whatever makes you think it won't be? I hope you're not allowing your intuition to work overtime."

She isn't prepared for his sarcastic tone.

"Your comment about the wall, whether or not it's still there, hit a nerve. I admit I've been worrying that the locals might have heard about my discovery. If the *tombaroli* get wind of it they could easily offer Concetta's son a small fortune for what's on that wall. Then it would be offered again to top dealers in Zurich where it would wind up selling for millions. It happens again and again in these villages."

Doubts begin to surface. "Are you sure you're not with the police?"

"I can assure you I'm not, Bianca, but neither am I in the business of tomb-robbing."

"So you're only a neutral bystander?" she responds almost mockingly. She can see by the set of his jaw that she's beginning to provoke him. Maybe he's just plain sick and tired of her company. And sorry he's asked for her help.

Scribbling his signature on the bill, he grasps her arm so tight it hurts and says, "Come on; let's get the hell out of here."

Ω

They leave the hotel and drive into the darkness. Even though the full moon hides behind the clouds and a heavy mist falls, Giovanni keeps glancing in his rearview mirror to make sure no cars are following. After a few miles on the main highway, past the local roadhouse, he turns down an unpaved, bumpy country lane winding up gradually around a hill. Intuitively Bianca begins to gauge the distance. By the time they come to a halt, they must have driven through at least two miles of ancient olive groves. Tall umbrella pines stand on the top of the hillock, sharply silhouetted against a star strewn sky now cleared by winds blowing in from across the Adriatic.

A *Vietato l'ingresso* sign is posted on the wood gate. A large van and a covered pick-up truck are parked on the side of the driveway, some distance from the *masseria*. No lights shine through its shuttered windows. The rambling limestone block structure is surrounded by high stone walls for protection. "The *masseria* is part of an ancient fortification for a farmers' collective. Considering its age it's in fairly good shape."

The dwelling is much larger than she envisioned.

"Concetta closes everything up tight, so it's always dark. Watch your step."

He grasps her hand as they trudge up the path to an open iron gate leading to the house. As they draw closer, she hears the bleating of goats and smells their distinctive scent. She pinches her nose. "Eew! Goats smell like old socks, don't they?"

"They stink when the male's in heat. This excites the female and activates her estrogen. My mother used to keep a herd at Sicchia, so I grew up with goats."

She's glad it's dark so he can't see her face. As they reach the dwelling she hears fiddles, the jingle of tambourines and singing, at first men's voices, and then, in a voice higher and more strangely pitched than the others, a woman's voice.

"Probably one of those R.A.I. variety shows." He reaches for the massive iron knocker and lets it strike hard against the oak. The music blares on. He tries again until finally he bangs impatiently with foot and fist. When the door finally opens, the eyes peering at them are dark, their whites yellowish. The old woman's face has the waxy, lusterless skin of someone who might have suffered from malaria. She thrusts her arm across the door in an unwelcome gesture and, when she greets Giovanni, speaks in a guttural, harsh-sounding dialect Bianca can't understand. Her gray streaked black hair is drawn back. She is dressed in black with a buttoned-up collar.

The music grows louder. More shouts, foot tapping, stampings. "Signora Lombardella tells me there's a *tarantismo* purification going on in there. Supposedly one of the farmhand's unmarried sisters was bitten by a spider this past summer. They believe the poison's still in her system." He raises a skeptical eyebrow. "It seems that *la Pizzicata*, the 'bitten one,' has been dancing for the past two hours. What you're hearing is a tarantella."

"It doesn't sound like the ones I've heard at Italian weddings in the States," she says "a hokey dance with tipsy old folks hopping around to *La lun' e mezz' u mare*. Certainly not the same music they played at the wedding in Venice."

"I can assure you this is something else. We can leave, if you want to, or I'll try talking Concetta into letting us watch. I haven't seen a *tarantismo* ritual since I was kid—and even then my mother usually dragged me off before the evening got too heated. Did you know the tarantella is supposedly a remnant of ancient culture here in Magna Graecia?"

"How do you mean?"

"Historians claim that it's one of the few remaining parts of the orgiastic rites of the Thracian Dionysos."

Shivers travel along her spine as her recent visions loom large in her mind. *I ponder which door to open. I see door handles. One is silver, the other, bronze. Is it Scythian or Thracian? A woman stands in the darkness, watching the ceremony...*

Concetta shushes them with a scowl and a shake of her finger, her hostile eyes sweeping Bianca from head to toe. Then, putting her finger to her lips, she beckons them to follow her into a room smelling of burning tallow and body sweat. Pulsing drum beats and the strangely pitched chants of old women reverberate to the ancient rafters. They stand in a far corner where they have a good view of the dancers. Bianca looks over the men and women, some young, some old, some standing, some seated on a long wood bench pushed against the wall. Over and over, a woman dips her fingers in a bowl of *neroli*-scented water, dispersing it in the air to dispel the smell of sweat and sex. In the center of the room, a woman is dancing, hands on hips, shoulders back, spine rigid. Ribbons, red, purple, bright green, saffron yellow, make a circle around her, marking her path as she dances in a trance, her glazed eyes fixed on a swath of scarlet silk placed before her feet. Bianca guesses the dancer's age to be about the same as her own.

The woman is wearing a black skirt and a white scoop-necked blouse. Lustrous, wavy dark hair falls halfway down her back. A black band tied around her forehead keeps the sweat from trickling into her vacant eyes. Her waist is wrapped with a red satin sash, coral beads encircle her neck, and a gold *cornicello*, a talisman to ward off the evil eye, dangles from a chain.

Her feet, in shiny slippers, mark heel and toe, toe and heel, to the haunting, rhythmic beats of the *tammore*, the drums tapped and slapped by two men. An elderly mandolin player plinks out a melody to the sounds of a flute, while two women in a corner shake tambourines as they sing, "*Pizzicata, Pizzicata*," the only words Bianca can make out.

Giovanni leans forward, his face now so close to hers she can feel his heat.

"The dance is supposed to cure the mythic 'bite' of the tarantula. She's trying to exorcise herself from the venomous demons the spider supposedly unleashes. When women worked in the fields, they claimed they'd been bitten by the wolf spider, but now psychologists tell us that it's more likely that they danced as a result of hysteria, sexual depression, or erotic desire. This part of the South, though once matriarchal and dedicated in ancient times to Aphrodite, has developed over the centuries into a stifling, patriarchal society."

"How long will she keep on dancing?"

"Until the demons leave her body. Or until she falls to the floor from exhaustion."

One of the older men leaps from his chair and thrusts a tambourine toward the dancer. Without missing a beat she grasps it, always swooping, spinning, shaking, tapping.

"She reminds me of a twirling maenad with a tambourine like the ones on your Apulian vases."

He nods. "Yes—like the frenzied maenads dancing the rites of Dionysos."

Suddenly a handsome young farmer jumps up and begins dancing by *la Pizzicata's* side. He's dressed in black trousers and a white t-shirt. With his back rigid, arms by his side, he dances with only his feet in motion, his gaze fixed in a vacant, trance-like stare, soon he's beaded with sweat, his shirt soaked. At last, spent, he falls onto the bench. But *la Pizzicata*, the bitten one, dances on, oblivious to everyone and everything—except the music. *"Pizzicata, pizzicata, hai, hai, hai!"* the women chant over and over, never letting the dancer forget the spider's bite. Her eyes half closed, Bianca listens to the beat, the insistent rhythm of the *tammora* and the jangle of tambourines. Pulling off her scarf she tosses it on Giovanni's lap. Suddenly she springs from the chair and comes forward to step over the ribbons into the circle. Her chin drops to her chest and she begins to roll her neck, round and around, feeling the weight of her head, her shoulders rotating. Her pelvis pulsates, fanning into flames a fever inside her. She yields to the motion, waves of rhythm wash over her body, her feet trapped in the succession of beats, dancing, dancing in her darkness. Now all longings, yearnings, cravings escape from the confines of her being.

Dance, Bianca, dance, musicians play faster and faster. Her hair comes loose, whipping around her face as she spins in her frenzy—endless shouts, thrumming drums, more and more insistent, stampings, turnings. She lunges forward. Giovanni leaps up to grasp her, but she falls to the floor as if she's been hit by a lightning bolt.

Bianca is free of the venom even against herself.

Giovanni helps the exhausted, unsteady Bianca to a sofa in the *salone* and Concetta covers her with a blanket. Bianca's dance, her raw, pagan emotions, and his response to them frighten him; at the same time, he feels wildly attracted to her, something he vowed he'd never let happen. He tells himself to take this night out of his mind. He'd better get her back to the hotel as soon as possible.

Bianca

When she opens her eyes, it's quiet; there's no music and everyone is gone. Only Giovanni and the old woman sit at a table drinking clear liquid from tiny glasses. Giovanni goes to her side and takes her hand in his. Then after gently kissing her forehead, he puts his glass to her lips for a sip of the potent grappa. She takes a sip and then another. Reaching for her scarf from his jacket pocket, she shakes it out, then presses her warm, damp face against the cool silk.

"How are you feeling?"

"Strange—revived, almost released, as if I came from some distant place."

"I should take you back to the hotel. We should be leaving. I don't want us to wear out our welcome with Concetta."

"Leaving?" she says, jumping up from the sofa. "Why would be leaving? What about your discovery—isn't that why we came here? I can't leave without seeing it! Please, Giovanni, you promised me!"

He turns to Concetta and mutters something in a dialect Bianca doesn't understand.

The old woman frowns, makes gestures with her hands before reaching for a key that hangs from a chain on her neck.

"Let's go, but you must be very quiet. Let her lead us."

They follow Concetta to the padlocked door. When it's pushed open, Bianca smells the aroma of antiquity, the same dank, musty odor of fungus and dust, that sweet-sourness she remembers from other ancient places, the Pyramids, the Catacombs, the Basilica San Marco on a wet day. He holds her hand as they step to the lower level of the *magazzino*. He aims his high-powered pocket torch on the far wall. "What can you see?" he asks, hoping that she'll be as surprised as he was the time he'd had his first look.

What's on the wall almost takes her breath away. "It's looks like a fresco-a painting of a man standing by a fire. He seems to be holding a hammer or anvil. A boy stands by with bellows in his hands."

"Hephaestus at his forge," he explains. "From the Archaic period—It amazes me that it's still so fresh as well as being so stylistically perfect for the period. Now come on over to this corner. This one isn't in nearly as good a condition but try to make it out." She moves closer to study the drawing of what appears to be a sketch of large vessel. "It looks like a mathematical sketch, with all those radial lines and angles, but I can't make out much more than that."

"It's Pythagorean, in concept. Pure mathematics. Although he was born on the island of Samos, Pythagoras lived and worked in nearby Kroton. I told you that Sybaris and Kroton were enemies. When I first saw this image, I was reminded of an object I knew, one that actually exists. The foundry couldn't have been far from this place; in fact it might have been right here—and here's one more thing I want to show you that should make everything clear."

She gasps, feeling the quiver of recognition, her heart thumping so hard that it seems as though it might beat its way out of her chest. For a moment she is frozen in place. She finds herself struggling for words.

"Before you show me any more, shall I tell you what I think?"

"Make it fast."

"It can't be possible that this sketch is the design for the bronze krater—the one in the museum at Châtillon-sur-Seine, *le Cratère de Vix*. But if it is what I think it is, you can't imagine what this means to me."

"How in the world do you know about the Vix Krater?" he asks, almost suspiciously.

Her heart is pounding away and she can hardly get the words out of her mouth. "Remember when I mentioned once that I'd been going to Burgundy on a project? I didn't want to tell you what it was about—and it was the same with you—not wanting to tell me about your discovery! If we hadn't made this trip together, I might never be standing here, stunned by what I've just seen."

"Bianca, Bianca, you never cease to amaze me. This synchronicity between us is incredible. Now tell me, do you remember the design of the handles?"

"It's etched in my memory."

"Then come and look at the fresco in the left corner."

He aims the torch at the other wall. "What do you make of this?"

"It's the snake-tailed gorgon—the Medusa—*mixoparthenos* on the Vix Krater!"

"Yes, a preliminary design for the handle. Take a mental snapshot and commit it to memory. Hurry up—Concetta is nervous and wants us to leave." He grabs her hand. "Let's go—and don't say another word until we get in the car. You never can tell who might be lurking out there."

Ω

Until they're well on the road, Bianca is silent, still overcome by the shock of what she has seen. Finally she says. "Think about it, Giovanni, neither of us wanted to go to that wedding. Yet we went anyway, mostly because of a feeling of obligation to do the right thing. You keep talking about synchronicity. How is it that we've been so affected by it?"

"Synchronicity can be about the relationship of minds, the relationship of ideas," he says. "When my last relationship ended, I decided to go into Jungian therapy. Not only did I leave restoration to go back to digging, I also began to dig down into my own psyche. As I progressed, I found that I was experiencing frequent coincidences. Before long I realized that that these were not at all coincidental occurrences. Jung also called it "selective perception." Once you become aware of something, you begin to notice it all around you. And with your dreams and your writing you obviously go deep into your mind for your work."

"Maybe that explains why we've both been involved—passionately involved—maybe even obsessed—with the Krater."

He went on." Synchronism manifests itself with meaningfully related simultaneous occurrences, and our case is exactly that. As you Americans say, we're on the same wave length."

"But how can you possibly avoid reporting this kind of find? It's far too important."

"I have my reasons. If it gets out that they're here, the fresco and the design might be hacked off those walls and sold to the underground trade. Then they'd wind up in a vault in Zurich. I've heard about furnished and carpeted vaults where unscrupulous collectors display their antiquities and spend the afternoon in a lounge chair gazing at them. And then Concetta knows very well that if we told the authorities, she'd be made to leave the house and then she'd be in trouble with her son-in-law. She made me swear to her that I wouldn't tell anyone. 'I'll put the curse of the evil eye on you.' She pointed her finger at me and made the sign of the devil's horns. I'm Southern Italian enough to admit I recoiled. Even now the thought gives me *pelle d'oca*. She told me that her son had considered removing them from the wall and selling them to the local *tombaroli*, but his wife kicked up a fuss insisting they save them to decorate their house. She'd visited the villas of the Veneto and admired the frescoes of La Malcontenta and Maser and wanted her *masseria* to have some of the same feeling. Since her husband doesn't need the money, he listened to her. I've helped Concetta cover the walls with canvas, as much to protect them as to save them from being seen and stolen by unscrupulous thieves. I also brought some bags of salt to absorb any moisture in the *magazzino*. This will help preserve them. But whenever her son is there, the signora removes the canvas and bags and hides them. Otherwise he would suspect that someone else has seen them.

"When I took a sample of dust from the floor to a lab, the technician who examined it found particles of bronze verdigris, unusual for a storehouse. The latest supposition about the Vix Krater is by the famous French bronze expert, Claude Rolley. He theorized that the Krater was made right here in Sybaris and not in Taranto, as was once believed. I would like to propose that not only was it made in Sybaris, but also it might have been cast on this very site. An announcement should be made at the right time—in mid January—on the date of the discovery of the Krater. That's why I'm keeping it quiet. I feel that it must have arrived at the oppidum in Vix circa 509 B.C.—not long after the fall of Sybaris in 510 B.C. We are now almost in 2008. Two thousand five hundred years ago."

"But are you absolutely convinced that the drawing on the wall is of the Vix Krater? What about the horses and hoplites? Are there sketches?"

"No, the horses were obviously cast separately and applied to the surface, perhaps later on. Soon after my discovery, I took measurements from the main gate at Sybaris to Strombi, where there were many artisans who couldn't work within the walls of the city. Bronze forgers made too much noise and too much heat and dust to suit the Sybarites who didn't like to hear even the roosters' wake up call. Their workshops were on the road from Sybaris, in the countryside around the polis."

Bianca is overwhelmed, dazed by these new-found revelations.

"Here's where you might be able to help me, Bianca. I am an archaeologist. Archaeology is a science so I'm supposed to be a scientist. Perhaps I'm making assumptions I shouldn't be making." He heaves a deep sigh. "Even though I'm convinced that this was the site of a foundry, I realize I've made a giant leap elliptically."

"How can I possibly be of help?"

"I don't have a mind like yours. Give me some of your insights. They might lead me in another direction—the right direction. Remember what Einstein said about the imagination-how it sharpens one's intuition?" He takes his hand from the wheel and reaches over for hers. "I have great trust in your imagination."

"So ask me, Giovanni, what you want to know." She closes her eyes and waits.

"Tell me how it happened. How did the Krater come to have been made here? By whom and for whom? What purpose did it serve? And how did it finally find its way to the Celtic oppidum at Vix, overlooking the banks of the Seine, then to its final resting place in the wheat fields of Vix?"

"Strange, though, that you didn't ask a fifth question."

"Oh?"

"You didn't ask me her name."

"Whose name?"

"The woman buried with the Krater. Who she was might give you the answer to your last question."

"I've been so focused on the sketch that I haven't thought much about the priestess-princess. Of course she had to have been a woman of great importance—maybe mythic importance—to be buried in her elaborate, bronze-wheeled wagon, with such fabulous gold jewelry and that immense Krater. This enormous vessel was like the never-emptying cauldron of plenty—the symbol of life everlasting for the ancient Celts. Imagine what the local folk thought about it, how important it must have been in their rituals and lore for hundreds of years."

"Now's not the time to tell you my own theory about the Krater and the woman. It's far too late and we're both worn out."

As he speaks, she closes her eyes and her mind begins to drift, to descend. When she opens her eyes, she can tell that he hoped she might have come up with a quick revelation.

"Where do *you* think the woman came from?" she asks. He puts his arm around her shoulder, and she's grateful even for that.

"I'm not sure." He ponders for a moment. "Mont Lassois was a citadel-trading post from the Celtic Hallstatt period in the sixth century B.C. She could have been from one of the local tribes, but she could also have come from somewhere else—these seem to have been a fairly sophisticated people judging by what was found in the grave of *la Dame de Vix*. The later, militarily-focused, La Tène Celts were a different lot from these early Hallstatt tribes who were farmers, successful traders, a traveling, aristocratic elite who were most certainly influenced by the Etruscans and the Greeks. Wine was probably their biggest import."

"When did the Celts plant their own vines?"

"Some oenologists claim the earliest vines were planted well before Julius Caesar's conquest of Gaul."

"What about weapons?"

"In the princely tomb discovered in Hallstatt, Austria, there were no weapons. There was only one gold dagger, obviously used for ceremonial purposes, yet these early Celts were skilled metal workers in bronze and in what was then precious iron."

"Later on, around 450 BC we have evidence that the later La Tène Celts swarmed down from the North, having made their way from the Danube across Europe and over the Alps.

They either overcame the Celts of Mont Lassois or they slowly merged with them. These new, perhaps 'hybrid' Celtic folk eventually found their way to the British Isles. The Celtic culture we celebrate today is derived from La Tène Celts, who were the same tough, ruthless and destructive Gaulish headhunters and plunderers who sacked Rome, as described by Greek and Roman historians—later on by Julius Caesar."

"But who this woman was, I don't know. Bianca, you're perhaps the only one who can answer that. Whoever she was, wherever she came from, pull her out from every fiber of your being—go ahead—reach for her soul."

"Maybe her soul and my soul are same," she responds solemnly, "I already know her name."

"Will you tell me?"

"Her name was Zato—but the Greeks called her Zatoria."

He looks thunderstruck. "When and how did you ever learn that?"

"I've known for quite a while. Before leaving New York, I woke up one morning with the name ringing loud and clear in my ears. Now you must really think I'm crazy."

He shakes his head. "To the contrary. I've read somewhere that the Kabala says 'a voice that rings loud and clear upon awakening is the voice of God within,' a voice you must listen to, take heed of... And don't forget, I was a student of Julian Jayne's when I was at Princeton." He laughs. "I don't need much convincing."

"If you really want to know more, I'll have to go inside myself—deep inside—to find out who she was and what she meant to her people."

"And while you're at it, give a voice to your visions—just as you do for the magazine."

"Since we've been on the road, I've been writing some articles to submit to Leonardo. Maybe the best way to do this would be to follow the famous short route the Krater might have taken from Sybaris to the other side of the peninsula, then continue to its ultimate destination, the village of Vix in Burgundy."

"How would you like to make the journey together? Since my Christmas break has already begun, I have free time off from the university."

"And I have no plans. I can't think of a better way to spend my holidays. But what's in this for you, really, Giovanni? Is it adventure you're craving, or recognition by your peers, or is there something about my company that you can't live without?" She hears both the sarcasm and the insecurity in her voice. "Why is it that you're so keen on helping me, or why I should be helping you?"

"It has to do with the connection we have."

"What connection?"

"The Italian Connection."

"You to me?"

"Yes, I've mentioned it before. The Norville connection. It's too late to talk about it now. Let's get off to an early start tomorrow. Get your bags packed so we can leave right after our visit to Sybaris."

Ω

It's well past midnight when they arrive at the Hotel Oleandro. Giovanni rings the buzzer to wake up the concierge who shuffles to the door to let them in. They climb the steps to their rooms. He bends to kiss her cheek, this time not formally twice, but once, gently. Though she longs to wrap her arms around him and draw him close, she realizes she's physically and emotionally exhausted and wants only to get herself into bed and have a deep and dreamless sleep.

Zatoria

> High fever rages through the city
> From a summer of rain and heat.
> In the temples, dampness oozes from the walls of
> the cella,
> Green fronds sprout between stones.
> Flying creatures buzz and bite, leaving welts
> Or oozing sores that turn the skin to yellow.
> Some Lokrians take to the mountains where the air
> is cool and fresh.
> Others must stay to watch over the temples of
> Aphrodite and Persephone.
> Many phases of the moon have come and gone
> Since the men of Lokri sailed to Miletus
> Where they trade for purple dye they will sell to
> rich Sybarites
> Who drape themselves in gold-edged purple
> tunics.

At dawn, I find my way to the temple to stand by the image of Aphrodite and take pleasure in the gentle breezes. I bring an offering, a clay dove, to put at the feet of the goddess. I hear footsteps and move into the shadows, not wanting to appear as a *hierodule.*

A tall Kelt enters the temple. His long hair, the color of wheat chaff, is combed back from his forehead and knotted. The southern sun has made his fair skin ruddy. His face is shaven like that of a Hellene or a Tyrrhenian, unusual for one of his people. Like other Keltoi I have seen, he wears trousers. Gold cords bind his felt boots to his ankles. He wears a birch bark hat with a peaked crown, the sign of a noble Kelt.

When I move from the shadows, he greets me in a deep voice, and is less hesitant than I with the language of the Hellenes. He tells me that he is a prince of the tribe of the Sequani, the River People, that his people have a trading post atop Latisco, north of Massilia of the Phoceans. He is in Lokri to barter for land with the King of the Dauni, whose territories are in the north of Megale Hellas. The Keltoi look to have a trading oppidum on the coast, beyond the land of the Sabine and Samnite tribes.

I tell him that my mother was a leader of a Tribe of the Gelonos, wheat growers by the Pontus Euxinus, and my father is the Thracian seer, Zalmoxis, teacher of Pythagoras of the Golden Thigh. When I say that we soon will be leaving Lokri for Kroton to visit the philosopher's famous school, I can see in his eyes that he is sorry. He tells me that he has been to Kroton and that there are many Hellenes who find the great teacher Pythagoras strange because he believes that the soul travels from this world to the Other. He tells me that his people, the Keltoi, have the same belief that death is a passage from this life to the other.

The Kelt is on his way to Sybaris where a master craftsman is forging a giant krater. The designer of the vessel is Eutropios, a student of Pythagoras. The Kelt ordered the great krater for his ailing father, the King of the Sequani, The River People.

I tell him I have heard the altars of Sybaris run with blood and there is feasting throughout the year, but that Pythagoras speaks out against this.

"Our bards and wise men tell stories of how the bull was honored. Pythagoras aims to change all that," is what he says to me.

Book V

Then the Lady Blanchefleur turned away her face
and bowed her head, and said in a voice as though
it were stifling her for to speak: "Percival…take
thou me for thine own, and then the castle and all
shall always be thine."
—Chrétien de Troyes, *Le Conte du Graal*

Bianca

The next morning when she looks out the window, the sky over once golden Sybaris is a cruel gray. Below, in the hotel garden, a light frost hazes the small patch of grass. She shivers from the dampness, turns on the wall heater, and calls the front desk for a double cappuccino. It arrives just as she's wrapping herself in a robe after a hot shower. As she sips the strong, steaming coffee through milky foam, she congratulates herself for having had the good sense to pack fleece-lined boots and warm gloves.

As soon as they arrive at the archeological site, Giovanni points out the excavated foundations, ancient paving stones, and the hunks of columns scattered about.

"It's hard to imagine this dismal place as the fabled Sybaris," she admits. She wonders if she can—or will—allow herself to envision it as it must have been. This morning the only thing golden about Sybaris is a network of bright yellow pipes connected to the motorized pumps that help drain water from the site.

He must be reading her mind. "Who knows how much gold is buried below in the mud of centuries—my father believed it would be a staggering amount—more than Mycenae, more than Troy—in fact, more than one could ever imagine."

"Sybaris was a city of 300,000—larger than Athens—a city where luxury and comfort were the norm. At least for the upper classes—but even the servants and slaves fared well."

"What about artisans," she asks, "like the ones who cast the Krater? Where would they have lived?"

"Outside the city—some only a few miles away—they've dug up evidence of potters' kilns and remains of houses of ordinary folk. Sybarites wouldn't have wanted to hear hammering or smell the odor of smelting metal." He drops his voice to a whisper even though there is no one else on the site. "Last night we continued north on that road to arrive at Concetta's son's *masseria.*"

Il Parco del Cavallo is closed to tourists because of the accumulation of heavy rain. But Giovanni knows the guards and they are allowed in.

"Why is it called The Park of the Horse?"

"Some diggers found a stone horse hoof and tail, so the supposition is that there might have been a large equestrian statue in this area. The horses of the Sybarites were famous."

After they walk look over the area for at least an hour, Giovanni leads her to the remains of a partially excavated wall. Set into the wall are carved marble panels of women dancers, each linked arm to arm, one to the other. "These stones are clearly from the Archaic period, about 510 B.C. They were probably found and reused in this later building. So it's here that you have tangible concrete evidence of life in Sybaris."

I lean against the wall for a moment and close my eyes. I see dancers in white peploses, criss-crossing back and forth in rhythm—their bodies swaying. Two dancers come forward to grasp the handles of a trapeze, swinging themselves across one corner of the room to the other, almost touching the ceiling.

She opens her eyes. The vision disappears. Giovanni hasn't noticed. He's busy examining the joints of the stones.

"The Orphics, contemporary with Pythagoras, also lived outside the city. Many of them must have been rich farmers who owned the lands where the famous cattle of Sybaris grazed." He reaches into the pocket of his coat and pulls out a small plastic square, slips out a silver coin. "Have a look—it's the famous stater of Sybaris, struck between 530-510 B.C. You can see that it depicts a standing bull with his head looking backward. They're not particularly rare."

She examines the coin, remembering the episode of her gold coin.

"There's a fine Archaic temple dedicated to Hera in Paestum, once Poseidonia, a Sybarite city, where citizens fled after the destruction of Sybaris."

"The hatred of the Krotoniates for the Sybarites had to have been fierce."

"The Krotoniates were the righteous ones. They thought they lived the pure life, dedicated to clean air, clean living. Pythagoras and his followers lived on grains and vegetables, and instead of offering the gods smoke from the ritual of cooking meat, they burned spices, myrrh and frankincense. It's said that Pythagoras lived on a diet of mallow and asphodel which probably kept him from hunger and thirst. It's been disputed that the Krotoniates never ate meat—they did, but in moderation.

"But it's also true that many Krotoniates were against excessive blood sacrifice and loathed the dissolute Sybarites for offering so many animals to Persephone, daughter of Demeter, an important goddess in a city whose wealth was derived from growing and selling wheat throughout the Mediterranean."

"What you're telling me doesn't sound very different from what goes on today. Two opposing ideologies—on the one hand, the avid vegetarians, recyclers, conservationists—and on the other, the conspicuous consumers of too many expensive goods."

"And later on it was Socrates who teaches that we must know to choose the mean and avoid the extremes. The earlier Sybarites had gone far over the edge with so much wealth, gold and purple dye, and such excessive, decadent luxurious living—*truphe* in Greek."

They wander the site for two hours, until the mist turns to rain. Since the museum is closed, Giovanni promises her that they will come back another time. The director is a colleague and she would be happy to show them around. They head for the car. He turns on the engine and the heater before unfolding a map to show her the route the Krater might have taken across the Italian boot from the Adriatic to the Tyrrhenian Sea to Massilia where it would have gone up the Rhone, then to its tributaries, finally to reach the oppidum at Vix.

"There's another theory that the Krater would have reached the Celtic oppidum on Latisco by way of a route over the Alps, but it doesn't make sense to me that it would have been hauled all the way to the North of Italy over the mountain range, then across to Burgundy. Especially when we're so close to the Tyrrhenian Sea on Italy's west coast and such a short way from here to Laus, in Calabria, another of the Sybarites' trading cities. It had to have been safer and quicker. The Krater was made in seven pieces which made the journey easier. Also there might have been a stop at Poseidonia where many Sybarites had fled; but most likely it was loaded on a boat as soon as they reached the coast, maybe at a port near Laus, in Calabria, then taken to Massilia, from there up the Rhone and to the Seine."

"I still can't get over this striking concurrence—our meeting because of the wedding was certainly not pure chance, but that both of us are obsessed by the Krater—now that's a remarkable coincidence." She shakes her head in wonder.

"In this case there's no such thing as coincidence. Again, it's synchronicity—events unlikely to ever occur together by chance. You see, Bianca, the culmination of synchronicity is its direct revelation of destiny, the design of the whole universe working itself out in the display of each unique human life. And since you delve so deeply into the unconscious, synchronism is activated and can occur frequently. Again, it's all that right brain business I keep talking about."

"Then how does chance figure in? I always wondered what the difference is between chance and destiny."

He smiles. "Chance may simply be a curious way the universe has of helping us to work out our destinies."

Ω

They leave the site of Sybaris and check out of the hotel at noon. She asks him about stopping at Kroton.

"Kroton would be a big disappointment to you. There's virtually nothing left of antiquity there. The city was devastated by an earthquake in 1905 and completely rebuilt. Not one of Italy's best architectural endeavors, I might add. Only one massive column from the Temple of Hera Lacinia remains and you can't get close to it because it's surrounded by an ugly chain link fence. And we don't even have a clear blue sky to take a good photo. Better that you see it in your visions, Bianca; imagine it as it was once. As for Lokri—it's the same story.

"Regrettably, the ruins of Lokri's most renowned shrine, the temple of Persephone, have not been found, but in the valley below they've discovered a large deposit of votive *pinakes*, so the conclusion is that her temple originally stood there.

"I suggest that we begin the journey of the Krater by driving through the mountains on one of the routes the Sybarites would have taken."

What is she letting herself in for? What might she lose? Or gain!

"Okay—where do we start—and when do we leave?"

Orphic *lamella*, Plural *lamellae*, Magna Graecia

Small gold tokens found for entrance into a golden afterlife: the deceased who were buried with them believed that they had earned Paradise.

Zatoria

We leave Lokri as dawn paints rosy streaks across the sky. I ask my father if we might go to Sybaris but he tells me that first we must make the two day journey to Kroton to visit the school of his most renowned student, Pythagoras. Often I hear Zalmoxis say that of all his pupils it is Pythagoras of Samos, who understands with mind and heart his teachings of the everlasting travel of the soul.

My father's fame has spread to Megale Hellas. They tell me that in Thrace he strummed his lyre and sang with Orpheus himself and that he believes that the soul lives past this lifetime. In his daily rites he says he travels from this world to the Other. Zalmoxis tells his followers that in their hearts they do not die, but their lives change time and place and so they go to their deaths happier than on any other journey.

And Pythagoras teaches his pupils about the principles of numbers and how to write the very sounds of music. And women are treated as respectfully as men.

Ω

When we arrive in Kroton, this most healthful city of Megale Hellas, we find rooms in a hostel of great comfort, where both men and women, students and acolytes of the most esteemed Pythagoras, dine together at long tables. As we stand at the entrance of the school, a servant announces the arrival of Zalmoxis, the seer of Thrace, and me, his daughter, Zatoria.

Pythagoras has not yet arrived. When he appears, I see how thin he is and that he is not as tall as I would have expected from a Hellene. He is dressed in a white tunic and wool *chalmys*; his skin is sun-bronzed, his beard as white as the hair on his head. As he stands at the portal, his intense blue eyes scan the room, as if to commit every face to memory. Following behind him are his wife, Theano, and his daughter. Theano is strong and stout, his daughter, Myia, the wife of the famous athlete, Milo of Kroton, is slender as a willow. Both women wear the soft white *chalmys* of his followers.

We eat well, but we have been served no meat, only greens, root vegetables and pulses, sweet figs from Smyrna, the dried red berries of Corinth. We are offered wine from the vineyards of the Oenotrians. A servant stands by with a krater half filled with thick dark wine, already strained and free from lumps of pine resin. Into it he pours spring water from an Attic hydria.

When the revered Pythagoras stands to speak, voices are hushed, the room becomes silent.

The great man welcomes us and offers his wisdom. "Man," he tells us, "may be divided into three groups. There are many whose goal in life is to acquire worldly goods, the pursuit of pleasure and the satisfaction of physical impulses. Many Sybarites fall into this class. Sybaris, the Decadent, Sybaris the Soft, is now the enemy of Kroton.

"The second, smaller group, gains success and fulfillment in praiseful enterprise or good works. Among these, are those who, for the glory of their polis, strive toward victory in Olympia. Milo, the Herakles of Kroton, was winner at the Olympiad six times.

"The highest and the fewest are those who love wisdom, those whose lives are devoted to pursuits of the mind—the philosophers, whose entire lives are given to searching for the true wisdom of the universe. Perhaps theirs are not only the greatest gifts, but also the greatest challenges.

"Yes, my followers, remind yourselves that all men may indeed assert that wisdom is the greatest good, but there are few who strenuously endeavor to obtain this good."

Then a student comes forward and presents to Pythagoras a basket of twisted willow. On a silken cloth lies a sheet of thin, flattened gold, what the Hellenes call *lamellae*. Pythagoras reads aloud the Orphic prayer incised on the golden sheet. "Address

Mnemosyne, mother of Muses, with these words."

I am the child of earth and starry heaven.
Come, give me cool water
Flowing forth from the Lake of Memory.
For it is memory that leads us
From one lifetime to another.

I, Zatoria, then and there committed these words to my own memory.

As we leave the symposium, strangers ask if Zalmoxis has taught me the ways of shamans. I tell them that I do not need to be taught things that are already within me, for, as my father often says, the surest way to become a shaman is to be born of one. I do not feel I am endowed with magic powers. My father does not teach me to bestow savage curses or work magic binding spells for unhappy lovers as the Hellenes are wont to do.

I think of myself as only a teller of stories, like mother like daughter.

Ω

At noon the cold, dreary sky has the muffled look of impending snowfall. Bianca starts to shiver and Giovanni turns up the heat in the car. She closes her eyes and listens to the steady hum of the motor, the alchemy of her mind all the while transmuting gloomy, gray Sybaris into gold.

Zatoria

As we leave Kroton and make our way to Sybaris, I gaze out at mountains in the distance, the shadows on the valleys and hills make me think of green lions, long limbs stretched out, their paws resting on mountain peaks.

Beyond the city walls lie the villas of the richest Sybarites, those who have herds of white cattle or vast wheat lands and vineyards. They ride in canopied wagons or in litters where they repose upon silk cushions shot with gold. To give them protection from sun and rain, awnings are stretched from side to side across the long, straight roads.

As I pass through the city gates, I think that I have entered the portal to the Otherworld, a golden, glittering, crimson, purple Otherworld. Its richness is something to behold, neither in Olbia nor in Sinope have I seen such wealth. Even the poor are rich, and slaves wear garments far better than those of any Hellene I have ever seen in Olbia. The colors, bright saffron, scarlet and the blue of lapis, are unlike the somber woven wool clothing of the Hellenes. The women paint their eyes in the manner of the Etruscans, lining their eyelids with soot, coloring their lips a lustrous carmine. They buff their fingernails with golden powder and wrap their hair in golden fillets adorned with jewels. Their chitons are sewn from *byssus,* a cloth woven of threads spun from the spit of whelks abounding on these shores, or they wear peploses of sheer flax cloth sold by sea traders.

We pass a woman dressed in a chiton of purple cloth gleaming like the skin of an onion. She is riding in a wagon under a white linen canopy festooned with branches of yellow acacia. Gold bracelets encircle her wrists, her lips are rouged, her cheeks flushed. On her head she wears a wide-brimmed hat of woven straw shielding her fair skin from the sun. A white horse with a golden harness draws her cart. On her lap she holds an ivory and gold coffer. Zalmoxis tells me that she is on her way to leave her offering at the shrine of Hera, the goddess much revered by the Sybarites.

As we are arriving at the house of our host, the Archon, we see a slave parading Hera's peacock about on a leash. The bird's silvery blue-green feathers are bound so that it cannot flare its tail. We watch as the slave unties the cord, and the peacock proudly spreads his tail wide for us. We admire its design of many eyes, the peacock's gift from Hera.

In Athens strangers are not welcome, but here, citizens of Sybaris welcome outsiders to their polis, as well as "barbarians," the name the Hellenes give those who do not speak their language. We enter the courtyard of the villa of our host. He greets us with courtesy, eager to hear the wisdom of Zalmoxis. Around the walls grow thick garlands of vines, heavy with clusters of purple grapes flushed silver, soon to be ripe for plucking. Beyond the plain of Sybaris our host's vines grow along the hillsides. When the grapes have been crushed and the wine is rich and dark, it flows through the pipes from our host's villa to the port, ready to be stored in amphorae to sell or to trade with the Keltoi or the Tyrrhenoi. The Phoceans of Massilia trade their wine and olive oil for tin and amber.

A woman of the household presents me with a

chest made of fragrant Phoenician cedar. Inside I find a white silk *peplos* and, to wear over it, a mantle of the whitest, softest goat hair bordered with ivy leaves of hammered gold so thin they tremble as I breathe. The women admire my hair and twist it with flowers and a fillet of gold ribbon. My bed is spread with a cushion of swans down, ample enough for me to lie on, and a cool silken sheet to cover my body. The beds here are so soft that the wife of our host is said to have complained that rose petals beneath her mattress ruined her sleep, but I think this is silly gossip spread by envious Hellenes from Attica.

Our host tells us that today Zalmoxis is to be the symposium's honored guest. He proudly shows us the tables already prepared for reclining. Their bases are supported by carved winged griffins, and they are covered with a finely-woven cloth so sheer it must have heavy gold weights in each corner lest the breezes cause it to ruffle. The plates and cups are gold, rubbed until gleaming by a slave who does nothing but polish gold. The Sybarites will have none of silver. Silver is for other Hellenes, the less rich Hellenes of Kroton.

The tables will soon groan with all manner of meat dishes, dishes normally eaten only on feast days by other Hellenes. Because Sybarites often lead their finest heifers to the altars, the flesh from sacrifice is standard fare. But fish is also eaten here, and the Sybarites excel in its preparation. They delight in the golden red mullet, cuttlefish stuffed plump with rare spices from faraway lands. Eels in anchovy sauce are a favorite delicacy, as are song birds baked in crust, buds of caper blooms, and lupine seeds preserved in wine vinegar to cleanse the palate. But the most precious dish is roast truffles, as they are said to be the food of Aphrodite. One chief household cook was crowned by the Archon for a dish he enjoyed more than any other, a recipe concocted with these fragrant *fungi*, a gift from the Tyrrhenoi, the traders whose sniffing pigs dig for them at the base of oaks. The Archon boasts that this fine dish has been deemed worthy of a patent, and no other cook is allowed to prepare it for one year.

The day has already gone into night. For it seems only then do these people socialize: the Sybarites dine all night and sleep by day. Their windows are lined with sheer linen panels to keep out flying insects and the *zanzari* that breed in the marshes. Before these people allow their guests to enter a dining room, they burn special herbs to keep away these tiny, flying demons. And the women of Sybaris and Poseidonia sometimes dine with the men—not only the *hierodule*, but also their own wives. At these famous dinners, the Muses are always honored: poetry is recited, lyres are strummed, flutes piped, and everywhere there are maidens whirling and swirling. Slaves pass golden bowls heaped with *klustre*, ribbons of coiled dough fried crisp in olive oil, then dribbled with honey and chopped almonds.

Tonight, only my eyes feast on the food. My stomach will have none of it. My father takes note that I am silent, distant, and that I do not eat.

Ω

Later, on my bed, I cannot sleep. My feelings are strong, and strange. Music must still be playing but I hear only shouting and screaming. I cannot quiet these sounds of pain and agony.

Now I hear the voices of men chanting paeans. I hear their marching feet. Where are they going, what enemy do they face? Suddenly terrifying visions appear. A giant leading thousands of men. He is naked except for a lion skin flung over his shoulder. He holds a club in his hand as if he were Herakles, the father of my people, he who planted his seed in the Milouziena. Are they marching to Sybaris? I shudder to think of it. Behind him march countless hoplites. Curved shields, each marked with the letter Kappa, press against their bodies, daggers, swords unsheathed to plunge into human flesh. Archers stand ready to rain showers of arrows down on their enemies.

Now I see that they are Krotoniates, led by the giant, Milo, ready for battle. I can see the cavalry of the Sybarites forming a border across the plain. Warriors astride white horses wear golden belts; their helmets flash in the bright sun. They wait still, confident, ready for the signal to charge. Drums beat, trumpets blare, horns wail. Then an eerie silence, a long moment of stillness as each army faces its enemy. Suddenly hundreds of the hoplites in the front flanks of Krotoniates put flutes to their lips and fill my ears with the sweetest sounds I've ever heard. At once the horses of their enemy begin to dance, leaping up on their hind legs, prancing on their forelegs, standing again on their hind legs, gracefully turning their heavy bodies, hopping on one front leg, then on to the other. Panic spreads among the ranks. Riders tumble to the ground. I hear bloodcurdling screams and the neighs of frightened horses. The giant gives the battle cry and rushes his phalanx into the melee of dancing horses. Javelins fly, swords swing, daggers plunge. Horses collapse to the ground as blood spurts from their bellies. The Krotoniates enter the gates of Sybaris. Shrieking women run with their children. Men rape screaming women on the steps of Aphrodite's temple, steal her golden cups from the sacred space. Blood runs from the altars of the temple of Hera.

The giant calls to his men to destroy this despised, decadent city. I see fire and flames, temples collapsing, the altar gutters running with blood, then water, like a bursting dam flooding the city, rising higher and higher until its temples can no longer be seen, until Sybaris the Golden is no longer.

I am shaking and weeping. Is this a prophecy? Why have I suddenly been given this gift, this curse?

Giovanni

They drive through the plain of Sybaris passing hectares of vineyards, here and there rows of tall black cypresses stand like mournful sentinels guarding the leafless vines. "These vines are descendants of those grown by the Greeks of Magna Graecia—a variety called Primitivo, thousands of years old, that produces an excellent wine. You call it Zinfandel in the States," Giovanni explains. "When we have dinner tonight I'll order a bottle. Maybe two."

About a half an hour down the road his cell phone buzzes. No one on the other line. He hangs up. A few moments later, another ring. It's Guiseppe Colaspada, the local *tombarolo*, on the line. The time has come to tell Bianca about Beppe, no use holding back, they're on this adventure together.

"The call was from a *tombarolo*," he says, "a pal of mine even though it may seem strange to you."

"What? How could you possibly be on good terms with a tomb robber! You of all people, a dedicated archaeologist, having a friend who digs illicitly! How can you possibly justify such behavior?"

"Beppe may be a *tombarolo*, but I've always found him to be a nice guy. You might be surprised—he's polite, soft-spoken as any clergyman—not one of those brash, sometimes crude and uneducated looters. I've known him for a while, met him when I was working here in Calabria. He's always been straightforward about his work—at least to me. One day over a glass of his home-made limoncello, he told me how he'd come to learn the trade. He was taught by his father. His family has been into plundering for a long time, even before the late Sixties when it became a thriving business. Over the years he's broken his way into hundreds of ancient burial chambers, found everything from Attic black-figure and Campanian red figure ceramics—

to bronze mirrors, gold jewelry, statuary. All of this he passes on to middlemen. Then the loot gets sold to collectors in the States and Europe. These guys have a well organized secret underground network so it's difficult to track plundered objects. That's where I come in. I have to make Beppe trust me, and, if the phone rings again, I'll stop to talk with him."

"What drives someone to keep on tomb robbing when it's a crime and so dangerous?"

"Beppe tells me, sure, he'd much rather be at home in bed cuddled up with his wife instead of screwing the earth for loot. But he has to have bread on the table. He has a mortgage to pay and two sons at university, one in Lecce, the other in Rome's Sapienza, plus he's also concerned about the guys who work for him. Only a few months ago he assured me that if he could make a deal with the *Soprintendente*, he'd take early retirement so long as he had a better *pensione*. He claims he knows an important necropolis and would lead me to it if I'd help him. I told him that maybe I could be of some help with the authorities, but he has to give me the signal. I just can't keep begging him to stop."

When the cell phone squeals again, he jumps out of the car and slams the door.

"Beppe—how the hell did you get this number?" Giovanni asks in Apulian dialect.

"From Sergio Battistoni's Milan office. His secretary gave it to me. One of the farmhands told me he'd seen you at the *masseria* belonging to that rich oil refiner from Taranto. You were with an American woman. Are you still with her?"

"She's sitting in the S.U.V.," he replies. *No use in telling the whole truth about the car swap. It might slip if Beppe should have a conversation with Sergio.*

"Then I'm warning you. Maddalena says Sergio's on the rampage. *Sentami*, Giò, whatever our differences, I want to make sure you get out of his way. Be careful. I'm warning you even though he's one of my customers. You're a decent guy, a *gentiluomo*, and I don't want to see you hurt. Or the signora. Sergio is outraged that you have his prime writer with you. He doesn't want her to know about him."

"But I've never told her anything—she has no idea," Giovanni tells him in an even denser dialect.

"You'd better tell her now."

"And what do you suggest I say?"

"Listen to me, Giò. *Per carità*! Avoid Locri and Siderno at all costs. They're a hangout for crooks, smugglers. You've got to take care or they'll do you in. You know as well as I that there's nothing much to be seen at Locri. No temples, only worthless little clay ex votos in the museum. I can find you better stuff any day of the week. *Gésu*! How many times do I have to tell you that we have nothing to do with Corona Sacra Unita or Ndrangheta! We don't use violence. We never have and we never will. We're loyal to one another, and we have our own code of honor and decency. Besides, you know as well as I that there's so much stuff under the ground here, enough to fill a lot of museums. *Di nuovo*, don't go near Locri or Siderno!"

"I'm not changing directions. We've already decided to head for Manella and the site of the Temple of Persephone. The signora wants to see it. She's familiar with the *pinakes* they discovered there." Giovanni is surprised as he hears himself fabricating a fantasy itinerary. There's no use pursuing the subject. Beppe doesn't know that he's already told Bianca that they will cross the boot of Italy on one of the shortest routes from Sybaris on the Ionian Sea to the Tyrrhenian Sea, the route of the Sybarites. So someone hot on their tail would be headed straight for Locri—southeast instead of due west looking for him in his trademark S.U.V. He breathes a sigh of relief that he left it in Sicchia and took the old Lancia.

But Beppe won't give up. "You've got to listen, Giò." Head for the mountains—drive *la signora* to Paestum, *per l'amor di Dio*, where at least there are standing temples and a museum with something to see inside!"

"Thanks for the advice—but I told you we're heading for Locri. Beppe, tell me, when are you going to get out of this rotten business? It's no kind of life for you and your family."

"Don't start that *porcheria* again, Giò. *Mannaggia*! I hear my wife yelling for me. I may check in on you again, but for now, ciao."

Giovanni gets back into the car. Once they're on their way, Bianca asks, "What did you mean when you talked about getting Beppe to trust you? Isn't he a thief, after all?"

"I want him to give his privileged information to the *carabinieri*—but first he must be guaranteed immunity and an increase in his retirement pension so his sons can finish their studies. I'm working on that. When the *carabinieri* confiscate a hoard and authorize or arrest tomb-robbers, they're usually consolidating somebody else's position and influence—so I need to be in control here to make sure that Beppe's sons can finish their education. He will lead me to this important necropolis which may be a major find from the Archaic period. It's not far off the coast of Kroton, and if it's anything like the treasure of Hera found near there, it is indeed of consequence, the kind of material for blockbuster museum exhibits."

"Do you think he has any idea about the drawing and fresco? Maybe the farmhands got wind of it the night of the *tarantismo*."

"I doubt it. I plan on telling the authorities about the wall right after the Christmas holidays—before Sergio learns about what else is going on at the *masseria*." The instant he mentions Sergio, he knows he has blundered.

"What Sergio are you talking about? Not my boss, I hope! How does Sergio fit in the picture?"

"I'll tell you when we can turn off the highway and I can pull over to the side. Right now I've got to concentrate on these slippery curves."

"Patience has never been one of my virtues, but I'm not going to plead with you. I'll wait. Besides, having already envisioned Locri, I don't mind not going there. I'd rather not have my visions destroyed by what my unmasked eyes might see today."

They don't speak until a half hour later when he finally drives off the main highway onto a dirt road and pulls over. He turns off the ignition and faces her squarely, eye to eye.

"Bianca, I'll be frank with you. Maybe I should have told you about this earlier, but I didn't want to upset you. You have a job at *Eyes and Soul*, a job you depend on. Your boss, Sergio, is an important middleman in the antiquities trade—he sells to collectors in New York, Switzerland, London. If you'd known that before you left New York, what would you have done? Would you have been able to call the police with no proof at all—only with hearsay as evidence?"

She unleashes her pent-up fury. "That dirty rat, that wretched, lying hypocrite! He used to infuriate me when he derided the South. It was as though I took it personally. Now I learn that all the while he's been plundering the patrimony and riches from the earth of Puglia and Calabria. The last time I saw him, I told him off and walked out. Now it's all clear. He was probably behind the break in—but what could he have been after? Nothing was missing so maybe it was only a warning—but what would he be warning me about?"

"The Sacra Corona Unita gang was warning you. Sergio obviously knew someone in the organization, maybe he's even part of it. Perhaps someone at the wedding noticed that we'd become friends—or maybe Leonardo found out and told him. When I learned about the painting of the Campanile, that it was in your possession, I didn't tell you that, from time to time, Leonardo visits my mother in Rome. She knows I don't approve, but she's strong-minded and set in her ways. Besides, she likes all Leonardo's fawning and flattery."

"I remember Leonardo telling me that he went to visit his widowed aunt on the Via Appia Antica."

"I can assure you that he's no blood relation. Leonardo is a direct descendant of the man our family dubbed 'The Writer.' The Writer bequeathed his *castello* in Sicchia to his lover, Margaret Norville, the Countess Bona Dea, the mother of Rose Alba, Nina's friend. The *castello* has come down to my mother and it will be mine one day—unless your great grandmother's painting of the Campanile comes into Leonardo's possession."

"What do you mean—comes into his possession? I don't get it."

"The Writer was sinister, always plotting and scheming. He played games with everyone, Margaret Norville, his own family. After the trauma of seeing the Campanile crumble into a pile of brick and dust before her eyes, Nina was in a state of shock—irrationally overcome with guilt. She thought she'd caused the Campanile's fall because of what she called her 'horrible supposings, her dark imaginings.' A few days later, Margaret Norville invited Nina and her mother to spend some time resting in The Writer's *castello* near Sicchia, in the Molise. But Nina became even worse during the visit, and her mother, along with Margaret, took her to a sanitarium in Vienna. The doctor told Nina to describe the traumatic experience, then asked her to paint the Campanile as she saw it that day. She followed the doctor's orders and, when she left Italy, Nina gave the painting of the collapsed Campanile to Margaret Norville, telling her that she never wanted to see it again. Not ever. And she didn't. Nina went back to the States, and later on the strange little painting somehow found its way from Margaret Norville to The Writer and then by descent to his family."

"I told you that I'd only recently learned that when Nina returned to Baltimore in September of 1902, she fell madly in love and had a child out of wedlock—my grandmother, but what you're telling me makes me wonder if... *"Suddenly she sees Nina in her green dress in the coffin, the man in the black cape over her. "And I will never write what I saw that day in Sicchia."* She feels a cluster of spiders on her body. Could it possibly be? Nina and the Writer? And not the dark, handsome young man from Baltimore? She lays her head back on the neck rest and closes her eyes, feeling nausea sweep over her.

Giovanni watches from the side of his eye as Bianca silently counts on her fingers and stops at the ninth. He knows what she's thinking, but he will never tell her that Nina's daughter, Bianca's grandmother, was born on April 3rd. He would not—ever—reveal this family secret. What purpose would it serve?

Finally she mutters, "The end of July to late April is nine months. Grandma's birthday was June 28." She releases a profound sigh of relief and the roiling sea in her stomach suddenly becomes calm.

She pulls herself together and says, "Most—but not all—of what you're telling me is written in Nina's diary. I had it with me that morning when we sat on the Piazza, but I didn't offer to let you read it because I didn't want to share it with someone I was just getting to know even if there seemed to be a connection between us. But what does my painting have to do with the one in Leonardo's possession?"

"Leonardo wants your watercolor desperately. He had Sergio, his old friend from Columbia, check it out to make sure you still had it whenever he came to visit you—so he knew it was hanging on your bedroom wall. Soon after, Sergio hired Leonardo as your editor so he could keep an eye on your whereabouts..."

"Again I ask you—what does my painting have to do with the one in Leonardo's possession?"

"Please let me finish! The Writer, with his tastes and dark. Byzantine mind, loved puzzles, conundrums and more than anything else he wanted control—in this instance control beyond the grave. In his will he specified that although the *castello* would be Margaret's, when—or if—the two paintings came together in the possession of one person, the owner of both paintings would receive complete and final title to the *castello*. He obviously took dark pleasure in imagining what his descendants might someday contrive as they pitted themselves one against the other, scheming, plotting, in order to get the painting from the descendants of Nina Evans. When you told me about your break in, about your painting and Nina's diary and earrings safe in the bank, I realized what the burglary attempt was about, that they were looking for the little water-color. Somehow someone knew you had it, had seen it in your apartment."

"Of course, Sergio saw it, even remarked about it once. He came every now and then to cook for me. Now I know why. He was always checking to see that the painting was still there."

"When you called me I remember checking the date with you to make sure yours was painted on the thirteenth of July, the day before the collapse—and it was. How relieved I was to hear that you'd already put it in a safety deposit box along with the earrings and the diary."

"I can assure you, Giovanni, it will stay there forever—or at least as long as I live." She sighs. "At least the mystery of the break in has been solved. But there's something else I want to know. That night in Sicchia I had a haunting vision of a man in a black cape with a black hat pulled down over his face. One night in New York someone dressed exactly like that followed me as I walked down Third Avenue. Then that night—very late—my doorbell rang. When it ceased ringing I tiptoed to the window I saw the same black-cloaked figure crossing the street. That was just before I called you. I wasn't sure what I saw was real. I feared it might have been a phantom from my overwrought imagination. Now I wonder if it could have been Leonardo."

"Maybe we'll never know, but at least we do know that your painting is locked safely away and he has no chance of ever getting title to the castle—he's completely out of the picture. And he's also out of *a* picture!"

Laughing at his word play, she says, "With my painting in safekeeping, the *castello* will someday be yours and no one will be able to take it away from you or your family. As far as I'm concerned, it will stay there in perpetuity."

"It's not a place I like or visit often, and, as you saw for yourself, my mother has eliminated some, but not all, of its weirdness. Besides, I've never felt the castle should be mine or that it should ever belong to my family. The *castello* should be yours, Bianca, because Nina painted the destroyed Campanile and gave it to Margaret Norville and then The Writer's family claimed it. If you possessed both paintings, you'd then have title to the *castello*."

"I certainly don't want to own it. What on earth would I do with it? I can just about manage a basement apartment, let alone a castle in a foreign country."

He doesn't respond. He seems concerned.

"But what about Sergio? I'm worried about him and what he might do."

"You're right. He can be dangerous. That's why we've got to get back on the road and head for the Tyrrhenian coast. I told Beppe that I wasn't going to disappoint you, that we were driving straight to Locri—so if someone wants to trail us they'll be headed there—or points south."

"You lied to him?"

"Of course I lied—even though I trust him. He might slip up, just as I did when I just mentioned Sergio. This is a matter of self protection, maybe even survival," he says angrily, shoving his key in the ignition, revving up the engine. "Let's be on our way—we'll begin our journey, the Krater's journey, to the oppidum at Vix. There are two good routes to the coast—we'll take the road through the National Park of Pollino. It's still early enough in the day—so if we push it we can arrive at Paestum before five."

"Why Paestum?"

"Because it was an important polis of the Sybarites. Many who fled the destruction of Sybaris headed straight for Paestum, once Poseidonia of the Sybarites, to give thanks at the Doric temple of Hera, and it wasn't long after their arrival that the other great temples were built. They're considered to be the most spectacular and best preserved Greek temples."

"So even though the later historians had much to say about the decadence of these Sybarites, they still had a lot of energy, power and money after the fall of Sybaris."

"You're right, Bianca, and they continued their heavy trading with Hallstatt Celts and Etruscans, as well as with Greeks from Massilia. They've dug up a fresco in Paestum—Etruscan stylistically—much like Hephaestus at the Forge at the *masseria*. I'd like to show it to you. After a quick look at the temples, we can choose our route to Châtillon-sur-Seine. Depending on the weather forecast, we can either drive to Marseilles, about fourteen hours—or take a ferry from Civitavecchia to Toulon—over twenty hours—and that's only if ferries are crossing in winter."

"Even if they are I don't want to get seasick—a problem I sometimes have."

"Well, that settles it then. We drive. Once we're in France we'll make our way north along the Rhone to the Seine, the village of Vix, and Mont Lassois—Latisco of the Celts. I'll try to map out the rest of our route tonight." He checks his watch. "It's already past one. I hope we can find somewhere on these roads to buy a *panini*. Are you hungry? I always keep a few energy bars in the car—just in case. Reach into the glove compartment to check them out and, while you're at it, pull out the Calabria Green Guide Map for Italy. It's about 220 kilometers to Paestum, but we're now at Morano Calabro—so we've already done forty kilometers. We're well on our way."

"On our own journey from Sybaris."

"I'll make sure you get to Châtillon in time for your winter solstice—and then we can surely make it to Venice by Christmas."

Ω

They drive through forests of Bosnian pines, seeded centuries ago by winds from the Dalmatian coast, past groves of silver-barked birches, through villages where Albanian from the 1500s is still spoken. Peregrine falcons dart and swoop against a sky already beginning to darken although it's not yet two o'clock. As they look out to the snow-peaked Apennines, he slows down to point out a golden eagle soaring above the dense forest. Snow begins to fall lightly, like feathers floating from the heavens. Before long, the roadsides are blanketed with white. Giovanni brakes when he sees a dead raven lying on the snow, drops of its blood splattered about. "I hope you're not superstitious about the bird—or sorry you've come on this trip," he says seriously.

"You Southern Italians are so superstitious," she says teasingly. "I don't take the raven as an ominous foreboding. Of course I'm glad I came. But this is not what I expected to see in the South of Italy—it's a different world up here—tall pines, oaks, almost Alpine, even without the snow."

"Trees from these forests supplied the Greeks and Romans with timbers for their galleys. Now it's reforested and will remain this way." He tunes in on the Park radio station for the weather and road reports. Heavy snow is predicted throughout the higher altitudes. Let's keep going. No stop for lunch—I want to get to the coast before it gets dark, then we'll turn inland and from there it's only a short distance to Paestum."

Bianca
Paestum, December 19

They arrive at six, later than they'd expected. The roads are slow until they're out of the park, and snow turns to light drizzle. The sky begins to clear and a ring surrounds the full moon.

Giovanni says, "Close to the temple site there's a little hotel, once an old mill, *Il Mulino di Grano*. How does that sound to you?"

"Perfect—do you think we can get rooms?" she says, emphasizing the plural.

"There's only one way to find out." He dials the number on his cell.

Will he ask for one room, or for two, she wonders, her heart almost skipping a beat as she waits.

He asks for two rooms. Her heart sinks. If not now, it will never be.

"Only one available room?" he inquires. "*Va bene*, I'll take it then. We'll be by in a few minutes." He hangs up and turns to her. "The owner said they just had a cancellation. The town is full—a computer company convention from the U.S. You heard the rest."

She doesn't detect much joy in his voice. Her heart now beats double time. "It's all right with me," she murmurs. "Don't worry, Giovanni, I won't try to seduce you." Then smiling wickedly, she adds, "I actually think you might be afraid of me."

"Don't be silly," he snaps back with a partly stifled laugh, "Of course I'm not afraid of you."

She is far from convinced when she notices his face turning red. "I'll admit I've not known many men in my life—and that I haven't dated for a long time. In my second year at college I had a heartbreaking romance so I left the States and went to live in Oxford—in England, not in Mississippi. I may even tell you about my time there. That is if you're interested."

"Why not tell me about it over dinner? This little inn serves a good *prezzo fisso* four course meal. I'll order a bottle of wine—the Primitivo from the Salento, and we'll have plenty of time to talk."

Ω

They drive up to the cobblestone courtyard of the old mill which has been sympathetically restored by its owner, a sprightly woman in her seventies who gives them a warm welcome. She shows them the library-sitting room before leading them up three flights of creaky wood steps to the former bell tower, now a round room. A four-poster curtained canopy bed with two large pillows of white embroidered linen stands in the center. The modern bathroom has double sinks and a separate loo. The signora pulls open the shutters. "Look, you have the very best view—the archaeological site," she announces proudly.

And there, in the distance, are the famous temples of Paestum, lit up by the full moon hovering above like a cloudy silver mirror. Bianca's never seen them at night, only during day trips from Naples. The majesty of the view fairly takes her breath away. Her eyes scan the room as she admires the soft patina of the old walnut furniture, the overstuffed armchair, its back casually draped with a mohair throw, and an ottoman large enough for Giovanni to stretch out his long legs. Maybe he plans on sleeping there, she thinks, a wave of disappointment suddenly washing over her. She vows to make the best of it—not to cave in to her feelings. It's as simple as simple can be—they will be sharing this room as friends, platonic friends. After all, they've only been together in Venice not even enough hours to make up a day—and now it's only three days since she arrived at the airport in Bari. Even though it seems as though she's known Giovanni forever, she realizes she hardly knows him at all.

After punching the mattress and checking out the bathroom, Giovanni says, "Nice room, we'll take it. I'll go down to the car for our bags."

The signora thanks him and then remarks, "Oh—I'm sorry to tell you this suite has no heat, but there are plenty of blankets in the top of the *armadio*. The TV weather reporter said the temperature may drop tonight."

Bianca quickly washes up, brushes her hair back, twists it behind her head and anchors it with the big tortoise hairpins she always carries with her. She slips into a softly gathered white blouse with long full sleeves and unpacks a crimson pashmina shawl to wrap around her shoulders in case the dining room is draughty. Rummaging around in her handbag, she finds the lustrous scarlet lipstick she'd bought at Bloomingdale's and has not yet tried. She draws it along her lips gingerly and looks in the mirror. Not bad, Bianca, with your pale skin and dark hair. *Drops of blood against the snow, hair as dark as ebony.* No, she won't allow herself to feel rejected. When he returns with the luggage, she smiles broadly and says, "Come on—now it's your turn to get ready. I'll be in the library-sitting room having a look through the newspapers."

Ω

He pours her a glass of rich, pomegranate red Primitivo. "Bianca, let's drink to our journey from Sybaris. May it be all we want it to be." He raises his glass to touch hers. She sips the peppery, powerful wine. "This is the first Primitivo I've ever tasted—I like it very much."

"My oenologist friend in Bari was the prime mover in the production of Primitivo."

The waitress materializes with a blackboard menu and recites the litany of specialties. "*Antipasto, mozzarella di bufala locale, la spigola alla griglia. Vegetarian choice, melanzane alla parmigiana.*"

They choose *la spigola*.

"You'll be sharing one large fish. And if you don't fancy ravioli stuffed with chopped artichokes, we can give you *spaghetti salsa pomodoro*," she says obligingly. "Our *dolce* this evening is the *specialità della casa, torta di fragolini*, wild strawberry cake."

Bianca studies the menu. "I'm starving. I almost could eat the fish *and* the eggplant. Do I sound greedy?"

"Not at all—you've eaten only one energy bar since early morning, so it's no wonder you're starving. As for me, I'm ravenous!" He asks the waitress to bring not one but two orders of the *melanzane alla parmigiana* with the antipasto. He offers to pay a supplement, but she tells him it isn't necessary. "Compliments of the chef."

They munch on super thin *grissini* and most of the crusty bread before the antipasto arrives. "If I drink wine on an empty stomach, I get either drunk—or sick," she says as she breaks off another crust of the *ciabatta*. She considers telling him about Oxford but she holds back, knowing that right now food seems of the utmost importance to both of them. After they feast on the comforting, plump pillows of ravioli, she'll feel confident, ready to tell him about Boar's Hill, her dark visions, Nina urging her to remove her veil.

Ω

Giovanni sits still, watching her intently, listening almost reverently as she tells her story. Bianca has no idea that at this moment he's thinking how beautiful she looks. When she finishes, he pulls his chair close and puts his arm around her shoulder drawing her to his side. By the tears in his eyes, she can tell he's moved. It's as though, in these few minutes, a barrier has been shattered and a bond forged. He no longer seems the formal, didactic, somewhat distant Giovanni she's known. Maybe she's been wrong about him. Maybe he's feeling something for her after all—if only compassion. Still, she will wait until they set foot on French soil. Then, on their way to Châtillon-sur-Seine, she will tell him her theory about the Krater, about Chrétien de Troyes and the Grail.

Ω

They climb the three flights to the tower. When he opens the door, she feels a rush of frigid air. The bed, curtained all around in crimson faux Fortuny, looks warm and inviting.

"Come on, Giò-shall we toss a coin?"

"No need to—you take it. The chaise is long enough for me, and there are plenty of blankets in the cupboard."

She reaches into her suitcase for the robe and nightgown. "Okay, I'll use the bathroom first, if that's all right with you."

"Go ahead, take your time."

When she crawls into bed, she shivers between sheets that have already been turned down on both sides. She leaves one folded down side undisturbed, hoping he might take it as an invitation to crawl in beside her. An image of red curtains banishing the black curtains flashes across her mind, wiping out, blotting out, the darkness.

When he comes out of the bathroom, he's dressed in striped pajamas with a matching robe. Typical, she thinks, always perfectly correct, dignified Giovanni.

He removes the extra blankets from the cupboard and pulls

up the ottoman to meet the chair. He sits reflecting for a few moments. Suddenly he leaps up and rips off his robe. He snatches the cover from the bed and jumps in, making the mattress squeak and bounce.

"Shouldn't we keep each other warm? It's freezing in here!" When he lays his head on her pillow she trembles as his tongue brushes the delicate shell of her ear. Reaching for her soft, graceful hands, he kisses each tapered, ringless finger, one by one. He cradles her head in his hands, looks into her smoky eyes, and says softly, seriously, "Bianca, Bianca, why has it taken me so much time, so much wasted time?" He draws the last curtain closed, grasps her shoulders, draws her against his chest, pressing his lips to hers, at first tenderly, then greedily. Pulling her gown from around her legs, he begins to stroke her thighs, her back, her breasts.

She opens her arms and enfolds him, returning his kisses feverishly, with abandon, releasing pent-up passions she has known only in her visions, in her dreams—only in the tarantella.

BOOK VI

Bianca and Giovanni

When the alarm goes off at six, they wake up in each other's arms. He calls for coffee, but the kitchen isn't open. He turns on the shower to make sure the water's hot. They stand, luxuriating in the warmth of the fine spray, while he lathers her back lovingly. Then she soaps his.

Soon they're in the dining room drinking strong black espresso savoring each other and the just-out-of-the-oven *cornetti* filled with vanilla pastry cream. As they sip their second cup he opens the map to show her the route he's sketched out.

"How long will it take for us to drive from Paestum to Marseilles?" she asks.

"With a hard push we can reach Marseilles in twelve hours. If we hit the road by eight, we can be there by nine or ten tonight. Certainly by nine if the traffic is easy—it's not tourist season and the weather looks good. Still, it's a long hard drive. Or—we can also take an interior road north to Châtillon-sur-Seine which goes through Lyon, avoiding Marseilles altogether."

"That's far too much driving in one day. I can't offer to drive. My license ran out in August and I forgot to renew it. There's no need for a car in New York. We're very close to Christmas and, if we time it right, we could be spending the winter solstice in Châtillon-sur-Seine."

"That's a great idea! Certainly the winter solstice was an important time for the Celts," he says enthusiastically.

"Somewhere I read that the Krater might have gone by pack mule through the Alps and not by sea. But why take such an arduous route when a sea voyage took less time and was probably safer?"

"In my opinion the Krater went by boat, probably in seven pieces to be assembled later *in situ*. It would have sailed, hugging the coast to ancient Massilia, then up the Rhone, the Saone, then a short distance overland to the Seine, and to Vix. Some historians disagree with me, but I think that sea transport in the spring or early autumn is easier and safer than the long haul north on pack mules through hostile territory and over an Alpine pass."

"Come on—let's be realistic! Whichever route we take, ours is hardly a difficult journey," she laughs. "Of course we'll take advantage of the time we live in—and be grateful that we can arrive there so fast and comfortably."

"Instead of driving straight to Massilia, why not make our first night stop San Remo? It's still a long drive, but if we leave Paestum around ten, we can get there by nine tonight. Traffic's light at this time of year and we'll surely make it to San Remo for a late dinner. Even if we take a lunch break at the Autogrill we can…"

She laughs, "Typical—food always on your mind."

He smiles ruefully. "And probably always will be. Let's walk to the archaeological site and have a look at the Temple of Hera built while Sybaris was still a city. Because they traded here, Hallstatt Celts would have seen this temple, and, by its size and grandeur, they would certainly have been in awe of it."

Giovanni and Bianca

The morning is crisp, the cloudless sky a cool, faded blue, a postcard perfect backdrop for their stroll. The guard knows Giovanni and allows them to enter even though it's only eight. The site is a compound of three temples, once a sacred area, the heart of the walled city of Poseidonia.

Giovanni clears his throat and speaks in his teaching mode. "We're looking at the earliest of the three temples. This one was dedicated to Hera although for years it was wrongfully called the Temple of Neptune because the name of the city was Poseidonia. It was built around 550 B.C. at the height of Sybarite power and wealth only a few decades before the Vix Krater was cast. The other temples on this site were built later, after the fall of Sybaris, by Sybarites who'd fled their city after Kroton destroyed it. I've seen many Greek temples in my lifetime but this one never fails to amaze me."

Daunting Doric columns loom, majestically supporting their massive burden. Sunlight and shade emphasize the fluting of the columns. He takes her hand as they mount the steps of the portico. "Look out beyond the colonnades and you can see how the temple faces those verdant, cone shaped hills, a site worthy of Hera. Once these three temples stood closer to the sea, but over the centuries the sea deserted them—as eventually it deserted the port of Sybaris. A temple in Sybaris would have resembled this one. Can you imagine such an enormous edifice constructed of local limestone painted to look like marble? The details of gods and goddesses in the frieze were picked out in vibrant blues, brilliant reds. What a dazzling sight it must have been."

"I remember how shocked I was to learn that the Greeks painted their temples gaudy colors," she replies. "I always thought of ancient Greek temples as models of simplicity, architecturally pure in concept, and so I guess I expected them to be pure in adornment, as well. It's even hard for me to imagine that they continued to paint them in the Classical era. Whenever I'm in London, I head straight for the British Museum to gaze at the Elgin Marbles, trying to envision the pantheon of gods and goddesses in Technicolor, but it's still hard for me to picture them that way. One famous decorator, I can't recall her name, seeing the Parthenon for the first time, cried out, 'It's beige—my color!' How disappointed she would have been had she seen the temples as they once were—in primary pigments!"

He laughs. "A few years ago I was here when the entablature was being strengthened. I climbed up the scaffolding almost thirty feet where I was able to walk around the *geison*, the cornice behind the frieze, under the eaves, so to speak. What a memorable experience."

"Even with my Nike-shod feet planted on terra firma it's still a memorable experience," she responds. "I'm glad we came here, the better to envision the Celts trading their salt and amber and furs."

"And don't forget coral—It was once plentiful along this coast and around the Bay of Naples."

For a few moments she reflects. "The Celts must have been awestruck by the Etruscans, Sybarites and Poseidonians—by their refinements—not to mention the immensity of their architecture. It's a wonder they didn't build something as grand as this temple in or around their citadel at Latisco. They certainly had the workforce to do so, as well as the wealth. And in Magna Graecia they would surely have found the inspiration—no need for them to have gone all the way to Greece, or to Olbia or Miletus."

"They may not have had such grand edifices, Bianca, but one way or another, however difficult, the enormous Krater found its way to Latisco. Most historians and antiquities experts think it was made as a tribute to a chieftain-king from a Hellene or from an Etruscan, but I'm not convinced. Are you?"

Ω

After they walk through the temple site, Giovanni leads her to the little museum to see the painting from the Tomb of the Diver. "I wanted to show it to you because it's stylistically like the painting of Hephaestus at the forge in the *masseria*. Before the Celts traded with the Greeks, they'd long been influenced by the twelve Etruscan tribes. The Etruscans were also expert bronze-smiths, so they had the art of metal working in common with the Hallstatt Celts, who were masters at forging bronze and iron. And the Etruscans, like the Celts, were believers in the afterlife: they buried their dead in *tumuli*, outfitted them with all they needed in the Otherworld. To this day objects from these tombs are looted all over Tuscany, Chiusi, Tarquinia. If only we could more thoroughly translate the Etruscan language, we might be able to understand not just the Etruscans themselves, but also the tribes they traded with—Celts, Illyrians, and later on, the earliest Romans. And we still don't understand where the Etruscans came from originally or if they were indigenous to the Italian peninsula. The study of haplogroups should someday find their deep ancestral origins."

"What on earth are haplogroups?" She shakes her head and laughs. "Come on, Giovanni, give me a break. You know that science isn't my strong point."

"You should know that it's a term used in ancient genetics."

"Maybe I should but I don't," she says unapologetically. "Come on, tell me about it but take it easy so it will sink into my left brain, my obviously deficient side."

He laughs. "Listen carefully and you'll catch on." There's the Y chromosome in the DNA that defines the male father to son, and the M DNA defines the genes passed down from the mother to child, the matrilineal—the DNA doesn't change from generation to generation. In some recent studies they've concluded that the Lebanese are descendants of the Phoenicians. As for the Etruscans, the last I heard is that they're now thought to be from Anatolia, in Western Turkey. When you think about it, Troy was also in Western Turkey, but no one to my knowledge has ever made a serious connection.

"The ancient Greeks, who had such a male-oriented life style, were aghast at the important place women held in Etruscan society, which, in fact, was also the case with the Hallstatt Celts, as we know from the Lady of Vix. The classical Greeks, however, were downright patriarchal."

"But why then did the ancient Greeks worship so many goddesses—from Hera to Aphrodite and Athena and Artemis?"

"In very ancient times the Great Goddess was worshipped all along the Mediterranean. After the Dorian Greeks appeared on the scene, they divided up her omnipotent power among several goddesses, Athena, Artemis, Aphrodite. No longer was there the one all-powerful Great Goddess of earlier times. And then with Zeus, Apollo, and finally Dionysos and Orpheus from Thrace, the patriarchy was on its way non-stop."

"It's like having a vice-president in a company and then allocating his authority among three or more vice-presidents."

He smiles. "That's a good way to put it in a contemporary context. Sometimes I think I must be boring you with all this information. I don't want to sound like a dry, dull professor."

"Not at all—you're educating me. Don't forget, I spent those two years at Boar's Hill where my reading was certainly not about Etruscans and their free and easy habits. I was reading Hildegard of Bingen's books of visions and Saint Teresa of Avila's *Way of Perfection*."

After surveying the site, Giovanni leads her to the museum to show her the fresco taken from the Tomb of the Diver. "I want you to see this because it's stylistically so much like the one in the *masseria*—so far the only example of Greek painting with a figured scene to survive in its entirety. Among the thousands of Greek tombs known from this time—roughly 700-400 B.C.—this is the only one decorated with a human subject. The fresco you saw at the *masseria* will be the second." After studying the painting of the young diver, his body in mid air about to plunge into the sea, she muses, "Do you think that he could have been diving for coral?"

He smiles broadly. "Or maybe for a lost earring."

Ω

As they leave the hotel, Giovanni asks, "Have you been to San Remo?"

"Years ago. On car trips with my parents, but not since. Because of my work I always seem to be drawn to museums, cathedrals, cradles of culture. And I usually stay away from holiday towns. I get bored lolling around on a beach in a bikini, getting badly sunburned, and never bronzing like Italian women."

"Even without a suntan you'd look fabulous, *stupende*, in a bikini."

In the past she would have demurred and muttered something about being too skinny and gangly. This morning she replies, "Thank you! I accept your charming compliment."

"The Ligurian Riviera has a sunny, mild climate almost the year 'round. San Remo is known as *La città dei fiori*. So, Bianca Fiore, it's a natural for you. The scent of carnations perfumes the air at this time of year. There are fields of them terraced on the hills from Genoa to Ventimiglia. When we have a rest stop I'll call and book a room."

By the time they reach San Remo, it's seven-thirty. Lights twinkle from boats in the harbor and the locals are making the evening *passeggiata*, strolling along the esplanade or Christmas shopping in the old town's crowded, narrow streets. They drive through avenues of palms and parks and olive trees until they reach the Hotel Costa Argentata. Giovanni called ahead to reserve. At the front desk the concierge checks out their passports, then hands the key to Giovanni. "I've upgraded you to a spacious suite with tall windows overlooking the beach and the sea. I think *la Signora* will be pleased."

When Giovanni opens the door, Bianca gasps. The waves of perfume are intense, pleasingly powerful. Vases of white carnations, vases of red carnations adorn every table.

"Happy Birthday!" he says with a wide smile on his face.

"How did you know it was my birthday?"

"Your passport. You left it on your bed table and I was curious."

"Now you know how old I am," she says jokingly.

"You're just the right age for me."

She throws her arms around him. "Thank you, thank you for this loveliest of surprises." She kisses him and whispers seductively, "I may not want to leave this room."

"No need to, we can dine right here. We're both worn out from the long day's drive. Why don't we order dinner right away? I just checked out the mini-bar and found a nice bottle of prosecco from Conegliano. I'll open it for us now."

"By the time dinner arrives, we'll be wrapped in our robes and cuddled up on the sofa with our glasses," she responds, thrilled at the thought. "While you're calling room service, I'll take a quick shower."

Looking over the menu, he chooses the sauté of *vongole*, local clams steamed-open in their stony shells, followed by chicken cannelloni with white truffles. *Gelato di frutto della passione* for dessert.

He reaches for the newspaper on the desktop, *Corriere della Sera*. Emblazoned on the front page is a photo of Sergio, captioned, *Siderno, Calabria: Sergio Battistoni, publisher of* Occhi e Anima *magazine, arrested for dealing in smuggled antiquities.*

"Come on out, Bianca—they've got Sergio!" he shouts gleefully. "Tonight we celebrate!"

After devouring dinner, downing the bottle of prosecco, sipping Ligurian limoncello, they tumble into bed and sleep soundly until five when the alarm jolts them awake.

Giovanni aims to arrive in Châtillon by six. It will take them about seven hours to reach Source-Seine. They can make it just before the sun sets on the eve of the winter solstice.

$$\Omega$$

December 21, the eve of the Winter Solstice.

As they're about to leave the room, he stops to pull out one red and one white carnation from the vases and presents them gallantly to Bianca. Although she seems sorry to be leaving her bower, he can tell she's excited that they'll soon be arriving in France, only thirty miles away. "When we reach the French border," he says, "we'll drive to Arles to get a good sweep of the Rhone, and then head due north toward Châtillon."

"Do you remember when I mentioned that I had something important to tell you?"

"I've been waiting for you to bring up the subject again."

"I wanted to wait until we set foot on French soil."

"Good—save it for Arles. We'll find a simple place by the mouth of the Rhone where we can have a coffee and a leisurely talk—and a good view. If we press on we can take another short break on the way, a stop to look at Source-Seine, a site considered a part of the City of Paris. From time immemorial it's been a shrine to the healing goddess, Sequana, a place of pilgrimage for the Celts. I've always wanted to see it."

"I've been there several times. I'll be your guide—for a change." She laughs. "I'm so happy to be here, Giò, so happy."

He's pleased that Bianca is elated about being in France.

"I love Italy, but, when I arrive in France, it feels as though I've come home."

He wonders why she feels that way but doesn't ask.

Ω

Before entering Arles they stop at a cafe on the Quai de la Roquette, the ancient quarter, now well on its way to gentrification. From the Quai they have an astounding view of the mighty Rhone, at once both benign and treacherous. A herb garden surrounds the old stone inn, and, even though it's late December, a hedge of lavender ready to burst into bloom billows over the pebble path. Bianca stops to pinch a sprig from a rosemary branch and holds it to her nose, inhaling the heady, aromatic scent. *"There's rosemary, that's for remembrance,"* she whispers.

"Pray you, love, remember." He finishes the quotation and puts her hand to his lips.

Ω

Once the coffee arrives, Giovanni asks, "Are you ready to tell me your ideas about the Krater? Until a few years ago it was one of the best kept secrets in France. Now Châtillon-sur-Seine has a booming tourist industry because of it—and *la Dame de Vix*." She takes a deep breath and begins. "On leaving Boar's Hill I decided I deserved the freedom to do what I've always loved—travel—whenever I had the chance. After I left Oxford, I rented a car and took the ferry from Dover to Calais. I was headed for Rheims because I wanted to see the cathedral of Joan of Arc. It was late afternoon so I stopped at a hotel in Arras, thinking that the next morning I could drive on to Rheims. That night I had a dream about Nina and Avallon."

"Do you remember it?"

She nods. "Nina is sitting by my side as we drive in a wagon toward a quay. Ahead, across the water, I see a dazzling sight. I tell Nina that beyond are the towers and turrets of Avallon. The vision is so vivid, so powerful, it still gives me goose-bumps. In my dream I know that Nina isn't really dead, and that it is she who has led me to this wondrous place. The next day, after visiting the cathedral I thought I'd drive southeast to Dijon to visit the museum. I have a happy memory of stopping there with my parents on our way to Bern. Anyway, while heading for Dijon I turned west instead of east, driving on country roads. I lost my way and found myself in the little town of Châtillon-sur-Seine. When I stopped to fill the tank, the attendant asked if I'd been to the local museum. I told him I hadn't, and he advised me not to miss the exhibit. This is the backstory. Now I'll tell you exactly when my ideas, my revelation—you might even call it an epiphany—came to me. I don't know why it took so long."

"Will you forgive me if I ask an impertinent question?"

"Sure—impertinent questions are the only kind to ask. Please go right ahead."

He laughs. "How did you get this 'Paul on the way to Damascus' flash of insight?"

"On the plane back to New York after the wedding, I was thinking about the Burgundy trip. By then I'd seen the Vix Krater five times since 1996. I sat there daydreaming while looking over the Michelin Green Guide map of Burgundy— for what reason I don't recall. As I studied the map, I noticed that Troyes was quite close to the little village of Vix where the Krater was discovered. And Avallon was close to both. I asked myself what Troyes was famous for. Besides the famous medieval fair, there was also Chrétien de Troyes, court poet to the daughter of Queen Eleanor of Aquitaine. Have you ever read Chrétien's *Le Conte du Graal?*"

"We read Chrétien in my French literature class—though I don't remember much about him or his Grail story."

"Since I write about ritual I'm very familiar with Jessie Weston's *From Ritual to Romance*. I've even memorized one of her famous passages. If you'll permit me:

That the man who first told the story, and boldly, as befitted a born teller of tales, wedded it to the Arthurian legend, was himself connected by descent with the Ancient Faith, actually himself beheld the Secret of the Grail, and told in purposely romantic form, that of which he knew.

"Weston is, of course, referring to Chrétien, the 'born teller of tales.' In his *Four Romances*, he was the first to tell the stories of King Arthur, Lancelot and Queen Guinevere, and Camelot, connecting them to the Arthurian Legend; Chrétien's *Story of the Grail*, his last, unfinished work is about the quest of Perceval. It's also about Perceval's romance with Blanchefleur."

"I vaguely remember Weston from T. S. Eliot's footnotes to '*The Wasteland,*'" he remarks. "The poet claims he is indebted to Weston. But what does all this have to do with the Krater?"

"Giovanni, just listen to me without butting in—and please don't laugh. Here goes, I believe—I *know*—that the Krater of

Vix was deep in the collective unconscious of Chrétien and other descendants of these early Celts. The Krater was buried in the grave of a woman near the village of Vix. Overlooking Vix was the important Celtic trading citadel of Latisco. Think about how, over the centuries, the local folk must have heard about this fabulous vessel, the symbol of feasting and abundance and immortality. I believe that when Chrétien told his story, the Krater was lodged in his ancestral memory, perhaps from the legends and the oral traditions of his Celtic forebears. Because the Celts had no written language, they had strong motives for keeping alive an active, collective memory. As the centuries passed, their tribal histories, stories, and legends were transmitted from father to son, from mother to daughter. And I'm convinced that the Krater is the very source of the story of the Grail. To make it simple, the Krater of Vix is the Grail, the pagan grail, the grail of Chrétien de Troyes. And he set his *Four Romances* in the Court of King Arthur, whose legends of fame and prowess and bravery were told and re-told orally in the lays and songs and sagas, and lingered on in the memory of the Bretons and the Gauls of Burgundy, When Chrétien wrote his stories, he wasn't writing about the Christian Holy Grail, as it later came to be called by subsequent writers, the so-called Continuers of Chrétien's unfinished story."

She looks him in the eye, waiting for him to laugh at her hypothesis. "I believe that I have found the link, the golden chain that connects ancient ritual to romance. If you don't agree with me, please, *please* don't try to change my mind because you can't now and you never will," she says decisively.

Giovanni doesn't laugh. He doesn't even smile. The look on his face is serious. "Bianca, have you ever studied Greek?"

She shakes her head. "I wish I had."

"You've obviously studied Latin."

"Yes, in high school for four years." She smiles. "Then later on I had a refresher course at Boar's Hill."

"Then maybe you know that the word for 'grail' is derived from the Latin *cratalis*, which in Greek is *krater*. The word *cratalis* evolved into a vernacular *cratale*, in old French, then eventually to *graal*, which rhymes with *cratale*. So the word '*grail*' is indeed a word originating from '*krater*.' There's nothing mysterious at all about the word 'grail.'"

She cannot believe her ears. "Let me repeat what you said. You're telling me that that the Greek word, *krater*, changes until it becomes *graal* and then 'grail' in English?"

"It's as simple as that, Bianca."

She shakes her head in disbelief. "I've been thinking of the Krater as a *graal*-grail, for quite a while. And did you know that Chrétien was also the first to link the Grail to Arthurian legend? And he was also the first to write about King Arthur and Camelot and Avallon. Giovanni, I believe that the Arthurian Avallon is right here in France, only a few leagues from Troyes. Avallon is a very ancient town of about seven thousand people. And Vix is perhaps a long day's horse ride to Troyes—but Troyes can also be reached by boat up the Seine. Remember that the Seine becomes navigable at Vix.

"There's no real place called Avalon in Britain, nor is there any indication that there ever was. But there is an Avallon in Burgundy and it has been there for well over fifteen hundred years. It doesn't make any sense that Avalon is in Wales or near Glastonbury. After all, Chrétien was court poet to Marie of Champagne, the daughter of Queen Eleanor of Aquitaine. He was influenced by the *trouvères* and troubadours of Eleanor's court and by the *jongleurs* and bards of Brittany, who spoke, and to his day continue to speak, a Celtic language.

"Unfortunately, and, strangely, the French have never made a concerted move to take back their heritage from the

British. And when they do, they'll begin to wonder, as I have, about the location of Camelot."

"Well, Bianca, given your theory—your marvelously intuitive theory—the French may change their minds and reclaim the mythical, magical Avallon as their very own. Then they can commence the search for Camelot."

BOOK VII

Sequana

Giovanni and Bianca

Giovanni is intent on reaching Sequana's shrine before dark. The sun sets around five thirty, making it one of the shortest days of the year. When they arrive at Source-Seine, they park on the side of a country road and stride briskly up a path to the fenced enclosure. In the late afternoon light, the dark, leafless branches of ancient oaks seem like arms reaching wide to welcome them. Beeches and tall, slender white poplars tufted with balls of mistletoe surround the park area.

They hurry down the path to a swampy pool and cross the small stone bridge toward a white stone statue of a river nymph reclining gracefully by the entrance of a mossy, man-made grotto framed by dangling vines. From this site trickles an obscure little stream that soon gathers force to become one of the most celebrated rivers in the world. An iron fence surrounds the grotto. They stop to read the sign, a decree by Napoleon III chiseled in stone: *"The source is the property of the La Ville de Paris."*

Bianca has been silent for a few moments, and then it's her turn to explain. "During the late La Tène period, this sanctuary of Sequana, the fast-flowing one, the healing goddess of the Celts, was taken over by the Romans, but most likely it had been a sacred place since the time of the Hallstatt Celts-or much earlier—since the Neolithic period. For centuries, these Gaulish Celts performed their rituals here, probably well into the Middle Ages." She then exclaims, "Giovanni—just imagine what it must have been like—throngs of pilgrims hoping for a cure from Sequana, the place crammed with food vendors, hawkers of votive images—ex votos in clay or wood, of arms, legs or breasts, internal organs, or whatever ailing body part a pilgrim wanted to toss into the pool for healing—or to give thanks for cures or favors already received. They've found thousands of these votaries, some obviously fertility objects— women with bulging bellies, swaddled babies, and, for those yearning for love or looking for a mate," her eyes meet his and she grins, "there are even images of entwined couples."

"I wonder how many thousands of pilgrims have stood at this quiet little stream to fill their cups with the sacred water of Sequana. When you think about it, it's not too different from Lourdes," she muses.

"Or from the grotto of Monte Sant'Angelo in Puglia," he adds. "Someday I'll be your guide there." He reaches into the pocket of his windbreaker to pull out a small, flat, collapsible cup. "I always carry one of these—just in case," he laughs. "Too bad we can't get closer to the spring. Together we could drink from the sacred stream of Sequana's Seine. But since we can't, a kiss—or two—will have to do." He pulls her close, and they stand mouth to mouth until the day begins to lose its light. Holding hands, they walk to the car and drive straightway to Châtillon.

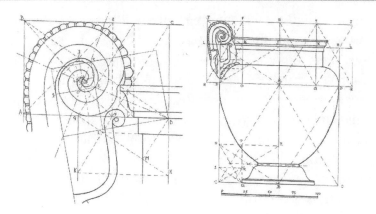

Sketch of the great Krater by Eutropios, student of Pythagoras

Zatoria

When the sun comes up, I find my father pacing the courtyard. I tremble as I tell him of my frightful visions and he confides that he too has such fears. Now, he says, is the time to leave Sybaris. "We must make haste." He thanks our hosts and tells them we will soon take leave of their ample bounty. He cautions that they, too, should forsake their home, for the future of Sybaris is at stake; he urges them to pass on this warning to friends and loved ones whose lives might well be threatened. Our hosts take heed of my father and make ready to desert their villa for a simple country dwelling in the midst of their vineyards and olive groves.

My father and I set out before the sun is high. We have not much to carry with us, just our clothing and my treasured *kylix* still wrapped safely in straw and sheepskin. When we are well beyond the walls of Sybaris, the cart driver turns down a country lane. He tells us that we will climb a hill to take a shorter, safer route to reach the other sea. On the way, he says, we will pass the workshop of a master craftsman who has forged a huge bronze krater, a vessel such as had never been seen in Sybaris. A slave runs ahead to announce our arrival. As we begin to approach the large stone forge, I hear ear-drum-bruising sounds, the clang, the rhythm of hammers beating metal. Plumes of smoke coil to the skies, but the acrid stench is not from the burnt offerings of sacrifice. Even from this distance we feel heat from the smelting oven.

When we enter the compound, we are welcomed by a man clothed in white. From his robes I know he is a follower of Pythagoras. Eutropios informs us that we cannot see the Krater. It is now in seven pieces, protected by animal hides and wood chips, each section ready to be hauled in its own wagon. After the Krater arrives in Latisco, it will be welded whole by a Kelt from Bribacte, since those Keltoi have great skill in working bronze and iron.

And as the master smith describes for us the long and arduous journey the Krater will soon make, I hear a voice behind me, not a Hellene's voice—yet one I have heard before. I turn to face the Prince of the River People. He greets us and tells my father that his fame has spread from Thrace to the wise men in Latisco, men called druids who also believe in an afterlife.

When we are taken to the hot, deafening foundry, we see a likeness of the Krater drawn on its lime-washed walls by Eutropios. The Kelt tells Zalmoxis that he has ordered it not only for his father, the ailing King, but for his people as well. The crops have been meager and there has been a drought for three plantings of grain. His people fear they will spend yet another winter without corn in the bins. In payment for the Krater, the Kelt has sent boatloads of tin and copper ore as well as gold for the Sybarites who revere the precious metal. He shows us the design for a gorgon with its gaping tongue to keep away evil spirits and the frieze with the horses and hoplites in parade around the rim of the Krater.

My father tells him of my prophecy, my visions, and of his own profound concern. He urges the Kelt to flee to Laus on the sea, then set sail north to Poseidonia of the Sybarites, where he is sure to be welcomed. The Kelt needs no persuading and, in very little time, he gathers his people, his belongings, his treasures. My father and I will leave with him and together we will cross the mountains to the other sea. The slaves begin to load the heavy cargo onto seven wagons drawn by mules. The Prince will furnish supplies and food, enough for each day that passes until we reach the coast where he will hire a boat to sail with us to Massilia of the Phocaeans.

We know we face hazards on the journey from Sybaris—bandits, harsh weather, bears, wolves, mountain lions—but the Prince of the River People will protect us. I trust in him.

Ω

After checking in at the Côte-d'Or in Châtillon-sur-Seine, they wash up and head straight for dinner in the hotel's popular bistro. The waiter leads them to a cozy corner table, and at

Giovanni's request, returns with a carafe of the *vin de pays*.

"I see someone I know— that man in the opposite corner," Giovanni says in a hushed tone. "Hermès Delaunay from the University of Dijon. A few years ago we dug with the Italian team at Ebla, on the Euphrates. I'm not sure he'll recognize me."

She glances toward the table. "He looks serious and professorial, even more so than you," she teases. "Strangely, he also looks familiar to me."

"Besides being an expert archaeologist, Hermès is also a brilliant historian of Burgundy." He pulls out his card, writes a quick note and hands it to the waiter.

"*Bien sûr*, Monsieur. Professor Delaunay is an *habitué*. In the summer months he works on the excavations at Mont Lassois and, whenever he's in Châtillon-sur-Seine for the *colloques*, he always comes here to dine."

When Delaunay reads the card, his face breaks into a broad smile. He leaps to his feet and makes his way to their table.

"My dear Giovanni, what a pleasure to see you here!"

"And for me to see you again, Hermès," he replies, throwing his arm around his friend's shoulder. Please join us for dinner."

"I accept with pleasure." He beckons the waiter to change his table.

"And permit me to introduce Bianca Caldwell—*nom de plume*, Fiore. You might have read her columns in *Occhi e Anima*."

When Bianca extends her hand, Hermès, the consummate Frenchman, bows, puts it to his lips, raises his eyes and gazes intently into hers.

"I am an admirer of yours, Madame," he says as though before him sits the loveliest, most desirable woman in the world. "I enjoy reading your imaginative column, but what I admire most is the way you have learned to take advantage of the most powerful source of your inspiration—although I might not always be in agreement with your intuitive insights."

Giovanni laughs. "Don't let his opinion bother you, Bianca. Hermès also considers my theories too subversively avant-garde for Greek ceramic scholars."

Delaunay seems amused. "Madame, Giovanni knows that, despite our differences, I have great respect for his instinctual perceptions. We used to have long, philosophical conversations after dinner during those work days in Syria. He might even recall that I am a follower of Henri Bergson, our French Nobel Prize winner who believed that intuitive knowledge is more significant than any other kind for understanding reality."

Giovanni, not wanting to be academically outdone, quickly responds, "His theory is more or less in agreement with Einstein's. But before we get to the subject of philosophy, perhaps we should order. I sense the waiter is becoming impatient. Bianca, Troyes is very famous for its *andouilettes*, tripe sausages, shall I order for you?"

Tripe has never been one of her favorite foods. "No thanks. I'm not all that hungry. I'd like the omelette and *pommes frites*, please."

"Are you here to visit the museum and *le Cratère de Vix*?" Hermès directs his question to Bianca.

"Yes, this will be my fifth time."

He seems surprised. "When was the first?"

"In 1996. I remember having the strangest experience. When I walked into the room, I was astounded by the Krater's size, by its anses with the grinning gorgons, their snake tails wrapping around the immense vessel. I had the place all to myself so I could study its details undisturbed. Suddenly the lights dimmed. I heard cymbals clash, the reedy sound of pipes, plucked lyre strings, then voices singing a paean in Greek. For a moment I was startled. I thought I'd traveled back in time. I felt faint. It almost took my breath away." She laughs. "I guess you'd call me hyper-impressionable."

Hermès smiles. "On the floor above, we were presenting a concert. A group of musicians from Munich was performing ancient Greek music on archaic instruments. When Giovanni introduced us, I thought that perhaps I recognized you from your photograph in *Eyes and Soul*. Now it's all coming back to me. I remember walking down the stairs to check on the exhibit. A woman was standing before *le Cratère*. She was pale and her hands trembled. It seemed as if she were in—or from— another world. I asked her if she was feeling all right. She broke out of her reverie and told me that she'd discovered *le Cratère* by taking a detour and then found her way to the museum."

"And then you kindly told me not to be frightened, that there was a live concert upstairs. I remember our conversation, very clearly now, even if I appeared to be far away."

"Have you ever written one of your imaginative meditations about *le Cratère or la Dame de Vix*?"

"None that have yet been published. When I left New York on a self-imposed sabbatical, I thought I'd be sending my monthly columns to the magazine, but a few days ago I decided to quit my job, so my vignettes might never be published. My last contribution would have been on the *mixoparthenos*, Milouziena of the Scythians, the melusina."

"Did you know that there was a cult of the Melusina, the double tailed mermaid, in this part of France? In fact, she was worshipped as a goddess throughout the early Middle Ages. She remains in our Burgundian folklore as Melusine. And you often see her image in many of our churches, including Vézelay, another of Burgundy's greatest treasures."

"Yes—I've seen the Melusina chiseled in a column in the Church of the Magdalene in Troyes—she's also in the mosaic floor in the cathedral of Otranto. And in Venice she can be found carved in the pillars of *Santa Maria dei Miracoli*—and many more sites in France, Italy and Spain," she asserts confidently. Since the Professor asks so many questions, she decides to ask a few herself. "Are you here on a winter dig?"

"No, Madame," he replies, still very formal. "I'm here for the annual *colloque* tomorrow afternoon, and to look over a site where my colleague, Bruno Chaume, and his Franco-German team have been digging."

"I remember that René Joffroy unearthed the Krater in the winter of 1953."

"You are correct. Joffroy deserves most of the credit for the discovery of the Krater and its treasures, and indeed his contribution is enormous. Then there was also Maurice Moisson, a local farmer who actually found the stones and the location of the tumulus, so he too deserves a bit of the glory."

Bianca then asks, "Why is this inland part of Burgundy called la Côte-d'Or —the Gold Coast?"

Hermès smiles, "In this case, la Côte d'Or means golden hillsides, perhaps more for the 'gold' of its vines than for its crops of golden wheat. There's evidence that the very first wines in France were produced from the vines of Burgundy. Perhaps you already know that tomorrow, December 22, is the winter solstice, the shortest day of the first day of winter, an auspicious day for the Celts. Although the formal announcement was recently published—on October 14—it was on July 31 that an astonishing discovery was made."

"Please tell us about it, Hermès." Giovanni says eagerly.

"Bruno Chaume and his team uncovered the remains of a town on the plateau of Mont Lassois, where there was once a Celtic trading citadel. The site covers an area of 120 acres and was built in the last years of the Hallstatt Celts, 520-500 B.C., about the time of *le Cratère* when...."

"Forgive me for interrupting," Giovanni remarks, "but I'm wondering why I haven't read anything about this amazing find—at least not in the Italian newspapers—but then I've been working on my own project in Calabria. What did you uncover in the town?"

"Plenty! We unearthed areas where there were once bins on stilts for collective grain storage, containers for water storage. The excavations also reveal a concise town plan, open and structured. We've also found the remains of three major buildings. The largest appears to have been a great hall over 35 by 21 meters, with a ceiling almost 15 meters."

Giovanni exclaims, "My God! He shakes his head in disbelief. "Larger than the archaic Temple of Athena in Paestum?! It's 33 by 14.5 meters. I know it well—I worked on some restoration there."

"Yes—and, to make it even more intriguing for you, Giovanni, the edifice was in the shape of a Greek megaron with an apse, and a stoa along the front. We call it '*le Palais de la Dame de Vix*.' Most likely *le Cratère* stood in the center of this 'great hall,' where we've uncovered evidence of feasting and ceramic utensils, some of them imitating bronze."

"Ceramics imitating bronze?" Giovanni asks, obviously hoping that this discovery might help to confirm the theory about Greek ceramics imitating metal.

"If you'd like, it would be my pleasure to show you the site tomorrow. You'll enjoy seeing it."

There is almost no reaction from Bianca. Finally she murmurs. "Thank you, Professor, that's very kind of you. Of course we'd love to see it. With you as our guide, and with your knowledge of historical Burgundy, it will be an unforgettable experience."

Giovanni

After dinner, Bianca is silent, hands clasped in her lap, eyes staring down at the starched, white tablecloth, as Giovanni and Hermès discuss the scientific details of the astounding discovery. Giovanni wonders what's going on in her head, what she might be thinking—envisioning, or digging up in that mysterious right-brain of hers. And suddenly it occurs to him. Bianca is stunned. She knows, and now at this moment, he knows, that tomorrow, together, they will see the remains of the *Palais de la Dame de Vix*. The Grail Castle. *Le Palais du Graal*. The Grail Castle of Chrétien de Troyes. He reaches over and clasps her hand tightly and murmurs "Yes, Bianca, from ritual to romance."

"Let's wait until we're up in the room before we talk," she whispers after they say goodnight to Hermès. He puts his arm around her as they trudge up the steps to their cozy room, tired but happy and excited. As soon as the door closes, she asks breathlessly, her words tumbling out. "Can you imagine what was going through my head when he told us about the discovery of the palace?"

He laughs and shakes his head. "I was sure that whatever was going through your head, was the same as what was going through mine. So what's your conclusion?"

She pauses to collect her thoughts. "Get ready for this, Giovanni."

He looks at her attentively. "I'm ready and waiting."

"I believe the *Palais de la Dame de Vix* was the Grail Castle of Chrétien de Troyes," she says slowly, deliberately, watching his reaction. waiting for him to laugh at her.

He's not at all surprised. "Certainly with the discovery of the castle, and because the Krater—the *Graal*—is now thought to have been used ritually there, it's not hard to come to this conclusion. It entered my mind as well."

"And—hold on to your hat—something else occurred to me while you and Hermès were in deep conversation and I was daydreaming."

"Tell me, Bianca."

"I am convinced that the Palais—the castle on the hill—was Camelot—imagine—Camelot! C-A-M-E-L-O-T! You Giovanni and I Bianca Fiore, have found Camelot! I have chills when I think about it. Chrétien de Troyes was the first *ever* to mention Camelot explicitly in his romance, *Lancelot, the Knight of the Cart*. In it he describes Camelot as a city on the hill overlooking a river, surrounded by plains and forests. Since then, Camelot has come to mean a place of peace, of culture and wisdom, of prosperity. For the folk in the countryside and villages around Latisco, I say that these remained as distant memories of a place that no longer existed, Camelot, their yearnings for and their remembrances of a golden age and a good life. Not for nothing were the Sequani called the Tribe of Sweet Goodness."

"You're going way too fast. Take it easy, Bianca, slow down! I want to hear every word of what you have to say."

She takes a deep breath. "This becomes all the more interesting because not only was Chrétien the first to write about the Grail, but let me repeat that he was also the first to write about King Arthur and his Court in his *Four Arthurian Romances*. Although Chrétien was writing in the twelfth century, it was way back during the late Roman occupation of Gaul, when a British general, Riothamus, the historical King Arthur, enters the picture. When Chrétien wrote his *Four Romances* and finally his last, unfinished romance, *The Story of the Grail*. I propose that he was writing from the memories of centuries, handed down for countless generations by storytellers, bards and druids! I've read that there were still druids in Gaul and in

Britain as late as Chrétien's time. History, folklore, fireside tales, characters, ideas, situations, places, images—all this I believe was embedded in the Celtic imagination of a medieval poet, Chrétien de Troyes, author of the first romance novels."

"Bianca—I think you've got something going here, but I'm wondering what Hermès would think about it. I'm sure that as a scholar of Burgundian history, he might be intrigued by your theory—and don't forget, as a follower of the philosophy of Henri Bergson, he wouldn't scoff at your imagination, your intuitive knowledge."

"I'm not sure I'll tell him about it yet. My ideas may be more effective if I send them to him as a saga—if I may be so overly generous to myself using such a word to describe my collection of vignettes."

"Your vignettes are your little vines—your golden vines."

"Strange, I never thought about the meaning of vignette."

"I'm sure it's occurred to Hermès, especially since he's a Burgundian." he replies.

"Maybe over lunch I'll ask his opinion about the historical Arthur Riothamus as the real King Arthur. Now—what are *you* going to do about the drawing of the Krater? You can't let your old friend and colleague read about it in *Le Figaro*."

"I thought about it during dinner—especially when I heard that the discovery of the Palace was made only a few weeks after I found the Krater's sketch. But I must first report my find to the *Soprintendente archeologica di Calabria*. I have an appointment with Professoressa Luppino on the fifth of January. When I leave her office in Sibari, my first call will be to Hermès."

Zatoria

The arrival at Latisco

The King of the River People begins his slow descent from the citadel to the river below. A harsh blare of horns rends the air. The road winding from the hill is soon cleared of barrows and wagons, and crowds scurry to make way for their silver-haired King, his fishing pole clasped tightly in his trembling hand as he attempts to hold it aloft as if it were a royal scepter.

Now the King watches from the river bank as the dark boats approach. When he sees the shining woman, her hair spread out in fiery points, he thinks he looks upon the arrival of a goddess, the incarnation of the goddess Sequana. The woman sits in a narrow black boat filled with gorse picked from surrounding hills by her attendants. She is dressed in fine white wool, a mantle fastened with a gold and coral brooch falls around her shoulders. A necklace of amber drops to her breast: her bright hair, more red than gold, is garlanded with mistletoe.

Behind her in a boat, young boys and girls play flutes. Seven barges follow, each poled by men wearing hats of thin, hammered tin that flash in the sunlight. Other men watch from the river bank. Their long fair hair is tied back. Some wear wide hats like cartwheels turning up in front and behind. Women, many with water vessels on their heads, are clad in robes patterned in squares and stripes of blue, red, yellow, and green. Hooded men in long robes stand with heads bowed, and strong lads, freckled by the sun, look on in awe. Helped by her attendants, she steps off the boat.

The King pulls the torque from his neck and places it on her head as though it is a diadem.

"Who are you if you are not Sequana?"

"My mother named me Zato, but the Hellenes call me Zatoria."

$$\Omega$$

Winter Solstice Latisco, December 22, 2007

The sky is a clear winter blue, the brilliant sun making up for the gloomy gray of yesterday, and for what will be the year's longest night.

Hermès comes by to pick them up at ten in the morning. Bianca and Giovanni are ready, eagerly waiting outside. As they drive north, they stop in the center of town to have a look at the Seine, ever widening as it rushes through Châtillon on its short journey to Vix.

On the way, Hermès relates the story about the days of the Krater's discovery by René Joffroy, the success of the dig almost sixty years ago. He has with him a few tear sheets from the *London Illustrated News*, the June 1953 Coronation issue. "You see, the British thought the discovery of the Krater so important that they thought it worthy to include in this famous, collector's Coronation issue. I have some extra copies and I would like to offer one to you as a remembrance of your visit here with Giovanni, my long lost colleague."

"Thank you, Hermès—I happily accept this memento of today," she says, scanning the article and its photographs of the Krater. "It seems fitting to read about the breathtaking discovery here, in this issue—as though the British regarded *la Dame de Vix* as a queen, an ancient Celtic Queen."

"Yes—these Hallstatt Celts spoke a proto-Celtic called

Q-Celtic, or Goedelic, a language still spoken by the young Queen Elizabeth's subjects, the Irish and Western Scots. So there is a linguistic connection here."

Ω

They turn off the road toward the village of Vix. From a distance they see Mont Lassois, also known as Mont St. Marcel, rising above.

When they drive over the stone bridge spanning the widening Seine and approach the village, Hermès responds to Bianca's question about its population.

"Now it's around a hundred people but in the summer many tourists make their way here. Until the mid-Nineties when the Internet helped the public take note of *le Cratère*, our great bronze was not very well known in Europe—not even in France. And in the States it's still hardly known at all. The last article about our treasure was in The New York Times, and that was about twenty-five years ago. Now, in the summer, besides tourists, we also have many student archeologists who work with Bruno Chaume and his French and German team."

They begin the gradual climb to the plateau of Mont Lassois. When they reach the summit, they stop to behold the rich farmlands of the Châtillonnais, precisely marked fields of tilled earth, ready for late winter seeding, as they have been for centuries. Hermès points out another tumulus, not yet excavated, close to the river, and the tumulus where the Krater was unearthed.

At the summit, Giovanni parks the car by St. Marcel, the little Romanesque church "Come—let us make our way over to the Palais—is very close by. Follow me."

They trudge up a steep road cut through the brush and trees. Bianca is wearing her Nikes and manages to keep climbing without slipping in the mud around the tire ruts. When they reach the top, she stops to look out toward the east, over the woodlands and forests surrounding Mont Lassois. There are the seeded plains in the distance, and the Seine is fast-flowing its way to Troyes to Paris and the Atlantic. She knows—she feels—she can see that she's standing on the earth that was once Camelot, exactly as it was described in Chrétien's own words, Camelot, a city on the hill overlooking a river, surrounded by forest and plains.

Hermès explains that the dig is covered in mid September to keep the work intact. Surrounded by a wire fence, the field of stones, once part of the palace, is protected by a waterproof canvas which clearly outlines its geometric form. Hermès points out the apse and its resemblance to a megaron, a Greek structure. "You can see here, by these symmetrical holes, how the palace was once supported by tall oak beams and how its pointed roof, covered in wood shingles, was able to withstand heavy snow. Of course, wood structures cannot withstand the test of time, but the depth of the holes, their spacing and the number of columns reveal a building of majestic scale. The entrance, facing east, was protected by an awning and the palace, from all evidence, was painted deep red. Archaeologists like to think that perhaps *le Cratère* stood in the center of this great hall, and personally I am convinced that it did. We have all the evidence of feasting here, thousands upon thousands of ceramic shards, evidence of foods—legumes, bones, grains. Can you imagine what the local folk thought about *le Cratère* in such a palace?"

Bianca nods, smiling, "Oh yes, I can imagine the stories they told and retold about the castle on the citadel and *le Cratère*."

"Hermès, before we leave the site why don't you tell us more about these Hallstatt Celts." Giovanni asks. "There are so few historical references to these people. Mostly what we know has come from fairly recent archaeological finds from the Prince's tomb in Hochsdorf, from Vix and other sites here in Burgundy."

"This ancient land, once Gaul, was a center of the Celtic lands that stretched from Anatolia to Hibernia," he replies. "Its peoples were linked by a common ancestry, a single speech. You already know that these Celts traded tin and salt from the mines near Hochsdorf for riches from the Mediterranean. Here, at Vix, they also collected tolls for cargos loaded or unloaded where the Seine became navigable. Besides trade, Hallstatt peoples engaged in agriculture, wheat crops and raising livestock, especially horses, sheep, and cattle. And then from the artifacts we've found, the Hallstatt tribes were certainly influenced by Hellenic and Etruscan culture."

Giovanni adds, "Anthropologists believe that there is a very ancient racial Hallstatt connection to Scythians, also horse breeders who eventually became wheat growers along the Black Sea, in the region of the Ukraine. Similarly, they buried their dead in wagons for the afterlife. This is not a casual similarity, it is profound."

"What about human sacrifice?" Bianca asks, then wishes she hadn't.

"There has never been any indication of human sacrifice in Hallstatt graves. And of course, there were no weapons in the grave of *la Dame de Vix*. War did not seem to be a preoccupation for these tribes—except to defend themselves. For instance, in one of the tumuli, the grave of a prince, only recently discovered in Hochsdorf, Austria, there were no weapons, only an impressive gold ceremonial dagger, part of the regalia of a Hallstatt chief or king. Other than these ceremonial artifacts, there was a lack of weapons, consistent with other Hallstatt princely burials."

"However, later on, around 480 BC, the La Tène Celts

appeared on the scene. They swept down from the North and spoke another form of Celtic called P. Celtic or Brythonic. Among these La Tène peoples were tribes staking out territories; they overcame or eventually merged with the Hallstatt tribes. And about that time, trade from Cornwall to Vix and to the western Atlantic lessened. The trade route from the Rhone to the Mediterranean had been weakened, either by these hostile invasions, or because of new trade routes to the Atlantic. The Phoenicians no longer had the monopoly around the Straits of Gibraltar, and so the trade routes from the Mediterranean to the Atlantic were now open. This meant, for these early Celts of the oppidum of Latisco, that there was not only dwindling trade but also the loss of revenue from the tolls at Vix. Gradually the settlement fell into disuse, eventually abandoned, and then we have also found traces of devastation by fire and its ultimate desolation."

"But then there are the war-mongering, cattle-thieving Celts—when do the ancient historians begin to write about those La Tène Celts?" Bianca asks.

Giovanni speaks up before his friend has a chance. "The first historical treatise was *History of the Celts*, by Posidonios, but it was lost, although there are quotes from much later writers such as Strabo and Tacitus who had read it. We have other later records: Julius Caesar in his Gaulish histories, writes about Celts first hand, some of it undoubtedly exaggeration."

Hermès nods and goes on. "And conversely, there are the Celtic legends, medieval Irish sagas. Indeed we do have two conflicting images of these tribes—on the one hand, the fearless Celtic warriors streaking into battle naked, screaming, terrifying and beheading their enemies, burning victims alive in wicker cages. Many of these were Celts who believed in the Cult of the Head, because to them the human head embodied the essence of being and imbued supernatural powers. They hung the enemies' severed heads as trophies or preserved them in cedar oil to show off to visitors. Even today, in a museum near Marseilles, you can how these Celts displayed the heads of enemies—set into niches on the facades of their dwellings."

Bianca shudders. "Gruesome!"

Hermès continues. "There are also the other mental images we have of Celts, nature-loving, wise, learned druids, intellectuals who contained the knowledge of generations— centuries of their people—and with no written language, everything was committed to memory. Not too far away from here, in the 19th century, at Coligny on the Seine, a bronze astronomical disc was discovered and only recently recon- structed. Some Celtic scholars consider this Sequani Calendar more accurate than the Roman Julian calendar. It must have taken millennia for these people to arrive at this knowledge of astronomy to explain it pictorially and in ancient Goedelic characters. It doesn't happen overnight, you know. This was real human achievement."

Giovanni adds, "If not millennia, centuries at least. Just think how many more centuries it has taken since then to achieve enough scientific knowledge to hurl a man into space and take the first step on the moon."

Turning to Bianca who has been listening intently to the two professors expounding their knowledge, Hermès says, "Now let us move forward from science to the human imagina- tion. Why don't you write one of your ritual vignettes about *le Palais*—like the kind we've enjoyed reading in *Eyes and Soul*?"

She responds with a smile. "I do intend to write a vignette on *le Palais de la Dame de Vix*, even though I have no intentions of ever returning to the magazine. I promise to send you a copy when it's finished. My story has become all the more intriguing because of the discovery of *le Palais*."

As they stroll around the remains of the Celtic town, they

listen in fascination as Hermès points out where the grain bins stood, the water cisterns, the tradesmen's houses. "The smith would have had a large house because of his important trade, working in metal, bronze and iron, especially. The *rix*, the king or chieftain of the tribe, would have rented his lands to the tenant farmers and animal breeders who lived in the country-side surrounding Latisco. Their houses would have been made of mud and wattle with peaked, thatched roofs. The houses on this site were made of wood, some painted. The larger, more important edifices were surrounded by palisades. The discovery of a Celtic town, a planned urban center, here or anywhere else in the ancient Celtic world, is unprecedented. We may have just taken a stroll around the first town in France."

Re Artù. King Arthur. From *The Tree of Life*, mosaic floor, Otranto Cathedral, Puglia, Italy. Designed by the monk, Pantaleone, in 1163, completed 1166-67. Chrétien died in 1180. Between 1160 and 1170 he was at the court of Marie de Champagne. The floor is contemporary with Chrétien. The story of King Arthur was most likely brought to Otranto by the Normans who had occupied what is now Puglia and Sicily since the early eleventh century.

Ω

At lunch Hermès asks the waiter to bring them a bottle of Romanée-Conti from his uncle's vineyard and explains, "This is still a young wine—2005—but it's supposedly the best year in memory. The local vintners claim that one day it will become legendary."

After a few sips of the garnet-red wine tasting of wild strawberries, Bianca relaxes and feels comfortable enough to ask Hermès, "May I ask if you agree with the theory that in Late Antiquity, the historical King Arthur, the British general Riothamus, was urged by the Romans in Gaul to get rid of the Visigoths who were besieging the territory?"

Hermès responds immediately, with deep personal conviction. "After losing the battle to the Visigoths circa 450 A.D,

Arthur Riothamus, which means king or chief, was taken to Avallon. This is not legend. It is historical fact.

"It was in Avallon that Arthur Riothamus died. I sincerely believe that our Burgundian Avallon is the true Avallon. *Aballo*, our Celtic apple isle, has always been here. There is no Avallon in Britain, nor has there ever been one. It is an imagined place."

"Thank you, Hermès. And I promise to send you the vignettes I've written from my imagination, while on our journey from Sybaris, along with some of my own ideas—intuitive revelations, you might call them."

"Intuitive revelations?"

"Yes, about *Le Cratère* and Chrétien de Troyes, Avallon and Camelot and *le Graal*. If I may ask, besides the historical information you have about General Riothamus, do you believe that your intuition helps you with your conclusions?"

"Without a doubt. I am convinced that there is a filament in our DNA which holds the memories of mankind and another filament which holds memories of the lifetimes we've lived. This, I truly believe, is the source of intuitive knowledge."

"Hermès," Bianca adds, "My intuition tells me that in your Burgundian DNA, you have the instinctive, accumulated knowledge of centuries of very wise and learned druids before you."

Obviously pleased, he responds, "Yes, I grew up only a few miles away from Vix. When I was a child, I wondered if there had ever been druids in my ancestry."

"Given your extensive, impressive knowledge, and your obvious passion and love of Burgundy and its history, my intuition tells me that you definitely have D for druid in your DNA."

Situla: Bucket or pail, is a term for a variety of elaborate bucket-shaped vessels used in ritual from the late Bronze Age, usually with a handle at the top. All types may be highly decorated with reliefs in bands or friezes running round the vessel.

Zatoria

The Winter Solstice Samonios, the New Year

The new palace is being readied for the ritual of the Feast of the Longest Night. Although the sun has not yet set, bonfires in the fields of Vix surrounding the citadel are already offering blazes to Arduina, goddess of the moon and forests. Farmers, cattle herders, horsebreeders and their families will spend the night under the stars feasting and carousing and storytelling. Both young and old will dance around the bonfires; the livelier the dance, the better the harvest from the yet unseeded fields. Before darkness falls, the older boys will run around the bonfires with flaming branches, imitating the course of the sun, and the revelers will look up to Latisco, all ablaze with the light of lanterns and torches, their shining citadel on the hill.

Mules and wagons heaped with logs for the cooking fires trundle up the winding road to the ramparts. There, in the center of town, on the road leading to the castle, boys tend the turning spits threaded with rabbits and fowl, boar and beef, slowly roasting over glowing, charred wood. This has been a year of plenty with enough food to feed the entire town, as well as strangers from distant lands who come to trade with the Tribe of the River People.

Behind the palisades, in the center of the new great hall, the Krater stands in its pride of place, filled with the dark, rich wine of Megale Hellas. To evoke the safeguard of woodland gods and green spirits, servants scurry about hanging boughs of holly and masses of winter-bare rowan branches still clustered with crimson berries. Others hang the ritual *situlae* and drinking horns on pegs along the wall. Youths hold torches aloft, shedding light in the great hall for the banqueters.

Sheep pelts cover the floor beyond the ring of the seated druids. The King and Queen will sit on bronze chairs sent as a gift from a chieftain of the Tyrrhenoi. A great round table, hewn from the trunks of lightning-struck oaks, is stacked with wood trenchers and bowls and flagons from Massilia. Baskets, woven from twigs of osier, will catch bones and bits of gristle to be thrown to the dogs.

The bards, storytellers and musicians enter. Trumpeters announce the arrival of the King of the River People, who stands tall, regal in trousers reaching the shivering thin gold plaques on his shoes. Upon his head he wears his crown, a pointed hat of silver birch bark. Zatoria, his Queen, is by his side, dressed in the white *peplos* of the Hellenes. Over her shoulders she wears a long wool cape woven in pattern of the tribe, red and blue stripes over green squares, pinned to one shoulder with a fibula of coral. The torque is a diadem, an arc over her russet hair, the polished gold gleaming in the soft light of the flickering flames of oil lamps.

The crowd disperses to form an aisle for them to pass, and the carnyx sounds to announce the hooded druids and the green-robed *Vates*. They enter solemnly and form a circle around the pit, a circle of fire, surrounding the great Krater. The druids of the tribe follow with Eutropios, the Pythagorean, who will teach the druids the philosophy of numbers, and the Thracian Zalmoxis, who will spend the last of his years sharing his learning with druids, the watchers of the skies, who carry vast knowledge in their heads but do not write their wisdom.

Next comes the smith, a most honored figure, for he is an artist as well as a worker in metals. Eutropios advised and helped him to weld together the seven pieces of the Krater and then encircle it with the frieze of horses and marching hoplites.

The carpenter enters with his wife. He is the master builder of the castle designed by Eutropios in the manner of the Hellenes. To reward the joiner for his considerable skills, the King commanded him to build a fine house with a pitched and wood shingle roof for himself and his family.

Before long the Great Hall is filled with villagers. Strangers are welcomed and speeches are made while the fire turns to glowing coals and then to ash. The carnyx wails again, and there is sudden silence. The ceremonies begin as the Arch Druid steps over the ashes. He approaches the Krater's lid, centered with a small image of Zatoria, her head draped in a mantle.

Four druids move forward to the great vessel and lift its cover. Another druid pours wine from the ritual *situla* through the strainer of the Krater, the cauldron of plenty, the cauldron of lives past and of lives to come. The Arch Druid tosses lumps of pine resin from the strainer into the fire making it sputter and hiss as the resin fumes, filling the great hall with fragrance for the feasting.

As the smoke rises, Zatoria, their Queen and Seer, also rises from her chair to recite a prayer to Arduina, goddess of the moon, of forests, of the earth, urging her to fill the bins with grain, imploring her to keep the tribe healthy, free from pestilence and destruction by the fierce, marauding tribes of the neighboring Senones and the Segobrigi of the Cult of the Severed Head, threatening those who live in Massilia of the Hellenes.

Now the sun has dropped into Mother Earth, the sky soon to deliver the moon. The druids begin their chant with the somber beat of large wood spoons on goatskin-stretched drums.

Arduina, orb of the night,
    of our earth
    and of our sacred oaks

Rise out from the cloudy sky.
Arduina, destroyer of darkness
Make bright our heavens,
Diffuse silver light
Amid the river of
Cold winter stars.
Stars shining through,
Clearing cloudy darkness
Freeing minds to open,
To gather knowledge,
To remember
So we may pass from this life
    to the Other
Holding the wisdom of mankind
For all the souls of mankind.

With these words the Arch Druid summons the Vates to step over the ring with the *situlae* filled with water which they pour into the Krater. The Arch Druid stirs the wine and water with a long staff made from the trunk of a sapling birch and topped with the golden cone, a gift from Zalmoxis, who had used it long ago, in the feast of Dionysos.

A druid stirs the wine in the *situla*, preparing to offer it to the Queen. Zatoria comes forward, her mother's black-figured *kylix* in her hands, and asks the Arch Druid to ladle wine into the cup. As she takes the first sip, tears fill her eyes. The fragile *kylix* has made the long and perilous journey from Sybaris together with the massive Krater.

There is celebration in the great hall but the druids do not partake in the bounty. They have passed from this world to the Other, and in silent stillness remain standing in the inner circle as the night passes in feasting and song, and revelers fill and refill their cups with sacred wine from the great vessel.

Before the sun rises, an elderly woman, the storyteller of the tribe, recites the story of her people from far back in Time Past to the Here and Now. She closes with these verses to honor Zatoria, Queen and seer of the Tribe of the River People.

> Over the mountains she fled,
> Fled from the flooded land,
> Her heart as wild as the waves,
> Crossed seas, sailed up rivers.
> And when at last she reached our gates
> Our people knew she was the Queen
> We'd waited for, and hailed her as our own.

With these words the woman comes to the end of her story. The great hall echoes with shouts and cheers for Zatoria, their long-awaited Queen, whose prophecy had spared the life of their Prince and the destruction of the King's Krater.

Now no carnyx wails. The great hall becomes quiet, with only sounds of strumming, plucking of the lyre, the high pitched melodies of reed pipes as the druids chant a hymn to the sun.

> Come, sun, rise, rise, golden Lord.
> Spread light upon our fields.
> May each planted seed
> Yield one hundredfold.
> Come out sun, come out sun,
> Do not keep us waiting.

Shine on us through time and tide,
Come out sun, come out,
Do not keep us waiting.
Rise, sun, rise from this too long darkness.
Warm us with your golden light.

Bianca and Giovanni

After lunch they walk to the Museum in the Maison Philandrier, originally a dwelling built during the French Renaissance. Hermès greets the ticket seller warmly. When the woman turns to Bianca and exclaims, *"Ah, Madame, c'est encore vous!"* Bianca tries hard not to laugh. *"Oui Madame, c'est moi,"* she replies airily but politely, "back again, this time after only six months." Pleased, she turns to Giovanni with a grin. "What did I tell you? They do remember me around here!"

They follow Hermès through the small, well lighted gallery filled with Gaulish ex votos found in the source of the nearby River Douix, a spring bubbling up from an underground cavern where amateur divers have discovered hundreds of votive offerings.

Giovanni studies the display he has never seen before. "Although these artifacts are mostly of the Gallo-Roman period, not as old as the ex votos we find in Magna Graecia, there's nonetheless a continuity of purpose, of similarity even, as the goddess Aphrodite becomes the healing Sequana in these rivers and streams."

Hermès replies assertively, "Not so long ago Hallstatt *fibulae* were found in the Source of the Douix, proof that it has been a sacred place for centuries, about as long ago as your finds in Magna Graecia, Giovanni—about the same time as *le Cratère*."

They climb the worn stone steps to the gallery of the Krater. Before entering, Bianca stops to reflect on two ancient stone sculptures, one a male figure, the other a woman wearing a torque. She remembers the couple from her previous visits and wonders if the woman might have been a representation of *la Dame de Vix*.

Hermès sees her studying the pair intently. "Bruno Chaume found them in 1994—his first day on the job! We took this as a good omen. And you have seen today what has happened since. Together with his team Bruno discovered *le Palais de la Dame de Vix*."

Bianca nods, closes her eyes, holds her breath and collects herself before entering the room. Then, with eyes wide open, she moves closer to the gleaming bronze vessel enclosed by glass, the wood chariot of *la Dame de Vix* by its side, its wheels placed along the wall. In the bier lies no priestess, no princess, now only jewels, the jewels of a queen, delicately placed on white linen. Giovanni and Hermès remain silent knowing that they have been left behind as Bianca is transported to her distant world.

Zatoria's kylix *from the Black Sea rests on the cover, a few inches away from the small veiled Kore, the silver phiale, the bronze flagon of the Tyrrhenioi, all used in the wine ritual. Her golden torque with its tiny winged horses, the amber beads and coral fibula, the schist bracelets once encircling her delicate wrists. And looming over the bier, the Krater, with it fierce, gaping-*

tongued Gorgons, their snake tails wrapped around the swell of
the vessel; the frieze of horses and marching hoplites of Sybaris,
immortalized by Eutropios, the Pythagorean.

Bianca closes her eyes and hears the voice of Chrétien's
grandmother reciting the words that Chrétien as a boy, might
have heard centuries ago.

> *And Queen she was until she left this world.*
> *She was buried with her cart.*
> *Around her neck, her amber beads,*
> *The golden diadem on her head,*
> *Not vanquished by time.*
> *Still she lies by her Sacred Cauldron,*
> *Cauldron of plenty that will never empty,*
> *Cauldron of life after death,*
> *From her we claim our descent.*
> *We hold the secret of all who come here to seek it.*
> *Our women are the guardians of the Grail*
> *That lies buried beneath the earth of Vix.*

When they leave the exhibit, Hermès glances at his watch.
"If I leave now I will be just on time for the *colloque*. It has been
such a happy surprise to see you again, Giovanni, and to meet
you, Bianca, and hear about your passion for *le Cratère de Vix*,
a passion you have had since the first time I saw you standing
before it."

"We've learned so much with you as our guide, Hermès,
not only about *le Cratère*, but also about Burgundy, the place
where the great *Graal* has remained for so many centuries
since its journey from..." she pauses and smiles, "since its journey from golden Sybaris to the golden hillsides of Burgundy."

"Sybaris? You must have read Claude Rolley's paper on *le
Cratère*."

"Giovanni has, but I have not." she responds. "Why don't we save Sybaris for our next meeting." She glances at Giovanni who graciously changes the subject.

"Hermès, my good friend, I also promise to save two weeks in August to help with the dig. But sooner than that, on the 5th of January, I'll be calling you with some news about a little find near Sybaris—after I've made my report to the Superintendent."

"What a fine experience it has been for me to show you our little town and its vast, highly important treasures. Until only a few years ago Vix was not very well known, not even in France, and before the discovery, Châtillon-sur-Seine was called a backwater place. Not even a train stopped here. Now it is worthy of three stars in the guidebooks, and its fame continues to spread."

They all embrace, kiss one another on both cheeks, and know, without a doubt, that they will soon have a reunion in Paris—or Puglia.

Ω

Giovanni and Bianca return to their room tired, but exhilarated. He puts his arms around her and says, "We'd better move on soon if we intend to be in Venice for Christmas Eve. We'll stay on through New Year's Day, then I must leave for Sibari and my appointment with the *Soprintendente*."

She sighs and rests her head against his shoulder. "Our journey together will have come full circle in Venice," she says wistfully, wondering what fortune might have in store for them after Venice.

Brushing away some wisps of hair from her face, he kisses her brow. "Certainly the fateful way we met—neither one of us wanting to be in Venice for someone else's wedding—was a meeting designed by destiny."

"When we're in Venice, I'll finish writing my Saga of Zatoria for Hermès, and as I write, I'll look out to the *pontile* where Nina's earring fell off. I'm sure when I'm home again, I'll tell and re-tell the story of the divers finding the gold coin gleaming in the mud of the Grand Canal."

He nods and says, "You can be certain that most people will think it's a tall tale. As soon as we arrive in Venice, I'll walk over to Nardi and ask Alberto to add a tiny gold plaque behind the earring engraved, '*retrieved from the Grand Canal on July 14, 2007*'. And then, when you take the earring from your ear to show it, they might believe your story."

"Believe it or not, this is a case where truth is stranger than fiction." Flashing her beautiful smile, she laughs, "Even stranger than the fiction I write!"

He responds seriously. "But most importantly, Bianca, we have discovered Camelot together. This is *fact* and not fiction. One day soon you must write about it."

Giovanni sits on the bed and pulls her down by his side. He looks at her face, turned up to him like a flower, a fresh, luminous flower. He takes his family's signet ring from his finger, poises it over her ring finger and, with his usual quiet dignity, proposes. "Bianca, would you consider becoming the wife of a professor? Living in Puglia would be a big change from midtown Manhattan but we can always visit New York in December and June to check out the antiquities auctions."

Her heart racing with joy, she blinks back the tears to study the porphyry intaglio, an engraving of the crenellated turret of the *castello* in Sicchia. Looking into his eyes she responds emphatically, "Of course I will marry you, and after we've repeated our vows, we'll own Nina's watercolor together. So the castle will always be yours." With her voice breaking, adds, "and—it will always be ours." He slips the ring on her finger.

Her bright, happy face awaits his kiss. "Yes, my darling Giovanni, from ritual to romance indeed!" He nods. "Here's to imperishable romance!"

ACKNOWLEDGMENTS

My acknowledgments and thanks go to countless good friends over the years (since 1994) who have been helpful to me with this book, either by listening to the sometimes circuitous route to discovering my narrative, or by their generous suggestions and sharing of information.

Infinite thanks to my dear friend and editor, Dr. Jenijoy La Belle, Professor of English Literature, Caltech, who shared with me her knowledge and love of the English language.

Dr. Kenneth Atchity, former professor of Classics, long-time friend, mentor, editor, literary manager and now my publisher— The Story Merchant.

Dr. Eric Haskell, Scripps College, Claremont, who, from the beginning, encouraged me to tell this story and was the first of my friends to read the finished novel.

Dr. Thierry Boucquey, Scripps College, Claremont for the novel's translation into French; Dott.ssa Paola Biscosi, for her translation into Italian.

Dr. Andrew Stewart, Professor of Greek Art, Berkeley, for alerting me to Claude Rolley's opinion on the origin of the Krater's casting in Sybaris.

Dott.ssa Silvana Luppino, archaeologist and Director of the Museo Nazionale, Sibari, Calabria, friend and guide at the sites of ancient Sybaris and Paestum, ancient Poseidonia of the Sybarites.

Professor Michael Vickers. the Ashmolean Museum, Oxford, for the use of the drawings of the Krater from *Artful Crafts*, Vickers and Gill, Oxford University Press 1994.

Bruno Chaume, archaeologist, discoverer of *le Palais de la Dame de Vix* for a personal tour of the site of the ancient Celtic palace on Mont Lassois.

Elizabeth Locke, designer of the Byzantine coin earrings, and who later inscribed my lost earring with the date of its retrieval from the Grand Canal.

With grateful thanks and appreciation to my friend Robin Tait, who, on our wine buying trip in 1994, happily agreed to the detour that led us to the wondrous Krater of Vix.

Hutton Wilkinson, dear friend of many years for his enthusiasm and encouragement.

Professor Manfred Kuhnert, always generous with his time, and for his dramatic and artistic insights.

Matthew White, friend and neighbor to whom I told Bianca's story even before I began to write it.

Georgiana Erskine, another first reader of the *Realms of Gold*, for her enthusiasm.

Warren Dennis, Kathy Offenhauser, Sassy Johnson, always ready to listen and suggest.

Fred Iberri, computer expert, for helping me in so many ways, and always by my side whenever there was a cyber emergency.

Chi-Li Wong, who brought my novel into the blogosphere: Realmsofgoldthenovel.blogspot.com.

Robert Aulicino for interior layout and design, bringing to life the ritual pages and book sections with the William Morris Kelmscott borders.

Brett Battles, for his beautiful formatting for electronic publishing.

Anjelica Casas, organizer of my historical library and files.

To Dennis, my devoted (and patient) husband who listened to all the twists and turns of the story as it was being woven in my head; Francesca, my daughter, a born writer and gifted novelist, for her writer's sensibility and loving support; Dennis, my son, of HBDesign, Singapore, for the striking cover of *Realms of Gold*; my dear sister, Eileen Olivieri Cassella, always there for me.

And to my beloved daughter Michaela, our "Cada," now in the Otherworld, for her extensive historical research at the Boston Public Library.

Made in the USA
Charleston, SC
01 July 2012